SHATTERED WORLD |
PARIS

SHATTERED WORLD I
PARIS

Scott M. Baker

A Schattenseite Book

Shattered World
by Scott M. Baker.
Copyright © 2020. All Rights Reserved.
Print Edition

ISBN-13: 978-0-9963121-9-6

Cover Art © by Joolz & Jarling – Uwe Jarling & Julie Nicholls 2020
Editing © Michele Thompson 2016
Map © Petar Dekic 2020

To my dear friend and colleague Alina,
You threw me a lifeline when I was going under and I will never forget that. Thanks.

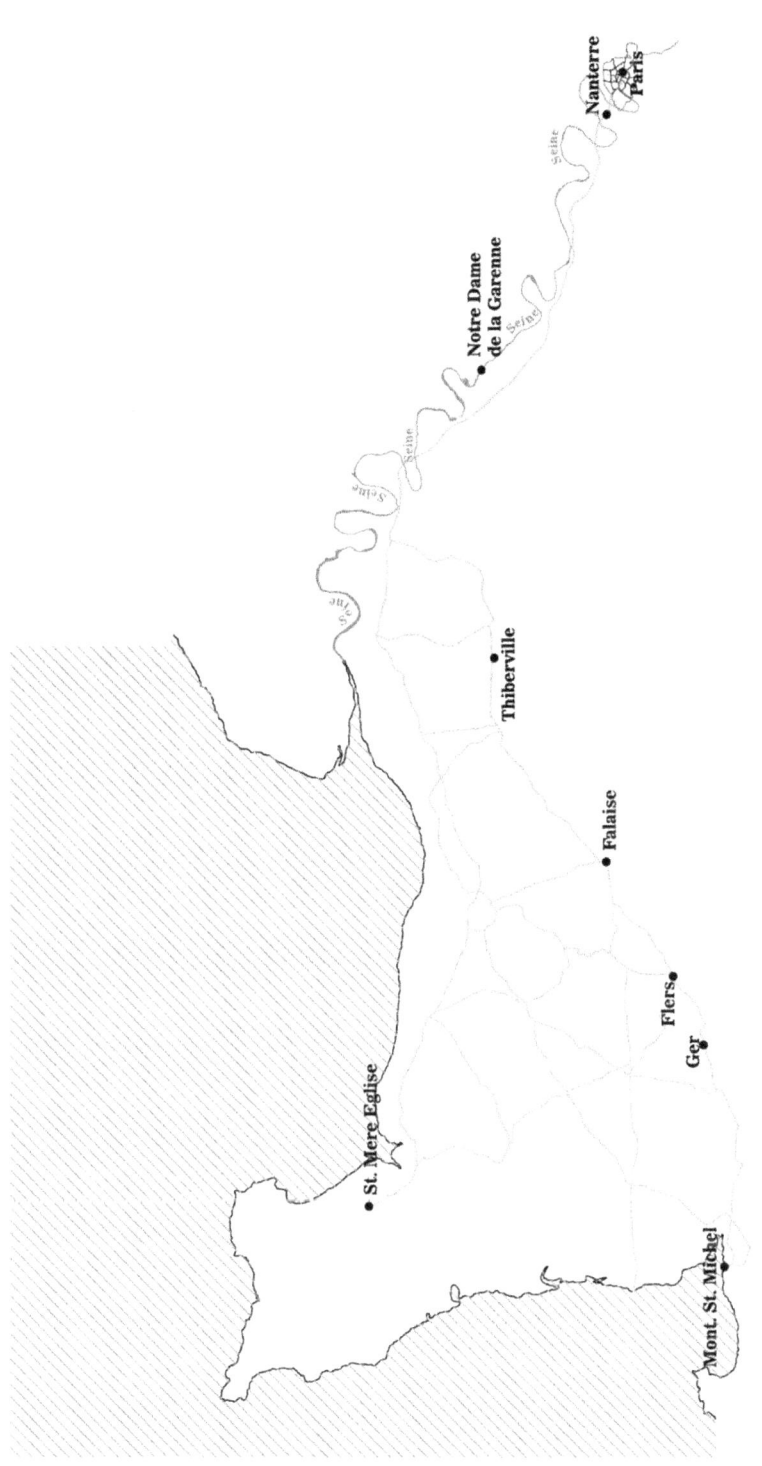

BOOK ONE

CHAPTER ONE

THE STILLNESS BELIED the danger that lurked in the shadows of every alley and doorway of St. Merc Eglise. Jason McCreary found it unsettling. Most of the towns along the Normandy coast had been abandoned long ago. Animals now flourished amongst the desolation, with livestock and wildlife replacing humans. That wasn't the case today. Even the birds had fled, plunging the town into an eerie silence that forewarned of an approaching evil. Experience had taught Jason that when the animals fled it was to escape from Demon Spawn. He made his way along the center of Rue Eisenhower, clutching his crossbow, ready to shoot if necessary. Despite walking lightly, his footsteps echoed through town, sounding like a dinner bell for the dead. His eyes scanned the buildings. Nothing moved except overgrown grass and weeds that swayed in the wind. The same wind tousled several blond strands across his face. Jason used his free hand to push them back behind his ears.

Jason took a deep breath to calm his nerves, holding it for several seconds before exhaling. It did little good. His heart still raced and his hands trembled, knowing that at any moment something demonic could lunge out of the shadows at him. He glanced down to the werehounds that stayed close by his side. Lilith brought up Jason's right flank. She looked like a large wolf with shiny black fur. Her head darted from side to side, seeking out anything that could be a threat. Occasionally, she glanced behind them to make certain nothing approached from their rear. Lucifer walked along on his left. He resembled a

Boxer. His ears stood straight up, listening for any noise that signified danger. When Lucifer saw his master staring at him, his stubby tail wagged. After the brief display of affection, he went back to prowling for Demon Spawn.

Jason sniffed the air to see if he could smell the demons. A tickle formed in the back of his throat, causing him to hack against the rear of his hand. Ever since the opening of the interdimensional portals, the air had taken on an unpleasant odor. Father Chirac referred to it as the brimstone stench of Hell. Jason had no idea what the priest meant. To him, the air smelled like the living room of his old house after his mother would build a fire in the fireplace, only mixed with the stench of rot and shit.

As he glanced from building to building, Jason chastised himself. He didn't like being separated from the group, yet he only had himself to blame for being the point man into a potential battle royale. Yesterday, a scouting party on horseback had reported Demon Spawn moving across the countryside toward St. Mere Eglise; they had been unable to conduct a proper reconnaissance because of the approaching dusk. A search and destroy team had been sent out that morning to assess the threat and deal with it. Jason was part of that team. A mile outside of town, the team had dismounted and left their horses with a rear-guard unit so they could proceed on foot. Andre had ordered Jason to go ahead and scout the area. When Sasha had protested sending him in alone, Jason had interrupted and said he wanted to take point. He didn't know if he had been trying to impress Andre or had been embarrassed by having Sasha fight his battles for him, not that it mattered. His stupid sixteen-year-old vanity had gotten the better of him. Now he was heading into a town probably overrun by Demon Spawn.

"And I wonder why they keep calling me Bait."

Lucifer looked up with his soulful brown eyes and whined, sensing his discomfort.

"I'm fine, boy. I need a bit more common sense than pride." He reached down and scratched Lucifer behind the ears. His stubby tail wagged.

Jason closed his eyes and concentrated. He could sense the others following half a mile to the rear. Most of the team registered as one signature, giving off an aura of concern over not knowing what to expect. Three auras stood out. Andre and Slava, both of whom who were excited about the possibility of combat, and Sasha who was afraid. Not for herself, though. She feared for Jason's safety. He grinned at the distant display of affection.

At the corner, the street opened. To the right sat a parking lot empty except for a few dust-covered vehicles. In the far corner of the lot sat St. Mere Eglise church, the one made famous when an American paratrooper got stuck on the belfry during the D-Day landings. He remembered seeing that in an old black-and-white war movie he watched with his dad. Red Skelton, or Buttons, or someone with a weird name like that had played the paratrooper. To the left was the Airborne Museum that commemorated the Normandy invasion. Jason veered off the street and into the outer edge of the parking lot. The werehounds stayed close.

He had approached to within twenty feet of the intersection of Rue Eisenhower and Rue de Gaulle when a single figure shambled out into the middle of the street. A flesh eater that fed off humans. These demons were slow and uncoordinated, so dealing with one or two was easy. However, a horde of flesh eaters could strip a man to the bones in minutes. Jason had seen hundreds like it during the past few months. Naked, emaciated, and with grey leathery skin dried out from the fires of the other dimension. It stumbled along, its gaze fixed on the road. The demon hadn't noticed him yet. Jason raised the crossbow and aimed at the skull above the right ear. Lucifer growled. The noise caught the flesh eater's attention. Its head shot up and its lifeless, cloudy eyes fixed on Jason. When its mouth dropped open, a mournful wail emanated from cracked, desiccated lips. Jason readjusted his aim and pulled the trigger. The arrow sliced through its left eye. It dropped to the ground, a final moan escaping from its lungs as its lifeforce drained from its body, creating a small eddy of blue light that twisted in the air for a moment before dissipating.

Jason reached around to pull another arrow from its quiver when the stench of decayed flesh filtered into his nose, a smell so overpowering his stomach heaved. As he swallowed back his vomit, a chorus of wails shattered the calm. A swarm of flesh eaters flowed out of Rue de Gaulle and filled the square. A fat female noticed Jason and screeched. The others turned and, spotting food, shambled towards him. At least a hundred flesh eaters emerged from the side street, all of them bearing down on Jason. Even worse, he saw four dark grey shapes darting amongst the horde. Though he couldn't get a good view because of the other demons, he recognized the bat-like bodies and bulbous, eyeless heads with gaping mouths.

Shit! Soul vampires!

"Come on, guys!" Jason said to Lilith and Lucifer. He ran for the church. Lilith stayed close to protect her master. Lucifer defiantly barked at the approaching horde before spinning around and sprinting away.

Reaching the door to St. Mere Eglise church, Jason tried the knob. It was locked. He rammed his shoulder against the door several times. It wouldn't budge. Placing his back against the wall, Jason scanned the area and weighed his options. Flesh eaters stretched out across the parking lot. They were still over fifty feet away and he could easily outrun them. Three of the soul vampires spread out behind the first line of flesh eaters, preparing to attack, and they would cut him down if he moved out in the open. If he stayed with his back against the church so he couldn't be surrounded, he might have a chance. With luck, the rest of the team would reach him before the flesh eaters did.

One of the soul vampires broke through the horde in front

of Jason and charged. The other two emerged thirty feet to either side. Lucifer growled at the one approaching from the left. Facing the demon, he began his metamorphosis. The fur on his back and legs receded, allowing the skin to harden into scales. Three-inch spikes tore through the muscles around his shoulders, and horns extended from behind his ears, giving his head the appearance of a bull. Lucifer's paws lengthened several inches and his nails became talons. To Jason's right, Lilith howled as she morphed into her demonic form. The shiny black fur stiffened like the spikes of a porcupine. The tail elongated into a five-foot appendage with a stinger on the end, much like a scorpion. Jason heard the snapping of bone as her jaw distended and her fangs lengthened. She crouched, ready to attack.

Lucifer pounced on the soul vampire moving in on the left flank, lowering his head and ramming the demon in its abdomen. His horns tore through its leathery skin and gouged open its stomach. It screamed and fell to the ground, its skeleton-thin hands clasping the wound to hold its intestines in place. Scrambling to its feet, the soul vampire tried to get away, moving slowly because of its wound. Lucifer jumped onto its back, pinning it to the ground with his hind legs. The were-hound's front paws slashed away at its neck and head, tearing away chunks of skin and fracturing the skull. The soul vampire howled and flailed its arm to drive away the werehound, yet Lucifer kept up the assault. With one final blow, his paw crushed the skull. A pathetic mewl escaped the demon's lips as its body went limp.

Lilith timed her attack precisely before lunging. She landed on the soul vampire's chest and toppled it over backwards. As the two hit the ground, her jaws locked around its neck, biting through skin and muscle. The soul vampire attempted to cry out, emitting a pitiful groan through its crushed larynx. It clawed at Lilith, shredding its hands on the porcupine-like spikes. Lilith's tail wrapped around her back and shoulder, and she plunged the stinger into the demon's forehead, injecting it with paralyzing venom. Within seconds, every muscle in its body went numb. With a violent twist of her jaws, Lilith severed the soul vampire's head and flung it aside. The head skipped across the parking lot.

Jason focused on the danger charging straight toward him. He aimed the crossbow at the center of its bulbous forehead and fired. Without eyes, the soul vampire's auditory senses were highly attuned. Hearing the projectile sailing through the air, it shifted to the right. The arrow missed and landed amongst the approaching flesh eater. Jason removed another from his quiver and reloaded. The soul vampire was ten feet away. Jason didn't have time to line up his shot. He raised the crossbow and quick fired. The arrow entered the demon's throat and punched its way out the back of its neck, lodging in its windpipe. It stopped and gasped for air. It reached up and tried to pull out the bolt; however, the protruding tip lodged it in place. Jason loaded another arrow into the crossbow and fired point blank. The arrow sliced into the center of its eyeless skull, scrambling its brain. The soul vampire collapsed to the ground.

Jason realized how precarious his position had become. The horde of flesh eaters was closing in, with the nearest one only twenty feet away. Lucifer and Lilith fell back so as not to be eaten, the latter whining to her master to warn him about their impending doom. And where is the last soul—

Jason sensed its presence closing in on his right along the front of the church. It must have circled around the parking lot while the other three distracted him. He ducked as the soul vampire lunged. It missed him. However, its hand clawed across Jason's shoulder, causing him to drop the crossbow. The soul vampire landed five feet from Jason and spun around, reacquiring its target. Jason had only a moment to react. Reaching down, he removed the machete from the sheath strapped to his leg. The movement caught the soul vampire's attention and it leapt. Jason rushed forward and plunged the machete into the demon's shoulder, pushing with all his might and impaling it on the church door. He pushed the weapon deeper, lodging the blade in the wood. The soul vampire's mouth opened, and Jason got a whiff of the acid vomit rising in its throat. He ducked a moment before it spewed the corrosive liquid. The bile splattered across the church steps, sizzling against the stone.

Jason's crossbow sat on the ground out of reach, with the closest flesh eater ten feet beyond it. He had to take the chance. He shoved the machete into the soul vampire's shoulder until it wouldn't go any farther, then rushed out into the parking lot. Snatching up the crossbow, he spun around and reached for an arrow. Shit, the quiver was empty. Several arrows lay scattered around his feet. He bent over to pick one up, stood, and reloaded.

A soul curdling cry sent a chill down Jason's spine. With an incredible effort, the soul vampire yanked itself off the door. The machete remained imbedded in the wood, carving out chunks of flesh and muscle as the demon pulled itself along the blade. Once free from the weapon, it acquired Jason's presence and snarled. Jason fired. The arrow struck the soul vampire in its open mouth, propelling it backward until the arrowhead lodged in the door. With a final spasm, the soul vampire died, its carcass hanging limply off the bolt.

A pair of dead hands grabbed Jason from behind. Before he could react, a flesh eater bit into his shoulder. He felt its teeth grind against the bone. Jason dropped the crossbow and grabbed its head with his right hand, holding it in place to prevent the flesh eater from tearing off a piece of his shoulder.

Another pair of hands grabbed Jason. He curled his left hand into a fist and started to take a swing, pausing when he stared into Andre's face. The Russian moved up behind them and pushed them away from the horde. When they reached the wall of the church, Andre removed a Glock 23 from his holster, placed the barrel against the flesh eater's temple, and fired. The demon's skull exploded. Jason felt the death grip on his shoulder loosen, and a second later the flesh eater dropped to the pavement, its lifeforce swirling into the air.

Andre shoved the teenager to the ground as gunfire erupted around him. Jason glanced up to see Gun Team 2 at the corner of the church firing their automatic weapons into the horde. Sasha stood in front, her red hair blowing across her face. She aimed her hand-held six-barreled GAU-17A minigun at the horde of flesh eaters and squeezed the trigger. A momentary whir cut through the moaning, followed a second later by the roar of the weapon as it engaged. Sasha swept the barrel back and forth. Fifty rounds a second tore into the front line of flesh eaters, ripping them apart. Her team advanced, stepping over body parts as they waded into the swarm.

More gunfire erupted to Jason's right. At the other corner of the church, Gun Team 3 fired into the horde, supporting Haneef as he used his own GAU-17A to decimate the flesh eater ranks. The two teams moved with precision, picking off the flanks and herding the remainder into a smaller grouping that could not withstand the massed firepower. It took only a minute for them to eliminate the horde, leaving shattered corpses and a mesmerizing blue eddy of lifeforces that shimmied over the parking lot. Silence descended across the area. Haneef stepped away from the carnage. Facing Mecca, he fell to his knees and bowed his forehead against the ground, repeating the prayer several times.

Andre grabbed Jason by the collar and yanked the teenager onto his feet. "Smart move, Bait. You put all of us in danger."

"I had no choice," Jason protested as he shrugged off Andre's grip.

"You couldn't outrun them?"

Jason pointed to the carcass impaled to the church door. "There were four soul vampires amongst the flesh eaters. I wouldn't have made it far if I had tried to run."

Andre studied the soul vampire hanging from the arrow and moved away without responding. "Okay, people. Stay alert in case there are any more of these things in the area."

Everyone followed the order. Andre noticed Haneef praying. "Haneef, what are you doing?"

"Thanking Allah for our victory." Haneef lifted himself off the pavement and brushed the dirt from his knees.

Andre shook his head in disgust. "We move out in three minutes."

Sasha came over to Jason. "Don't listen to him," she whispered. "You did great."

His heart skipped a beat. He wanted to say something cool, something that would impress her. He could only come up with, "Thanks."

Lucifer and Lilith plodded up to Jason. Both animals had changed back into their animal forms. Jason crouched down to pet them. Lucifer licked his face, happy that his master was safe. Lilith sniffed Jason's wound and whimpered.

Sasha noticed the blood on Jason's shoulder. "Oh my God! You're hurt!"

Jason twisted his head and saw the bite for the first time. The teeth marks were deep, and he could see bone through the gash. Thankfully, it was a clean wound, and the bleeding had slowed. Now he noticed the pain.

"It's not that bad," he lied. "I'll have Doc fix me up when we get back."

Sasha spun around toward Andre. "Did you know Jason was hurt?"

"Yeah. So?"

"We need to get him medical care."

"He'll be fine. Maybe next time the idiot will be more careful."

Sasha started to respond. Jason placed a hand on her arm and stopped her. "It's okay. I'll be all right."

"Well, you won't be if you keep letting Andre push you

around." Sasha stormed off.

For a moment, the blow to Jason's pride hurt worse than the pain in his shoulder.

Andre shook his head, a sour expression on his face. "Let's move out, people. I want to be well clear of this area before nightfall."

CHAPTER TWO

NIGHT HAD FALLEN by the time the team approached home. No one had spoken on the journey back because everyone had tried to forget what had happened at St. Mere Eglise. Jason knew that each one of them would try to quash the recollections either by tamping them down deep into their psyche or drowning them in alcohol. Suppressing those memories had become difficult. Attacks like the one this afternoon occurred with greater frequency, and over the past few weeks had involved an increasing number of Demon Spawn and losses among the teams. Today had been the worst attack yet and they were lucky to have survived. What Jason realized—what all of them realized, even if they refused to admit it—was that their luck would not last forever.

Jason had his own coping mechanism to deal with his brushes with death, preferring to allow guilt to consume the fear, even if it ate away at other emotions in the process. It didn't work in this instance. He could not forget the afternoon's events because the pain from the bite in his shoulder served as a constant reminder of his encounter with the flesh eaters. What had started out as an isolated ache now spread down his left arm and across his back until every step his horse took made it throb. He didn't need to see the wound to know it had become infected.

The injury didn't hurt as much as the silent treatment Sasha had given him after leaving St. Mere Eglise. During a scouting expedition, she usually would check on him, or at least look at him with that full-lipped smile that always made him feel warm inside. Not tonight, though. Sasha had taken a position ahead of him and had not glanced back once. Jason had tried to catch up with her a few miles west of Avranches, but she spurred her horse ahead, so he gave up and fell back in line. Doc would be able to give him something for the bite. Only time would heal the dull void in his chest.

Around nine o'clock, the group arrived at the area surrounding Mont St. Michel. The road to their right ran for a hundred yards before ending at a beach. Half a mile offshore sat the island city, which had been their home since shortly after the opening of the portals. Even in the dark, the city inspired awe with its buildings and structures casting tall shadows into the star-lit sky. The 11th Century abbey towered three hundred feet above the bay, partially blotting out the moon. Candlelight flickered from hundreds of windows.

In front of them stood the refugee encampment that had developed around the motels once used by tourists. Five and six families shared rooms barely large enough to fit four people, and they were the lucky ones. Those who couldn't find space inside had set up a makeshift tent city that spread for acres across the campgrounds and deep into the forest. Jacques, the mayor of Mont St. Michel, had stopped counting refugees when their number reached five thousand almost four months ago. Their ranks had nearly doubled since then as survivors made their way to the only sanctuary in the region. *Some sanctuary*, thought Jason. These people had to scavenge for what little food and water they could find, all the time sitting in the shadow of a well-stocked and relatively comfortable town. Jacques refused to let them onto the island, stating that to do so would put everyone's safety at risk. He had provided the refugees with a few desalination stills, though they barely produced enough drinkable water to keep the refugees alive. Jacques had also posted armed guards to roam through the camp, ostensibly to keep the peace, although everyone knew that, in reality, he wanted to keep an eye on the refugees and stop any plots to take over the town.

As the search and destroy team passed by, hundreds of envious, spiritless eyes followed their every move.

On approaching the coastline, Jason spotted Gruber's team on horseback. Jacques had sent them to the outskirts of Geneva two weeks ago to check on the original interdimensional portal at the European Organization for Nuclear Research, or CERN. When Gruber's team had left camp there were eight members; now Jason counted only three. Andre maneuvered his horse beside Gruber's and said nothing. The rest of the team fanned out around him. Lucifer and Lilith lied down beside Jason's horse, both animals exhausted from their long walk.

A man emerged from the shadows wearing a long, dark grey pea coat. He stepped up to Andre. "Is this all of them?"

"We didn't lose anyone this time." Andre nodded at Gruber in sympathy. The German responded in kind and lowered his head in despair.

The man in the pea coat trudged to end of the causeway. He used a match to light two lanterns, picked them up, and held them over his head, swinging them back and forth. The signal meant that those approaching the city had a right to be there and should be given safe passage. A few seconds later, a return signal came from the main entrance at the southwest corner of Mont St. Michel. The man stepped over to Andre.

"You're clear to go. Be careful of the quicksand."

Andre led his horse down to the beach. Most of the causeway had been destroyed seven months ago to prevent anything, or anyone, from swarming the town. Any potential siege would only last a few hours before the incoming the tide rushed in and drowned or drove away the attackers. That meant scouting parties had to cross the sandy floor of the bay to get home. The weight of each horse and its rider caused the hoofs to sink into the wet sand, each step accompanied by a squish. Lilith and Lucifer made the crossing with ease, although the former whined several times over having to wade through the muck. Everyone kept an eye on those around them, ready to go to their aid if one of the horses stepped into one of the quicksand pits that formed without warning. No one wanted to die so close to home.

Jason examined the city's defenses. Every thirty feet, an armed guard stood sentry on the outer wall, most of them men too old or weak to go out with the gun teams. For added protection, Jacques had engineers weld four-foot-long metal spikes into the top of the wall at one-foot intervals, each pointed down at a forty-five-degree angle to prevent anything from scaling the outer defenses. It would hold off humans, flesh eaters, or soul vampires. However, if even a fraction of the rumors he heard about other Demon Spawn proved accurate, these defenses would not be enough to stop the other demons from making their way into Mont St. Michel. Jason spotted the top three stories of *Le Mere Poulard Hotel* extending above the outer wall. The hotel sat between the two main gates into town. Jacques had reserved it for the three gun teams and the gate guards, wanting the main defenders to be close to the entrance in order to protect the city. The hotel had its own kitchen and enough space for every member of the team to have his or her own room, which presented a sharp contrast to the living standards of the refugees across the bay.

After five nerve-wracking minutes, the group reached the cement landing in front of Mont St. Michel. A dozen armed men stood with rifles at the ready, only dropping their guard when they saw that those approaching were their own people. The horses maneuvered up the embankment, past the guard outpost, and through Boulevard Gate. One hundred feet ahead of them stood King's Gate. Massive steel doors had been constructed on either end of the archway. In a crisis, these doors could be sealed shut, locking out any enemies.

The team dismounted and a band of young women gathered up the horses. A blonde girl pushed her way pass Lilith and Lucifer to grab the reins of Jason's horse. When Jason slid out of the saddle and dropped to the ground, a bolt of pain shot down his arm, causing him to wince.

The werehounds plodded over and sat beside him, each staring at their master. "Are you all right?" asked the blonde.

"Yeah," he grunted. "Thanks."

She smiled and led the horse through the portcullis to the stables.

Sasha stepped up beside Jason. He hoped for an apology for the way she had ignored him on the trip home. Instead, her tone was cold and professional.

"Get that shoulder taken care of. I'll take Lucifer and Lilith to your room."

Andre sneered as he slid from his saddle. "I hate the idea of having those things stay in the same hotel as us."

Lilith leered at him, her ears folded flat against her head and her lips curled up to expose her fangs. The Russian reached for his Glock.

Jason jumped in front of him. "Leave them alone. They're not a threat."

Andre dismissed Jason with a shake of his head and walked toward the hotel. "Tame that bitch before I put her down."

Slava passed by Jason, purposefully shoving him with his backpack. "I think it says a lot about Bait that he keeps Demon Spawn as pets."

Although Slava constantly picked on him, this time his taunt hit home since it came closer to the truth than Jason let on.

Sasha waited until the two Russians had entered the hotel. "Don't listen to them. A lot of us wouldn't be here if it wasn't for Lucifer and Lilith."

"Thanks," Jason said half-heartedly.

"I'll make sure they're safely locked in your room. You go see Doc. Now." Though meant as an order, she spoke with the hint of friendliness. Jason wanted to ask Sasha if everything was okay between them to make certain that her feelings toward him had not changed but thought better of it. He already felt that he seemed pitiful in her eyes. Jason watched as Sasha led the two werehounds inside. Once she entered the lobby, he passed through King's Gate and headed for the abbey.

CHAPTER THREE

T HE INFIRMARY WAS located on the top floor of the abbey. To get there, Jason had to make his way across the city. The only access to the structure passed between twin towers stretching over one hundred feet into the night sky that guarded a flight of steep stairs between the ancient walls of the abbey and the outer defensive wall. The walk and the climb did not do his shoulder any good. By the time he reached the top, he could barely move the fingers in his left hand due to the pain. Using his right hand, Jason pushed aside the entry door to the abbey. Even that minimal effort caused his wounded shoulder to ache. Passing through the Romanesque nave to the opposite bank of doors, he opened the one farthest to the right and entered. The Gothic architecture towered above him, only heightening his feeling of inadequacy. Two rows of floor-mounted candelabras ran along either side of the central nave. Their light reflected off the stone arches and windows, yet penetrated only thirty feet, leaving the vaulted ceiling in shadows. Jason veered right and passed through a set of curtains into the room used as an infirmary.

The soft glow of fluorescent lights washed over him. Most of Europe had lost electricity when the portals opened. Doc had told him that they had emitted an electro-magnetic pulse, whatever that was, which burned out anything that ran on a motor. It explained why they had no cars, no televisions, no radios, and no computers, nothing that most people equated with modern living. In a matter of minutes, Europe had been plunged into a void the continent had not experienced for centuries. Jacques had somehow obtained half a dozen solar-powered generators; however, they produced minimal amounts of energy, so only the most vital parts of the city—the infirmary, the command post, and the kitchen—used them.

Their primitive existence served as a constant reminder of his guilt.

"Is Doc around?"

"Hey, Jason." Neal glanced over his shoulder and acknowledged the teenager with a nod. His eyes widened upon seeing the wound. He dropped the scalpel into the sink, grabbed a towel, and dried his hands. "What happened?"

"I got bit by a flesh eater in St. Mere Eglise."

"Hop up the exam table. I'll go get Doc."

Jason complied and Neal raced out of the infirmary. While he waited, Jason slid off his jacket. His left shoulder throbbed as he pulled off his shirt. The skin around the bite flared red, and yellow pus had begun to form around the edges. Jason pushed the top flap of dangling skin aside to get a better view. His face contorted in pain as the rancid skin folded back.

The curtains to the infirmary pushed to one side and Doc entered. Doc's real name was Eric Fisher. He had no medical background, having worked as a physicist alongside Jason's mother. Being the only person in Mont St. Michel with a doctorate, by default he had become the city's physician. Jason liked Doc, and not just because Doc had been watching out for him since that fateful day outside of Geneva. He reminded him of one of those befuddled doctors from the movies, over six feet tall and lanky, with a full head of neatly combed hair. The only thing about Doc that bothered Jason was the left arm missing above the elbow, yet another reminder to haunt Jason.

"Evening, Jason," said Doc.

"Hey."

"Neal says you were bitten by a flesh eater."

Jason nodded toward his shoulder. A few strands of blonde hair fell across his face, which he pushed aside. Doc examined the wound from several angles and pushed aside the loose flap of skin. Jason jumped from the pain.

"I'm afraid it's infected. Lie down. I'll stitch it up."

Jason maneuvered himself lengthwise onto the examination table. "Will I be okay?"

"It's going to hurt for a while but in a few days you'll be fine. I'll give you something for the pain." Doc raised the head of the table so Jason could sit upright and then stepped over to a cabinet that contained medical instruments. "Neal."

The young man poked his head through the curtains. "Yes?"

"I need two hypodermics with penicillin and morphine."

"Coming right up."

Neal crossed over to the makeshift pharmacy and prepared the injections. A minute later, Doc returned with a tray containing a hypodermic needle, a bottle of rubbing alcohol and gauze, and a suture kit. "I'm going to inject the area around the wound with Lidocaine. It'll hurt for a few minutes. You shouldn't feel anything when I stitch you up."

Doc stuck the needle into the skin around the bite and squeezed the plunger a quarter of the way down. Jason winced. It felt like a hornet had stung his shoulder. The pain soon disappeared as numbness settled in. Doc repeated the process three more times until he had saturated the area around the wound with Lidocaine. He dropped the needle onto the tray.

"Neal, help me suture him up."

"Yes, sir."

Doc stood by the exam table. "How does that feel?"

"Pretty good. The throbbing is going away."

"In a minute you won't feel much of anything." Doc opened the bottle of rubbing alcohol and stood over Jason. "I'm going to disinfect the wound."

Jason gritted his teeth, preparing for a searing pain when Doc poured alcohol into the bite. Instead, he only felt pressure as Doc dabbed away the liquid and wiped off the pus. He figured it should only take a minute or two to clean. After five minutes and a dozen pieces of gauze, Doc still hadn't finished.

"Everything okay?" asked Jason as he strained to see what Doc was doing.

"The wound has a nasty infection. I caught it in enough time that you shouldn't feel anything worse than a slight fever for a few days. I'm going to put you on a heavy regime of antibiotics. It should knock it out of your system in a week."

"I thought we were running low on antibiotics?"

"We are. You're a special case."

Jason bowed his head. "Because of what happened to my mother?"

"No." Doc's voice sounded firm yet caring. "Any member of the search and destroy teams is entitled to it. However, it will run out quicker than I want if you keep making yourself a Demon Spawn Happy Meal."

Neal sighed. "What I wouldn't give for a Happy Meal."

Someone entering the room caught their attention. It was Monique, one of the pre-teen girls who served as a runner for Jacques. Doc glanced up. "How can I help you? You get bit, too?"

"N-no, sir," she stammered, confused by the question. "Jacques sent me to tell you that he wants you at a meeting tonight in his quarters."

"What time?"

"Midnight."

"Why so late?"

"I have no… I mean, he didn't say."

"That's okay. Tell him I'll be there."

Monique spun around and raced out. Jason grinned. He could never understand why so many of the others didn't like Doc. Jason enjoyed being around him and Neal. They didn't judge him like everyone else in the city. In the infirmary he felt at ease, which is why he spent so much of his free time helping around the infirmary.

Neal sewed up the wound because Doc couldn't manage it with one arm. It took thirty-six stitches. As Neal washed off the shoulder one final time with rubbing alcohol and applied the bandage, Doc came over with a metal tray containing two hypodermics and two orange plastic bottles.

"What's in the needles?"

Doc pointed to the one on the end. "This one is morphine. It'll deaden the pain for a few hours and help you sleep. The other is Zithromax. The flesh eaters' mouths are Petri dishes of disease, especially clostridium, so I'm giving you the most powerful antibiotic we have to be sure we kill whatever infected you." Doc handed over the plastic bottles. "This is Zithromax in oral form. Take two pills a day until the bottle is empty. The larger bottle is Motrin. Take two as needed if the pain gets bad."

"Yes, sir."

"Stop calling me sir. We've been through too much together."

That's for damn sure, thought Jason.

CHAPTER FOUR

JASON STRUGGLED TO make it back to *Le Mere Poulard*. Not because of the pain, which he no longer felt, but because the morphine kicked in as he left the abbey. He hated that the way to the hotel led down a dark, steep flight of stone stairs and through poorly lit streets. He took his time, concentrating on staying awake, and trying to block out everything else around him.

It didn't work. Everything about Mont St. Michel reminded him of what his life had become.

Thanks to the accident at CERN, overnight Europe had been tossed back to the Dark Ages. Without electricity, the citizens of the city were forced to rely on fireplaces to heat their homes and candles to provide light. Things he had taken for granted like smart phones, laptops, and television were relics of the past. He always overheard the adults complaining about how every task had to be done by hand since there no longer were machines to help them. Jacques gave pep talks about how hard work was good for the soul, and other crap like that, although no one believed him. Whenever Jacques was not around, Jason heard the adults mutter about it being easy for Jacques to say these things because he never did any of the work himself. Jason couldn't relate. As a member of the protective force, he was not required to participate in the daily chores, so he felt he didn't have the right to complain about the lack of electricity. Still, he missed surfing the Internet and playing video games.

He would gladly give up for good all those long-gone luxuries if only he wouldn't be treated like an outcast.

Jason made his way down Grand Rue. A group of four men had gathered by the steps to the Parish Church, chatting and laughing. When he approached, one of the men pointed in Jason's direction. They stopped talking and stared. Jason lowered his head and quickened his pace, rushing pass the men and hoping no one would say anything. Only after he had moved on did they resume the conversation, speaking in loud whispers that carried far in the night.

"Is that him?"

"Yup. That's Jason McCreary."

"Poor kid."

"Screw him. We wouldn't be here if it wasn't for his mother."

Jason continued and pretended not to hear. Not that it mattered. Everyone in town felt that way. That was now his lot in life, to be Jason McCreary, the son of the woman who opened the interdimensional portals.

A few minutes later, Jason entered the lobby of *Le Mere Poulard*. The guard at the front desk stopped reading his weathered book, scowled upon seeing him, and went back to reading. Jason climbed the three flights of stairs, followed the candle-lit hall to the far end, and entered his room. Sasha had set the candelabra on his desk so he would have light. Maybe she wasn't mad at him after all.

Lucifer and Lilith were curled up by the open window. Lilith raised her head and, upon seeing her master, lowered it on her paws and went back to sleep. Being more protective, Lucifer raised himself off the rug and came over to check on him. Jason bent down and scratched the werehound behind its ears, receiving a face bath in return. The werehound plodded back to the window and lied down beside its mate.

Jason pulled off his boots and stripped out of his green, military-style flightsuit. Taking the candelabra from the desk, he brought it into the bathroom, peeled back the bandage, and checked himself in the mirror. He grimaced at the sight. The bite covered most of his shoulder. The stitches reminded him of something from a monster movie, and the skin around the sutures had already begun to turn black and blue. He had been banged up enough to know that it would hurt in the morning despite the drugs.

There were a lot of scars on his body from previous battles. Three scratches stretched across his chest from where a flesh eater had clawed it three months ago. A two-inch wide burn marred his left forearm below the elbow where he received splash back from a soul vampire's acid vomit. Of course, there was the embarrassing one—a gouge taken out of his right shoulder where he had accidentally raked an arrowhead across his skin while first learning how to use a crossbow. Jason hoped they made him appear tougher. God knows he needed all the help he could get. Despite eight months of conflict, the image that stared back at him still was that of a teenager, with a soft and child-like face and gentle green eyes. Worst of all, that scraggily blonde hair with several strands hanging loose. Even covered with the grime of battle, he still appeared younger than his age.

Pouring water from the porcelain pitcher into the accompanying bowl, Jason splashed handfuls across his face and chest, using his palms to wash away the dirt and sweat, and being careful not to get the stitches wet. He finished by scraping his hands clean in the brown-tinged water. Pulling a towel off the rack, he dabbed it across his body and stepped back into the bedroom. Moving to the open window, or least as close as he could get to it because of Lucifer and Lilith hogging the floor, he gazed out. The abbey's southern façade dominated the view. From his room, he could see the soft glow of lamps lighting the abbot's lodging where Jacque maintained his quarters. Jason didn't have a watch, so he assumed that the midnight meeting must be underway.

He closed his eyes and mentally reached out to Sasha, figuring as the leader of one of the gun teams she would probably be in attendance. He could pick up only the barest hint of her aura. Sasha seemed concerned about something, although he could not determine what caused the emotion. He assumed Jacques was briefing them on some half-assed suicide mission that would put them all in harm's way, with Jason on point. If that happened, he would find out soon enough.

Jason crawled into bed and threw the covers over him. Nestling into his pillow, he closed his eyes and drifted off due to a combination of exhaustion and drugs. With luck, he'd get a good night sleep and not relive the nightmare that had changed his life forever.

CHAPTER FIVE

J ASON BLINKED AGAINST the flashing of cameras and the glare of klieg lights. He lowered his head and stared at the floor of the make-shift stage set up in the dining hall. The metal chair was uncomfortable. He tolerated it, knowing his mother would be upset if he fidgeted and ruined her big day. She stood before him at the podium, wearing a black skirt and cream-colored blouse, with a white lab coat covering her clothes. Long red hair cascaded down her back and draped over her shoulders. Doc sat in the folding chair beside him. Several other scientists occupied the remaining seats, although he had never bothered to learn their names. In front of the stage, more than thirty reporters and cameramen crowded around, hanging on his mother's every word, anxious to talk with Dr. Lisa McCreary, the lead physicist for Project Discovery.

His mother smiled for the cameras. "Project Discovery is the most ambitious undertaking yet in the field of anti-matter research. The intention is to generate more anti-matter at one time than has been attempted previously. At the same time as we here at CERN will be generating our own continuous stream of anti-matter particles, our sister facilities in Russia, China, Japan, and the United States will do the same. We hope to exponentially increase our knowledge of anti-matter and, once the separate facilities combine our research, develop a better understanding of the physics involved in the creation of our universe. There are so many vistas of particle physics not yet explored that we—"

Jason tuned out his mother and let his mind wander to

things he would rather be doing, which included almost anything. He had no idea what she was talking about. She always used scientific terms that were way over his head. Even at home, during what little quality time they spent together, she discussed her work. Rarely did they ever talk about him, and then it was mostly about his grades or how he was doing in school. She never asked him about his friends or his social life, neither of which he had. This was the first thing the two of them had done as mother and son in years, and even now he served as window dressing for his mother's moment in the spotlight.

Doc leaned over and nudged Jason with his left elbow. "How are you doing?"

"Okay, I guess."

"I know this is boring. It's even boring for me. Try not to yawn or you'll get me going." Doc gave him a conspiratorial wink.

Jason liked Doc. He paid attention to him at his level. Doc would often drop by the house on nights his mother worked late, which was usually every night, to chat with him about girls and movies. Once he even played *World of Warcraft* with him. Doc was really good at solving the puzzles in the game, although he sucked at boss fights.

Lisa stepped away from the podium and motioned to Doc. "Let me give up the floor to Dr. Eric Fisher. He's the true mastermind behind the technical aspects of this project and can do a better job of answering your questions than I can."

Doc stood up and patted Jason on his shoulder. "I'm on."

Jason considered Doc the closest person he had to a father since his parents divorced when he was ten. Although neither his mother nor his father discussed the details with him, from the pieces of arguments he overheard from his bedroom he thought they split up because his mother had spent as little time with his dad as she did with him. Even after the separation, Jason and his dad had been close and did things every other weekend until two years ago when his father moved to Tokyo to head up the Japanese portion of Project Discovery. Since then, they only talked via text messages and the occasional Skype call. Although Jason never admitted it to anyone, that hurt him as much as his parents' divorce. He could never shake the feeling that everyone who mattered in his life found their jobs more important than being with him.

A bustle of activity around the stage snapped Jason back to the present. The news conference had ended, and the reporters headed off to the viewing area to watch the experiment via closed circuit camera. Lisa turned to those behind her on the stage, her face beaming with pride.

"All right, everyone. Are we ready?"

The scientists followed her to the control room attached to CERN's Antiproton Decelerator Facility, an off shoot of the primary accelerator loop where the anti-matter would be created. The decelerator would slow down the particles enough so they could be captured and stored in an electro-magnetic containment chamber situated in the adjacent room. A thick glass partition built into a heavy steel wall separated the two areas. Jason maneuvered around the horde of scientists and officials to get a glimpse inside. The glass-enclosed containment chamber sat on a platform in the center of the decelerator room. It measured three feet in circumference, with a series of giant electro-magnets encircling it. This is where the anti-matter would be captured. Jason shrugged. It seemed like an awful lot of time and effort to produce something so small.

As she always did, Jason's mother took charge and began ordering everyone to their tasks. When the others were in place, she switched on the intercom so they could all hear the conversation between the control room and the other facilities.

"United States, are you ready?" asked Lisa.

"Ready when you are." The voice spoke with a New England accent, the "are" sounding like "ah."

"Russia?"

A thick Russian accent came over the speaker. "We're ready."

"Japan."

"All set to go, Lisa," answered his father.

"And China?"

"We're ready."

"Then let's make history."

Jason pushed closer to the corner of the glass, ignoring the commotion around him and focusing instead on the containment chamber. A white mist like cigarette smoke swirled into the chamber and then vanished as the massive vacuum pump beneath sucked out all gases, leaving the interior void. A few seconds later, a spark lit up the interior as the first particle of anti-matter collided with one of the remaining matter particles. Jason blinked. When he opened his eyes, a series of sparks flashed throughout the containment chamber as anti-matter destroyed the last of the matter. Then the interior went black, a dark so intense it reminded Jason of the photos he had seen of deep space. Whoops and applause filled the control room.

Doc yelled out. "We achieved anti-matter containment!"

Lisa asked the other facilities, and the same chorus of voices applied in the affirmative. Several of the officials rushed over to shake her hand. For the next several minutes, the celebratory atmosphere continued as an increasing amount of anti-matter filled the containment chamber. Jason was pleased. He could not remember the last time he had seen his mother this happy.

"*Merde.*" A young man sat in front of a computer screen, his eyes wide with fear. Jason knew something had gone terribly wrong. "Dr. McCreary, we have a problem."

The congratulatory spirit evaporated. Lisa joined the young man. "What's wrong?"

"The magnetic containment field is destabilizing."

"Are we about to lose it?" Lisa leaned forward and began punching code into the keyboard.

"No. I think the field will hold if I can increase the cooling to the primary mag—"

Before anyone could react, the containment chamber erupted. The blast slammed into the glass partition and knocked Jason off his feet. He landed on his back and slid several feet across the floor. Though winded, he didn't feel like he had been hurt, which surprised him considering the pane had fractured into a spider web of cracks that scoured its surface. Jason rolled onto his knees, his ears still ringing from the concussion. Most of the others had also been knocked down. Lisa and the other scientists climbed back to their stations and worked at the control panels, each occasionally casting a frantic glance toward the decelerator. The officials got to their feet more slowly. Some moved to the rear wall of the control room while others ran for the exit. Jason crawled over to the control console and, using the edge for support, pulled himself to his feet. Finding a place where the partition had not been fractured, he peered through the glass.

The decelerator room was in shambles. The breach had destroyed the containment chamber and blasted the monitoring equipment into the far corners, leaving it in smoldering piles of twisted metal. Fortunately for everyone in the control room, the heavy partition wall had deflected the explosion and vented it against the weaker structures inside the room. The left wall had been breached, a huge gash nearly thirty feet long having been gouged out of the metal surface. A large hole twenty feet across had been cratered in the cement floor beneath the containment chamber, and above it a large portion of the ceiling had been blown away. Jason barely noticed that damage, his attention focused on the cause of the destruction. A swirling vortex with a two-foot wide hole in the center filled the space where the containment chamber had once stood. Black smoke poured from the opening and formed an ominous cloud around the circumference. The hole glimmered like a mirage. Jason gazed through it, expecting to see the opposite side of the decelerator room. Instead he stared at a dark, barren landscape. The only light came from rivers of lava that cast an eerie glow onto a blood-red sky. In the background, strange figures lumbered through the shadows, approaching the opening. The vortex pulsed every few seconds, and with each pulse it increased a few inches in diameter.

"Mom, you might want to see this."

"Not now, Jason."

"But the hole is getting larger."

"I'm busy at the—" Lisa stopped in mid-sentence when she saw the vortex. "What are the radiation levels in there?"

"There's no way of knowing, Dr. McCreary. All the instruments were destroyed in the blast."

"I'm going to check it out. Nancy, Andre. You're with me."

"You can't risk it," said Doc.

Lisa ignored Doc. As she passed by, Jason grabbed his mother's arm and held her back. "Don't go in there," he pleaded.

"I'll be fine. I have to get a closer look." Placing her hands around his wrists, she tightened the grip until he released her arm. Her hands slid into his palms and squeezed gently. His mother's touch felt reassuring but did little to quell his fear that he might lose her.

"Please," he cried.

"I'll be right back." The tenderness in her voice was offset by the stern look in her eyes. Lisa let go of Jason's hands and walked over to the decelerator room.

The partition door had been warped by the blast, and it took the three scientists several attempts to open it. When they did, their lab coats and hair blew in the wind as a steady undercurrent of air flowed into the decelerator room. Jason heard a low rumble that sounded like an approaching thunderstorm. The scientists stepped inside and cautiously approached the vortex.

"What do you see?" Doc asked from the doorway.

His mother's voice trembled. Her eyes darted around the

decelerator room, wide with fear and uncertainty. Jason had never seen his mother like this before. "It's a portal of some type."

"A portal? To where?"

"I don't know. I've never seen any place like this before."

The vortex emitted a heavy pulse and expanded, doubling to almost six feet in diameter and accompanied by an increase in the tempo of the rumbling. The wind grew in intensity, sucking the three scientists toward the portal. Nancy and Andre were yanked off their feet and flung through, their screams cut off when they passed through the vortex. The two scientists were tossed nearly fifty feet into the other world. Neither got back up. The wind dragged Lisa toward the same fate. She reached out at the last second and grabbed a twisted piece of the console still welded to the floor.

The vacuum sucked air out of the control room, generating a whirlwind of papers that flowed into the decelerator room and through the portal. Doc threw himself against the wall inside the control room. He pulled against the force of the wind toward a fire hose anchored on the opposite wall, unwound the hose, and wrapped one end several times around his right arm. As Doc inched his way toward the partition door, he yelled above the roar of the vortex. "I'm going to save Lisa. Drs. Kim and Bernard, stay here and pull me back. The rest of you, get out now."

"Let me help," said Jason as he rushed toward Doc.

Doc grabbed Jason by the shoulders. "You stay here."

"She's my mother."

"I don't have time to argue." Doc pushed Jason back against the partition wall. "Promise me you won't move from this spot."

"I promise." Jason stayed put, watching the rescue attempt through the fractured glass.

Doc stepped into the doorway and was dragged across the decelerator room by the roaring wind. Jason thought he would be sucked into the portal. At the last minute the hose grew taut, jerking Doc to a stop a few feet from the opening. He maneuvered over to Lisa, held out his left hand, and clasped it around her wrist. She hesitated, too scared to react, then released her grip on the console and wrapped her hands around Doc's arm.

Another massive surge occurred, and the vortex's size increased again, along with a similar increase in the flow of the wind, which yanked the hose out of Kim's and Bernard's hands. Jason gasped as he watched the airflow suck his mother toward the portal. Doc still held on but was pulled along behind her. His scream of "No!" could be heard even over the roar. A second later, the hose grew taut again as it reached its full length. His mother was on the opposite side of the vortex, her legs dangling in the air as the wind tried to yank her away. She still held onto Doc's arm, which extended through the vortex up to his above his elbow, the rest of him still on their side.

Doc yelled, "Pull me back!"

Bracing his feet against the wall, Kim pulled on the hose. It wouldn't move. Bernard joined him. They two pulled with all their might. Finally, the hose moved back a foot.

In the decelerator room, Doc screamed. As his arm emerged from the portal, the exposed skin blackened and exploded into a cloud of ash, severing it above the elbow. With nothing left to anchor Lisa in this world, she was sucked into the other realm, still clutching the other end of Doc's severed arm. She landed alongside Nancy and Andre.

Jason rushed to the door. Kim noticed him at the last second. Dropping his end of the hose, Kim wrapped his arms around Jason.

"You can't go in there. You'll be sucked in, too."

"I have to save my mother."

"It's too late for that."

As Jason struggled to break free, the wind died out. The swirling papers floated to the ground and the hose went slack.

Doc dropped to the floor, crying and writhing around in pain. An eerie calm settled over the facility. Bernard took advantage of the lull to race into the containment room and help Doc to his feet. Despite Doc's arm being severed, it didn't bleed. In fact, the end appeared cauterized.

"Jason!" The voice belonged to his mother, although it sounded muffled and far away. He turned to the portal. He could see her on the other side. She had helped Nancy to her feet and, as the young woman stumbled toward the portal, bent over to assist Andre. After a second, his mother lowered her head, patted Andre on the shoulder, and set off after her colleague.

Jason moved toward the portal. "Hurry up!"

"Send them back," huffed Doc as he leaned against the doorway.

"What are you talking about?"

"They'll never make it through."

"Of course they will. The wind has died down."

"No." Doc held up the remains of his left arm. "They won't."

Realizing the danger his mother and the other scientist faced, Jason stood in front of the portal, waving his hands and yelling for them to stay back. Neither woman listened. Nancy reached the portal first and jumped through. She never made it. Her body crumbled as it passed through into their side, becoming an ashen silhouette that fell to the cement and erupted into a cloud of dust, showering Jason in ash. On the other side, Jason's mother stopped short of the vortex. Her gaze scanned the circumference as if trying to find a way to cross back. Jason knew there was no way for her to do so and survive.

An inhuman moan sounded from behind her. Their eyes both focused on the silhouettes that had been in the background, only now much closer and more threatening. When his mother turned back to him, a single tear streamed down her cheek.

"Jason, get out of here while you can."

"I'm not leaving you."

Her voice became calm and soothing. "There's nothing you can do for me now. I'll be fine. I promise to find a way out of here. I need to make sure you get to safety. I love you."

Without waiting for his response, she ran out of his line of sight, away from the approaching figures. Jason went after her. If he couldn't get his mother out through the portal, the least he could do is join her in the other realm and protect her. A hand clutched his arm. He spun around to see Kim holding him. "Leave me alone."

"Don't be an ass. You'll only get yourse—"

The wind picked up again, only this time it blew from the portal into the facility. It increased in intensity, pushing the loose papers across the floor of the decelerator room. Jason couldn't hear the gusts because the sound was drowned out by the moaning that came from the dozens of silhouettes on the other side. Jason could finally make them out. They reminded him of walking corpses, naked and emaciated, and with pale leathery skin. They were within a few yards of the portal.

Doc stepped over to Jason, standing between the teenager and the vortex. "We have to get going."

"Wh-what about…?"

"You can't help your mother if you're dead." Doc reached out his remaining hand and placed it on Jason's shoulder. "We'll figure a way to rescue her, but we have to get out of here first."

They darted into the control room. Before Jason exited into the corridor, he stopped, hoping to catch a glimpse of his mother. The portal's façade vibrated, causing a shimmering effect.

"Hey, you should see this. Something weird is happening."

"Come on!" yelled Doc.

Jason had started down the corridor when a massive pulse

exploded from the portal. It shot through the building, knocking over everyone in its path. Jason sat up, dazed and unable to see a thing. He thought maybe he had gone blind in the blast until Bernard flicked on a lighter, allowing them to see. They would need it. Doc and the others got up and ran, with Jason right behind them.

For the first time in his life, he thought he might not live through the next few minutes.

It would not be the last time he felt that way.

CHAPTER SIX

SASHA STOOD ALONG the right side of the conference table with Andre and Haneef on her left and Gruber on the right. On the opposite side, Doc shifted his weight from one foot to the other. Father Chirac glanced over at Doc's fidgeting, the usual displeasure spread across the cleric's puffy face. Jacques had not yet arrived, which didn't surprise Sasha. Keep everyone waiting so he could make a grand entrance and remind the others who was in charge. Even after the world had come to an end, some people still needed to display their status and show off their rank in the social order. Sasha wondered if others noticed that Jacques made the political members of the group stand along one side of the table and the military along the other, as if separating them by caste. The important and the unimportant. Those who gave orders and those who carried them out.

Those who were not expendable and those who were.

Sasha crossed her arms across her chest and huffed, drawing glances from the others, who then averted their gaze. In all honesty, Sasha didn't blame Jacques for categorizing people the way he did. There were only a few at Mont St. Michel who possessed the skills to keep the survivors alive, Doc being one of them. Almost everyone at the sanctuary were college students, salesclerks, lawyers, businessmen, and a whole host of other careers whose occupations, like so many other things, had been swallowed up by the portal. Most ended up doing menial tasks around the city, like tending the stables or growing crops. Those who were capable and foolhardy enough to fight the

Demon Spawn joined the four search and destroy teams Jacques had created to defend the city. Youth, strength, and courage were the only things the military members brought to the table.

She glanced over at the other team leaders. Andre was the overall commander as well as one of the team leads. He stood six-feet-one-inch in height and barely weighed one hundred fifty pounds, giving him a lanky appearance. He cropped his blonde hair into a buzz cut, and he bore a scar on his right cheek from a knife fight in the streets of Moscow. Sasha thought he was in his early twenties, although Andre never said. A Russian Jew from Siberia, he had moved to Moscow at sixteen to make a living. With no education or skills, he soon found himself enmeshed in the organized crime that had taken over the city following the collapse of the Soviet Union. Andre and his best friend, Slava, had run a drug and prostitution ring until they crossed paths with the local crime lord who had ordered their execution. They emigrated to Chartres where they had hoped to re-establish their criminal empire. The opening of the portal had put an end to that plan. Andre's behavior hadn't changed much at Mont St. Michel. He bullied everyone under him, especially Jason. However, he knew how to organize a fighting force and had proven himself fearless in combat, so Jacques had placed him in charge of the search and destroy teams. Behind the Russian's back, Jacques referred to Andre as "a necessary evil."

Haneef, the other team lead, was Andre's polar opposite. He stood five-feet-seven-inches and possessed a quiet, personable demeanor. A devout Muslim from Sudan, he had shunned the Jihadist movement that plagued his country and gone to Paris to study international law. He had been in his third semester of college when the portals opened. Despite everything, Haneef never lost his faith and still prayed to Mecca whenever possible, although he did shave his head and forewent facial hair to show his disdain for Islamic fundamentalism. He had once told Sasha that the portals were Allah's punishment for the extremism that had taken hold of the three main religions—Islam, Christianity, and Judaism—and that he felt himself lucky to be among the righteous who had survived.

Sasha studied Gruber, realizing only then that she didn't know anything about him other than he was a German student from Bonn who had graduated from college and been taking some time off to explore southern France when the world came to an end. His team usually stayed behind to defend Mont St. Michel when the others went out on raids, so he readily volunteered for the reconnaissance mission to Geneva. Less than half his team had returned. She remembered Gruber as being an optimistic and outgoing guy, wondering what had happened to make him so sullen.

Her own story had not been that much different. After graduating from Salem State University with a degree in elementary education, she had decided to join her boyfriend, Norman, on a six-week tour of Europe. The romantic vacation ended prematurely in Florence when Norman dumped her for some Italian whore he had met in a nightclub. Angry and heartbroken, she had decided to fly home, and had been waiting for her connecting flight at Leonardo da Vinci International Airport when the portals opened. Following the flood of panicked refugees away from Rome, she made her way to Mont St. Michel and eventually had become the leader of one of the gun teams.

The door to the private quarters swung open and Jacques entered accompanied by Bishop Fiorello, the religious leader of the city. All eyes focused on the two men. To Sasha, it seemed as though central casting had put out a call for someone to play the lord and bishop of the manor. Jacques appeared older than his sixty-plus years, mostly because of the burdens of trying to keep Mont St. Michel safe. His long, scraggily hair had turned white over the past few months. Wrinkles creased Jacques' face and dark circles shadowed his eyes, and he walked with a slight hunch. However, on seeing his trusted companions, the barest hint of a smile pierced his lips. Bishop Fiorello, on the other hand, bore the perpetual stern visage he always wore around the city, part of his "God is punishing us for our sins" demeanor. It did not help that in a city where the food supply neared starvation levels, his paunch strained against the fabric of his cleric uniform.

"Thank you all for coming at this late hour." Jacques stood at the head of the table, with Bishop Fiorello behind and to his left. "Gruber, we'll start with you. What did you find at Geneva?"

The German stood up straight and took a deep breath. "We made it to CERN without incident. We encountered only a few Demon Spawn, mostly flesh eaters that had wandered down from the north. There were none at the facility, so gaining access was easy."

"How bad was the damage?" asked Jacques.

"It was confined to the control and decelerator rooms. The portal was just as Doc described it. Thirty feet in diameter with a pulsating surface, like water on a pond."

"So, you were right," Jacques said to Doc. "It stopped growing." Doc shrugged. "That's one thing in our favor."

Jacques turned his attention back to Gruber. "If there were no Demon Spawn at the facility, what happened to your team?"

"We didn't see anything moving on the other side of the gate, so Hans, Greta, Francois, Andrea, and Robert crossed over—"

"Damn it!" Doc pounded his fist on the table. "I warned you not to do that."

"They wanted to see if they could locate Dr. McCreary," Gruber yelled back. His anger subsided as quickly as it had flared, and the sullenness resumed. "When they tried to come back, they... they..."

"Disintegrated?" asked Doc.

Gruber nodded. Doc involuntary reached up to massage his missing arm.

"I'm sorry," Doc said softly.

"I am, too. I never should have let them go."

Father Chirac crossed himself. "At least they're with God now."

Or stuck in Hell, thought Sasha.

Jacques ignored the priest and glanced at Doc. "Your theory about the gate being a one-way portal was correct."

Doc nodded. "Sadly, we lost five good people proving it."

"What theory?" Gruber asked.

"It's why I warned you not to send anyone over to the other side. The theory came to me when I saw the technician who had been sucked through try to escape back into the facility, and when I lost my arm. It's a one-way portal. It allows you to cross into the other realm but won't let anything to come out."

Gruber bristled. "You could have been a bit more specific! I wouldn't have allowed my people to cross over if you had warned me that could happen!"

"Enough." Jacques said it in a soft manner, like a father admonishing his children. "Doc feels your loss as much as I do—"

"And me," interrupted Fiorello.

Jacques ignored the bishop. "Thank you, Gruber, for all you've done and for the sacrifice you made. You're excused."

Gruber stared at the three men for a moment, anger flaring in his eyes, and then exited the conference room. Jacques waited until the German had departed and continued his conversation with Doc.

"If you're theory about the Geneva gate being a one-way portal is correct, that leaves only one possible answer as to where the Demon Spawn are coming from."

"I'm afraid so," replied Doc. "There has to be a second gateway allowing these things into our world."

CHAPTER SEVEN

S ASHA LOOKED BETWEEN Doc and Jacques, uncertain if she had heard correctly. "What do you mean by 'a second gateway'?"

"Let me explain." Doc walked over to Jacques' desk and removed a letter opener and a plastic gallon-sized bottle of water. He grabbed a waste basket off the floor and brought the three items back to the conference table. Placing the basket on the surface, he asked Haneef to hold the plastic bottle above it. "My theory is that the other realm is self-contained and separate from our world. Under normal circumstances, there is no connection between the two. Now, think of this bottle as the other realm and the area outside of it as our world."

Using the letter opener, Doc punctured the top of the bottle near the neck and held the letter opener in place. "This is the portal we punched open in Geneva, the entry gate."

Sasha nodded. "Okay."

Doc shoved the letter opener deeper into the bottle until the tip poked through the bottom. When he withdrew it, water flowed from the hole. "Our anti-matter experiment also punched an exit portal from somewhere into our world. That's where the Demon Spawn are coming from."

"It makes sense," said Jacques.

"Where is the exit portal?" asked Sasha.

"I can't be certain," Doc answered as Haneef put the leaking bottle of water into the waste basket and placed them both on the floor. "Normal geometrical equations are useless in a situation like this."

"In English, Doc," said Andre.

"There's no scientific way to determine it. My best approximation is somewhere in Paris."

"Why Paris?" asked Sasha.

"Based on the eyewitness accounts of the few survivors who were in Paris at the time, and based on the migration pattern of the Demon Spawn that we've tracked over the past several months, I'm speculating that the exit portal is located somewhere in the downtown area. I don't know exactly where, and anyone who saw the portal open probably didn't make it out alive."

"It doesn't matter," said Jacques. "It should be easy enough to find."

"What are you going to do once you find it?" asked Haneef.

"Close it."

A moment of awkward silence passed before Sasha asked, "How?"

"With the bomb Doc has made."

All three team leads stared at Doc.

"It's not actually a bomb," he explained. "The device contains anti-matter. When it hits the portal it will disintegrate, releasing the anti-matter inside. Once the anti-matter inside the device connects with the anti-matter portal, they should cancel each other out and blast the portal shut."

"And you *know* this will work?" asked Andre.

"No." Doc shifted his stance from one foot to the other. "However, the theory is sound. If I can introduce the device into the portal, I'm confident I can close it."

"Besides," added Jacques. "What other choice do we have?"

"We sit tight." Andre pointed to the windows. "Our defenses here are good, and we can safely ride out anything the Demon Spawn throw at us. If you send my teams into Paris, it'll be a miracle if any of us come back, let alone succeed. Don't get me wrong. I'm not a coward, but I didn't sign up to die needlessly. What's the worst that could happen if we do nothing?"

"This." Doc reached into the basket and withdrew the plastic bottle. It was empty. "Theoretically, every Demon Spawn in the other realm could cross over to our side, and then how long do you think we'll survive? Our only chance of rebuilding society is to close that gate and stop the flow of demons into our world. Then we can take care of the Demon Spawn that are already here and maybe take back this world."

Andre made eye contact with Sasha and Haneef. She knew what he wanted to ask. They all wanted to ask the same question yet were afraid of the answer. Finally, the Russian summoned up the courage. "I doubt you're going to send Doc off alone into Paris to close the portal."

Jacques forced a smile. "Your three teams will accompany him."

"You're not seriously considering sending *all* of us to Paris to find that damn gate?" asked Andre.

"Of course," replied Jacques.

Andre grew frustrated. "You realize this is a suicide mission?"

"My son," said Bishop Fiorello. "You must have faith that the Lord will provide for your safety."

"Perhaps you'd like to come with us, Bishop?" Andre snarled, his Russian accent becoming heavy. "We'd have a much better chance of survival if we had a direct link to God through His Holiness."

Fiorello stepped away from the table. The two men glared at each other, one out of contempt, and the other out of fear.

Sasha felt that a cooler head needed to prevail. "Jacques, I understand your desire to make sure we close the portal. Sending all three teams to Paris is risky. If we don't make it back, Mont St. Michel will be left defenseless."

"I know that, my child. And I will do everything I can to ensure your success."

"There has to be another way," added Haneef.

"I wish there was. We have no other choice." Jacques stepped over to the bay windows that faced south and motioned for the others to join him. Everyone except Bishop Fiorello complied. Off in the distance, along the shoreline, sat the refugee camp. Sasha had never seen it from the city's heights before. The camp covered more than fifty acres. Fires dotted the landscape, more than she could count. Jacques kept his attention focused on the coast as he spoke.

"We cannot protect those people. We're barely able to keep them alive. It's only a matter of time before the Demon Spawn make their way this far west. Then what? We can't take them in, and we can't hold off the Demon Spawn indefinitely. Your three teams will die anyway. If we ever hope to survive and get back to a normal way of life, we most close that portal. Would you rather die saving the world or getting slaughtered in a hopeless last stand?"

"I'd rather die on my feet then live on my knees," responded Andre with his usual bravado.

"It's Allah's will," answered Haneef with less enthusiasm.

I'd rather not die at all, thought Sasha. However, she replied, "I'll go."

"Then it's settled." Jacques stepped away from the window and faced his team leads. "Rest up tonight. You'll prepare tomorrow and leave at dawn the following morning."

"One request," Sasha interjected. "Jason is too young for a mission like this. I'd like to request that we leave him behind."

Andre huffed. "You want to protect your boy toy?"

"That's not it." Sasha realized she responded too quickly and forcefully. Her face flushed with anger. She tried to keep her reply calm. "He's only sixteen. There's no need for him to die like this. He'll be of much better use staying behind and helping establish the new teams to replace us."

Jacques deferred to Andre. "How about it?"

Andre shook his head. "I need him."

"You want to use him to lure out the Demon Spawn," Sasha spat.

"He's a good fighter. And he has some weird sense about these things. He knows when they're around before we even see them."

"That's true," added Doc. "The opening of the portal disturbed the balance between the two worlds. The same pulse that wiped out our electrical systems also enhanced the paranormal attributes of those predisposed to them."

"You mean Bait is psychic?" asked Andre.

"He's prone to psychic ability."

The Russian nodded. "All the more reason he needs to go along. I can't count how many times Bait's saved our lives by warning us about danger."

Sasha was taken aback by Andre's answer. "Then why do you always ride him so hard?"

"Because he's still a kid." Andre held up his hand, cutting off Sasha. "I used to be like him. Young and naïve. I had to toughen up otherwise the streets of Moscow would have eaten me alive. I bully him for his own good. He'll either learn to be a man or he'll die as a boy. In any case, he's going with us."

"It's settled." Jacques words ended further argument. "Go prepare your teams. Take whatever supplies you need. And may God be with you."

I doubt even God will be able to help us once we reach Paris, thought Sasha.

CHAPTER EIGHT

J ASON USED HIS fork to push the scrambled eggs around his plate and flip over the strips of bacon. Every few minutes he would use it to shovel some into his mouth. He wasn't hungry yet ate in spite of that. With rations scarce, and only the military teams and the top leadership being fed such luxuries as bacon and eggs, Jason didn't want to waste food. Despite his not having eaten in over twenty-four hours, he had no appetite and merely went through the motions.

"How's your shoulder?" Neal walked up from behind with his own plate.

"It's okay right now. I took four Motrin a little while ago."

"Be careful with that stuff." Neal sat down opposite Jason. "If you misuse it, you could ruin your kidneys."

"I doubt I'll live long enough for that to happen."

Neal focused on his plate, embarrassed by Jason's pessimism. An awkward moment passed before he looked up. "Things were pretty rough yesterday in St. Mere Eglise?"

"Yeah."

"What was it like?"

"I don't like to talk about it."

"Come on. Give me details."

"Why are you so curious?"

Neal leaned forward and lowered his voice. "I'm stuck in this place. I haven't been off this damn island since I got here. The most exciting thing I've done is fight an outbreak of diarrhea within the refugee camp."

Jason sighed. "I don't know."

"Come on," Neal begged. "I live vicariously through you."

Unlike Andre and Slava, Jason hated talking about his experiences. He didn't see his actions as heroic, but as a penitence. However, Neal was his friend, so he indulged him. Besides, it gave him a good excuse not to eat. Halfway through relating the story, Andre approached. Jason knew nothing good would come out of it.

The Russian stepped up to their table and leaned forward, resting his knuckles on the wooden surface. "Bait, when you're done, I need you to go to the stables and check on the preparation of the horses."

"Sure. Are we going on another search and destroy run?"

"More like a suicide run." Andre's demeanor did not express his usual enthusiasm for a fight. "Long story short, Gruber's team discovered that the portal in Geneva is only an entry gate. Jacques thinks the exit gate is somewhere in Paris. Doc has a device that he claims can close it and stop the Demon Spawn from entering. We're supposed to make sure Doc gets a chance to play the hero."

"Who's 'we'?"

"All three gun teams." Andre glanced over at Neal. "You're going, too."

"Why me?" Neal blurted out.

"Doc says you're the only other person who knows how to use the device, so you're his back up." Andre smiled the familiar sneer he used when bullying people. "Scared?"

"Damn right. I'm not a ground pounder like you guys. I don't even know how to use a gun."

Andre laughed and patted Neal on the shoulder. "My team will protect you, Little Doc."

Neal lowered his head. "You know I hate it when you call me that."

Andre turned his attention back to Jason. "Your girlfriend tried to have you left behind until Jacques overrode her. You've got to nut up a bit if you want to see if she's a natural redhead."

Jason ignored the rude comment, more incensed by Sasha's attempt to have him excluded. "What did she say?"

"Looks like I touched a nerve." Andre chuckled. "She said you weren't tough enough for this mission. Don't worry. I stood up for you, so you're going. Now your girlfriend will have her boy toy along for the ride."

"She's not my girlfriend," Jason said defensively. *Though I wish she was.*

"You'll have plenty of chances to prove yourself. Make sure the horses each carry a seven-day supply of food yet aren't weighted down too heavy. It's a long way to Paris. We're moving out at six tomorrow morning. See you ladies then."

Andre marched off. Neal waited until the Russian was out of earshot before mumbling, "I can't stand that asshole."

Jason agreed, although he said nothing. Right now, he was more concerned about why Sasha didn't want him along.

AFTER CHECKING ON the horses as Andre had asked, Jason made his way to the armory, which had been set up in the parish church of St. Peter. As he climbed the front steps to the main door, he could hear the metallic clicking of ammunition being loaded into magazines and weapon bolts being checked. He paused for a moment to collect his thoughts.

All morning he had played over in his head what he would say to Sasha, rehearsing his lines and preparing a response for every possible come back. In every scenario he dominated the conversation, proving to Sasha just how much of a man he was and winning over her affections. He needed to get this perfect. Her comment had wounded his feelings as well as his pride. Of course, this was assuming that Andre had told him the truth and wasn't screwing with him. Even so, the very thought that Sasha considered him not tough enough bothered him. He had been on as many search and destroy missions as her, and had faced as many Demon Spawn, except he usually did it alone with only a crossbow and a machete. Unlike her, he didn't have a minigun to protect him. That type of bravery should count for something. What bothered Jason most was the thought that Sasha didn't want him along. Although too shy to ask her out, he still considered Sasha his girlfriend. Sure, a seven-year age difference existed between them. However, such niceties had been sucked into the interdimensional portal along with the rest of civilization. Jason hoped she felt something for him. She always treated him nicer than she did any of the other guys, and her eyes lit up when she saw him. Her smile was the only thing that made this miserable existence bearable. That was why trying to have him scrubbed from the mission hurt so much. Sasha should be supportive like a girlfriend. Instead, she made his decision for him, just like his mother would.

Taking a deep breath to calm his anger, Jason pushed aside the door and stepped inside.

Most of the gun team members sat around workbenches either cleaning their weapons or preparing spare magazines of ammunition. The weapons the search and destroy teams used were 5.56mm FAMAS F1 automatic weapons liberated from an overrun military camp they had stumbled across near Caen a few months ago. Firearms reserved for local defense included a collection of rifles and semi-automatic weapons carried by those who had migrated to the city, and which Jacques had confiscated. Side arms consisted of pistols of various makes and calibers. A huge selection of melee weapons hung from one wall of the church and included almost every type of instrument that could be useful in hand-to-hand combat: hunting knives, bayonets, crowbars, clubs, axes. Most team members, however, preferred machetes. The area behind the nave contained larger items raided from museums all over the area, everything from pikes and glaves to maces and morning stars, although these were reserved to defend Mont St. Michel in case any Demon Spawn breached the city's walls.

The mainstay of the teams' arsenal consisted of the two miniguns, which they had confiscated from abandoned vehicles inside the Caen military encampment. The chief gunsmith had taken great care in adapting them for personal use. He had developed back packs that carried close to ten thousand rounds of 7.62 mm ammunition in one continuous belt, enough for nearly two minutes of constant firing. The miniguns were easily reloadable, so each team assigned two members to carry spares packs. Even using lightweight material where possible, each backpack weighed over thirty pounds. Sasha and Haneef had the added burden of carrying the miniguns, which weighed thirty-five pounds each. Jason had no idea how they lugged around so much gear. Sasha had let him try on her minigun once, and he could barely stand let only move.

Sasha stood at one of the workbenches, feeding a belt of ammunition into one of the backpacks. The sight of her made his heart skip, and for a second he almost forgot his anger. Jason took another deep breath and approached from the opposite side of the workbench.

She saw him and beamed. "Are you here to pick up a firearm?"

"I'm fine with my crossbow, thanks. I wanted to talk to you about last night."

The smile melted from Sasha's face. "That little shit Andre told you what I said at the briefing?"

Jason nodded. "It bothers me that you don't think I'm tough enough to go to Paris with the rest of you."

"That's not what I said." Sasha leaned forward so the others could not hear the conversation. Auburn hair fell across her face. "I said you were too young."

Of all the answers Jason had planned for, he had not expected this one. He stumbled for the right words, and instead let his emotions get in the way. "That's supposed to make me feel better?"

"It's nothing personal. You're a good fighter. But most of us

53

probably won't be coming back from this one. If we don't, somebody who knows what they're doing has to stay behind and train the next generation of fighters."

"Bullshit!" Everyone turned to Jason at his outburst, and then nervously looked away and pretended nothing had happened.

Sasha stiffened yet tried to remain calm. "Jason, please don't do this."

"Don't do what? Stand up for myself?"

Sasha lowered her head, breaking eye contact.

"You think I'm only a kid."

"That's not it."

"You're treating me like I'm your little brother."

"I'm trying to protect you."

"My mother always tried to protect me. A lot of good that did." Jason's venomous response surprised himself.

He paused, waiting for a reply. Finally, Sasha mumbled, "I didn't mean to hurt you."

"You know I have to go with the rest of you."

"Why?" snapped Sasha.

"I bear responsibility for opening this portal. I should be the one who closes it."

Sasha folded her arms across her chest. "You need to stop taking the guilt of the world on your shoulders. You are *not* responsible for opening the portal. Your mother is."

The comment about his mother struck Jason hard. He felt his face flush with anger. He wanted to lash out, to say something cruel that would hurt Sasha as much as she had hurt him. The words never came. All he could think to say was, "You're supposed to be my friend."

Sasha lowered her arms and bowed her head. "I am. Only a real friend would tell you the truth."

Jason stared at her for several seconds, hoping for an apology. None came. He noticed that the others were glancing up from their work to see how he would react. Only then did he realize that Sasha had made a fool of him in front of everybody. The one person he felt affection for, the one person that gave him a reason to get out of bed in the morning, the one person who had made him feel like a man rather than a teenager, had just emasculated him in front of others. He had come here to set things straight and now felt worse than before as well as humiliated. Mustering what dignity he had left, Jason spun around and stomped away. As he stormed out, he said, "I thought you liked me."

Hurrying down the church steps, he headed back for the hotel, holding back his tears.

SASHA WATCHED JASON barge out of the church and disappear into the courtyard. She wanted to run after him and apologize. As a team leader, it would not have been appropriate. It would have shown weakness on her part, and she couldn't afford that, especially with what lay ahead of them. She had only wanted to protect Jason and instead had upset him.

The confrontation also pained her. Though she never would admit it to anyone, his last words had struck home.

You have it all wrong, you jerk, she thought. *I love you.*

CHAPTER NINE

T HE SEARCH AND destroy teams gathered outside of King's
Gate, jammed in between the front façade of the hotel and
the city's perimeter wall. The horses snorted and shook their
heads. Every few seconds, one of the animals would shift its
weight from one set of hoofs to the other, bumping into the
horse crammed in beside it. They were anxious to break free of
the confined area and get out into open country. Even Lucifer
and Lilith, who crouched underneath Jason's horse, seemed
eager to get moving. Jason didn't share their enthusiasm. For
all his bluster that afternoon to Sasha about needing to go with
them to Paris, at this moment he would be quite content to stay
here. He knew that once the group left Mont St. Michel, most
of them would never make it back.

Positive way to start a mission, he chastised himself. Jason tried
to push that thought from his mind, although the prospect of
death weighed heavily on him. Not that they hadn't placed
themselves in harm's way before. For the three search and
destroy teams, it had become a weekly occurrence. Yet those
were calculated risks, carefully prepared missions undertaken in
terrain they were familiar with that probed the countryside
looking for and eliminating Demon Spawn. This trip to Paris
was insanity. Jacques was sending them into the heart of a
major city, more than likely overrun with Demon Spawn, to
close the portal despite not knowing its location or whether
Doc's device would work. A shiver ran down Jason's spine at
the prospect of what they would face. Drawing in a deep
breath, Jason held it until he tamped down his fear. He had to

make sure this mission succeeded no matter what the cost. He had to close the portal to rectify his mother's mistake and to clear her name as well as the family name. That's what a dutiful son would do. That's what a man would do.

A gust of wind blew several strands of blonde hair across his face. Jason pushed them back behind his ears. He examined each of his teammates, wondering who would survive the next few days.

In addition to himself and Slava, Andre's team consisted of some of the toughest men in the city. David had been a security guard at CERN who had escaped with Jason and Doc and stayed with them all the way to Mont St. Michel, protecting them until they made it to safety. David had maneuvered his horse to be beside Jason as he had done on every previous mission. On the other side was Antoine, from Morocco. He towered over Jason, standing at six-foot-four and weighing in at close to two hundred and fifty pounds. Though quiet and unassuming, in combat Antoine was a fierce and violent fighter. Only Sook-kyoung, the exchange student from the University of Seoul, seemed out of place. Tall, slender, attractive, and quiet, no one had assessed her as much of a fighter. However, her black belt in Taekwondo made her as tough as the others. Usually Sook-kyoung let her brunette hair hang loosely around her shoulders, only tying it in a ponytail when she expected to go into combat. He noticed that this morning it hung in a single tight strand down her back. Doc and Neal rounded out their team, the former carrying a large saddle bag containing the device.

Haneef's team stood next in line. Franco sat off to Haneef's right. After Doc, Franco held the distinction as the oldest member of the group at thirty. He had olive-colored skin, dark hair, and a weathered visage. Because Franco had once been a sergeant in the Spanish army, making him the most skilled soldier at Mont St. Michel, Jacques had asked him to train the four search and destroy teams in combat tactics, which he did with all the sadism of a Hollywood drill instructor, and with a vocabulary that would have made the sergeant from *Full Metal Jacket* cringe. Although no one liked Franco, they all knew that they were alive today thanks to him, and thus he had earned their begrudging respect. Ray came from Texas. Short and muscular, he talked with a thick southern accent. Jacques had included him in the team because of his military training. Ray and Franco each carried one of Haneef's spare ammunition backpacks. Petra had been an Italian flight attendant who fit the part, a tall woman with short blonde hair pinned back with bobby pins. She was willing to defend the city, and as a flight attendant had been trained to calmly respond to crises, earning her a spot on the team. Renato had been touring western France and had been unable to make it back to his hometown of Florence, eventually making his way to Mont St. Michel. Short and stout, he didn't know any English, which didn't matter since Haneef considered him one of his toughest fighters. Philippe rounded out the group. Only a few months older than Jason, Philippe was a native of Mont St. Michel and had volunteered to defend his city. Jacques agreed because he thought it appeared appropriate.

Sasha's team brought up the rear. Three American college students who called themselves the Gainesville Mafia, because they all came from the University of Florida, dominated the team: Shane, the older of the trio, a mid-Westerner of average height and build; Bill, an amateur boxer from Key West with a muscular body and close-cropped black hair; and Josh, a stocky Georgian five-foot-six in height and with a boisterous personality that more than compensated for his short stature. Shane and Josh carried Sasha's extra ammunition backpacks. Bald and lanky, Reinhard was the opposite of the three Americans. The German never smiled and rarely spoke and, when he did, he used short, curt sentences. Christophe rounded out their team. He had been an Austrian student, tall and thin, with wavy blonde hair and a pair of glasses that constantly slid down his nose. Sasha rode at the end of the group. She looked like one of those warrior princesses in the comic books that he used to fantasize about. She wore the same green flightsuit they all did, although Sasha filled it out much better than even Petra and Sook-kyoung. The minigun rested in a special mount strapped to her right leg. Her auburn hair fell down her shoulders and across her chest.

When Sasha saw Jason staring at her, she smiled. His body tensed. Damn it, Sasha didn't have the right to be angry at him on a whim and expect him to be okay with it, and then expect to be forgiven so easily, especially after the way she had insulted him in front of everyone. Jason had good reason to be mad at Sasha and was not ready to forgive her yet. He turned away.

The head guard for the outer wall defenses walked up to Andre. "Are you ready?"

"Let's do it."

The guard strolled to the opening that led to the bay. He grabbed a pole-mounted lantern, stood at the end of the walkway, and waved it back and forth. Jason pictured his counterpart on the opposite coast responding in kind. After a few seconds, the guard placed the lantern against the wall and motioned them on. Andre spurred his horse forward. One by one, the others fell in line. As each one passed, the guards on duty gave them thumbs up or wished them luck. The head guard shouted, "May God be with you."

The group left Mont St. Michel and crossed the bay in single file, with twenty feet between each horse. Everyone remained on edge, half expecting to see a swarm of soul vampires or other Demon Spawn charging at them from out of the darkness. Lucifer and Lilith stayed on either side of Jason, their attention focused on the bay. Soon they made landfall and navigated up the remains of the destroyed causeway, the horses moving more assuredly once on dry land.

A throng of refugees had gathered along the side of the

road to see them off, though no one showed enthusiasm. Maybe they realized that the city's sole defenders were going off on a suicide mission. If they had any idea what the teams were about to face, none of them showed it. They all stared at the group with the same hollow, blank expression that had become normal. Only a little girl about six years old with curly blonde hair and a tattered dress offered any type of emotion, waving to the teams as they passed. Jason waved back. He wondered what type of world they'd be leaving her once they completed this mission.

Andre followed the road to the left and headed away from the camp. The others followed. Jason looked back at Mont St. Michel before he entered the tree line, knowing he might never see that monstrosity of a city again.

Off to the east, the first rays of dawn tinted the clouds a beautiful shade of reddish-orange.

BOOK TWO

CHAPTER TEN

N O ONE SPOKE for the first few hours of the journey, which suited Jason. He enjoyed the serenity, which allowed him to be alone with his thoughts. The morning was pleasant, with a warm sun complementing a cool breeze blowing in from the English Channel. The clopping of the horses' hoofs on asphalt competed with the chirping from flocks of birds that nestled among the trees. As they approached the village of Montitier, the horses startled a family of deer grazing by the roadside. Each one bolted and made a mad dash across the field, eventually disappearing into the high grass. Jason grinned. With humans having been almost completely wiped out, wildlife now began to flourish and repopulate the countryside.

Of course, that would all change when the Demon Spawn finally made their way into this area.

The route that took them into central France was all too familiar. Andre had designed it to avoid large towns and major highways, both of which offered too many opportunities to be ambushed. South of Bas Courtils, the group got on to Rue de Mont St. Michel and followed it west to Le Pommeray where they picked up the D113. They passed north of Pontaubault and, shortly after, crossed underneath the A84. Normally at this point they would head northwest for the Normandy coast via Avranches. This time they headed northeast, winding along back roads until they reached Ger approximately thirty miles away. Ten miles beyond that sat the town of Flers, their first scheduled stop.

Jason sat upright in his saddle and began to be more attune

to his surroundings. Most of the others did the same. Lucifer and Lilith sensed the tension and moved in closer to Jason. This was unchartered territory for all of them. Jacques had limited their previous search and destroy missions to the coastal region, reasoning that any Demon Spawn that entered the area would follow the contour of the land. No one had ventured this far out in over six months. Only wildlife populated the countryside. Occasionally, the group passed an abandoned vehicle that had died when the EMP hit, yet they never saw any signs of the former owners. At one point, they came upon a tour bus sitting on the shoulder. The main door was open, although it didn't seem as though the occupants left in a hurry. Jason wondered what happened to those who had been stuck out here in the middle of nowhere.

They entered the southwest outskirts of Ger when Andre raised his palm in the air for the others to halt, and then swiped his hand across his neck several times, gesturing for everyone to remain quiet. The reason for the sudden stop became apparent when the wind shifted, blowing the sickeningly sweet odor of rotting flesh in their direction.

Flesh eaters.

Andre came back to the others. He spoke so softly they could barely hear him. "There's trouble ahead. I can smell them from here."

"How many are there?" asked Slava.

"I have no idea. Judging by the how strong the stench is, I'm guessing there's a lot of them."

"What do we do now?"

"I want to check it out. Slava, take the others and fall back about a mile and wait for me. If I'm not back in half an hour, circle around south of town and head for Flers. If I don't catch up to you in two hours, take command and continue on without me."

Slava's eyes widened. "What about you?"

Andre forced a grin. "If I don't catch up to you in two

hours, it's because I'm dead. Now move before those things see us. Have Sasha join us."

"Okay."

"Bait, you're with me."

"Okay."

The Russian motioned toward Lilith and Lucifer. "Leave them here."

Jason ordered the two werehounds to go with Doc. Lucifer stared at him with his brown eyes and whined, yet both animals did as they were told. Jason set off after Andre.

Sasha rode up a minute later. Her features were hardened into a grim determination, what she referred to as her battle face.

"Slava says there's a swarm of flesh eaters up ahead," she whispered.

"I don't know how many. That's why I want to check it out."

"You're not planning on engaging them, I hope."

Andre shook his head. "I want to get an idea of how many there are and in which direction they're heading. I don't want to be camping out with a swarm of those things roaming the countryside. At the first sign of trouble, we'll fall back with the others."

"Gotcha."

Andre brought his horse around and sidestepped up to Jason. "Bait, you sense anything?"

Jason closed his eyes and concentrated. He felt the presence of flesh eaters not too far from here, but they already knew that much. There were too many auras, all of them blending until they overwhelmed his senses. He cleared his mind of all thoughts, yet he still could not get an accurate picture of where the Demon Spawn were or how many they numbered. Finally, he opened his eyes and sighed.

"I can't get a thing. Sorry."

"Don't worry about it. If you get a sixth sense that we're

about to be attacked, don't even bother telling me. Haul ass out of here. We'll be right behind you."

With that, the three headed toward the center of Ger.

CHAPTER ELEVEN

THE THREE RODE into town at a slow, steady pace to maintain their stealth. Andre took the lead. Sasha stayed to his left and Jason to his right, each three horse lengths behind. Jason kept a cautious eye on his surroundings, searching for any movement in the shadows that might forewarn of danger. He divided his concentration between scouting the area and listening to his sixth sense that would hopefully warn of an impending attack. Sasha had removed the minigun from her leg mount and clutched it in her right hand. Her left hand still held the bridle, although she would be ready to fire her weapon in less than a second if need be.

At the juncture with the first road they came upon, which was on the left and two hundred feet from the center of town, Andre paused and raised the binoculars to his eyes. Jason watched as the Russian's features tightened. Andre handed the binoculars to Jason. A large roundabout dominated the main square where all five major roads into town converged. A swarm of flesh eaters at least a hundred strong filled the roundabout, moving in a slow shamble from north to south. God only knew how many were in this swarm. None of the demons had spotted them yet.

"Do you notice anything unusual about them?" asked Andre.

Jason studied the flesh eaters more closely. The demons swarmed like all the others they had encountered. And they looked the same—emaciated bodies and leathery skin. Half were naked. The other half wore a variety of outfits, though at this distance he couldn't determine what type of.... Then it hit him.

"They're clothed."

Andre nodded and removed the map from his jacket pocket. "It's the first time we've run across any of these things with clothes."

"What do you think it means?"

"Your guess is as good as mine, and anything I'd guess would probably be wrong."

Sasha moved up between the two. "Is it bad?"

"It's about as bad as it gets," replied Jason.

"Shit," said Sasha. "What now?"

"Wait here for a minute." Andre pointed on the map to the road on their left. "Bait and I are going to scout down here."

"We can't afford to split up. It's dangerous."

"Relax, girl. I'm only going down to the bend. I want to get an idea of how many there are. If you see any of those things start to head this way, scream your pretty little head off and we'll come running."

Sasha seethed with anger. If Andre noticed it, he didn't care. He headed off down the side road. "Come on, Bait."

The two traveled to the bend and paused. Andre scanned the area with his binoculars. Jason's blood ran cold. At the end of the road, a mass of flesh eaters dragged themselves toward the center of town. They packed the main street for at least a mile, and that was what he could see. He had no idea where this stream of demons began and ended.

Andre passed him the binoculars. "Want a look?"

"No. I've seen enough."

"Then let's not push our luck any more than we already have."

The two made their way back and picked up Sasha and the three of them left Ger.

CHAPTER TWELVE

J ASON INHALED DEEP, sucking the aroma into his lungs. His mouth salivated. He scooped up a forkful of chicken and scrambled eggs, sighing with delight at the taste. He usually didn't eat much but could not pass up this. It had been months since he had chicken. Considering how the others around him were wolfing down their dinner, he assumed they were enjoying the meal as much as him.

It was a pleasant end to an eventful day. After running across the flesh eaters in Ger, the group had backtracked a few miles before Andre ordered a rapid dash south across the countryside, hoping to cross the road ahead of the swarm. They succeeded without incident and made it out of the area undetected. Even so, Andre drove on for another few miles, wanting to get as far away from danger as possible. Though no one said it, they all realized how well their luck had held. A few hours later, and the swarm would have blocked them from their destination.

Then they found the farm. It sat along the side of the road surrounded by fields overgrown with tall grass. There were still a few hours of daylight left. However, the horses had already traveled well over thirty miles since leaving Mont St. Michel and needed to rest, so Andre had ordered everyone to dismount and set up camp. Sook-kyoung and Petra put the horses in the barn and gave them hay and water from a nearby well while Haneef's team checked out the farmhouse. While scouting around out back, the Gainesville Mafia had discovered a fifty-five-gallon drum cut in half to form a makeshift barbecue as well as several dozen chickens milling around the remains of a ramshackle coop. Within an hour, the three Americans had prepared a hot meal. Andre had ordered everyone to eat in shifts, with him, Slava, David, Franco, and Antoine manning the perimeter first while the others ate. The group dined by an old tractor, with Lucifer and Lilith spread out near a pile of hay, devouring the whole chickens Josh had cooked for each of them.

"This is great." Neal raised his plate. "Much better than what we get back at the abbey."

"Thanks," said Josh. "It comes from years of tailgating."

"Do you guys always eat this well in the field?"

"Hardly," Josh snorted. "We usually don't eat on search and destroy missions."

"We usually don't spend more than one day in the field," added Shane.

"On a suicide mission," chimed in Bill.

Neal felt guilty for creating the sour mood. He decided to change topics. "How did you all get here?"

"Jacques ordered it," Ray said with a smirk. Josh and Shane laughed.

"No," said Neal. "I mean how did you arrive at Mont St. Michel?"

Bill seemed confused by the question. "We're here because the portal opened."

"I think he's asking what happened to us after it opened," said Sook-kyoung.

"Exactly."

She placed her empty plate on the ground in front of her. "I was an exchange student from Seoul University getting a bachelor's degree in history. When classes were over, I decided to spend the summer in Europe and see the things I had been studying about for so many years. I was at Rheims when the portal opened. I made my way to Brest, hoping to find a ship that could take me home, but none were working because of the EMP. I followed the coast until I came across Mont St. Michel and Jacques took me in."

Sook-kyoung glanced over at Petra. The Italian contemplated whether to tell her story, and then gave a slight shrug. "I was on an El Italia flight from Paris to Rome and was on the taxi way when the gate opened."

"Did you see it?" asked Sasha.

Petra shook her head. "We knew something bad had happened, but we had no idea what. Our flight had been delayed twenty minutes. At the time we didn't realize how fortunate we were. I was watching a JAL flight take off, a 747. The plane made it about two hundred feet into the air when the EMP hit. Its engines cut out and nose dived into the runway. I doubt anyone survived the explosion. Not that it would have mattered. There were no emergency vehicles to help them. Anyways, our pilot evacuated the plane and led us back to the terminal. By then, everything was chaotic. Airport officials had no information on what happened."

"How did you wind up here?" asked Neal.

"I didn't stay at the airport long because it became too dangerous. People began to panic. Fights broke out. Some people looted the food court. I even saw one teenage girl being assaulted. When we heard about the Parisians evacuating the city, five of the flight attendants and I decided to get out while we still had a chance. We headed for the highway and joined the mass of refugees heading west." Petra's voice trailed off and she lowered her head.

"What happened to the others?" prodded Sook-kyoung.

"We lost Maria and Theresa in the crowd on the second day. They became separated and we never saw them again. The rest of us were afraid to stay on the highway since the situation was becoming tenuous, so we set off cross country. We eventually found an abandoned farmhouse with a well-stocked pantry that we held up in. Unfortunately, Raphaela gave up and committed suicide on the second night. Gabi wanted to stay put in the farmhouse, so I left her there and set out on my own. I kept on walking until I reached Normandy and one of Jacques' search and destroy missions rescued me." Petra paused and shrugged her shoulder. "Here I am."

"I'll never top that story," said Ray, trying to add some levity to lighten the mood. "I had finished a NATO exercise in Germany and had stopped by Normandy to tour some of the battlefields. When everything went south, I headed for Mont St. Michel because it was the closest, most fortified location around. I'd do anything to get back to the States."

"We all would," said Shane.

"I have a wife and two kids back in Fayetteville, and I have no idea whether or not they're safe."

"Sorry," Shane whispered.

"Don't be. It is what it is. I'm not the only one who doesn't know what happened to their loved ones."

"Not much to tell on our end," said Shane. "The three of us were vacationing in Nice. When the shit went down, we tried to make our way to the American Embassy in Paris, until we learned that the city had been evacuated. We wandered around France until we heard rumors of a sanctuary being set up at Mont St. Michel. The rest is history."

"And you?" Neal asked Christophe.

"I'd been vacationing in Lisbon and was on my way back to Vienna when the gate opened." Christophe slid his glasses up his nose. "The EMP stopped our train outside of Tours. Since everyone I ran into was heading west or north, I went in that direction and eventually made it to the city."

Neal turned to Renato yet did not ask since he could not understand English. The Italian grinned, trying to hide his embarrassment.

"What about you, Reinhard?"

"Vat does it matter?" Reinhard practically spat the words. "The vorld vent to hell. *Mein* life vent to hell. And now I'm going to hell. Literally."

A strained moment passed as the German glared at Neal. Thankfully, Philippe broke the tension. "I have the most boring story of all. I was born in Mont St. Michel."

Josh laughed, and most of the others joined in. Reinhard stood up, flung the remnants on his plate to the side, and walked away. Neal waited until the German had walked out of earshot before asking, "What about David and Antoine?"

Jason shrugged. "All I know about David is that he was one of the security guards from CERN. He helped Doc and me get out safely and stayed with us as we made our way out of Switzerland and into France. He's never talked about himself. As for Antoine, rumor has it that he belonged to a crime syndicate in Lyons and barely escaped the city when Demon Spawn over ran it. No one dared ask him about it, though. We're too afraid to."

"Wow." Neal glanced down at his plate. "I never knew."

"That's why most of us don't talk about our past," said Petra.

"It's too painful," added Ray.

The sound of approaching footsteps caught the group's attention. Andre stepped up and slid his FAMAS onto his shoulder. "If you ladies are done gossiping, let's switch out so the rest of us can get a meal."

"Roger that." Ray stood first, followed by the others.

"I want everybody bunked down in half an hour," said Andre. "Sasha, your team will sleep in the house and mine will take the barn. I don't want us to be surprised by any Demon Spawn tonight, so each team will take a four-hour shift. Haneef, your people will stand watch until ten o'clock when Sasha's team will relieve you. My team will take the watch from two until dawn."

"Gotcha."

"First, I want to chat with Doc and the team leads. The rest of you are dismissed. Bait, you stay behind, too."

CHAPTER THIRTEEN

ANDRE WAITED FOR the rest of the team to leave before moving closer to Doc. He talked soft so his voice would not carry. "I'm concerned about that swarm of flesh eaters we ran into earlier. They're getting too close to Mont St. Michel."

Doc shrugged. "We knew that sooner or later the Demon Spawn would find us."

"It doesn't bother you?"

"Of course, it does. But there's nothing we can do about it, besides making it to Paris and closing down the portal."

"At least they were heading south," chimed in Jason. "Away from us."

Sasha made eye contact with Jason, hoping to engage him in conversation. "I wonder where they came from?"

"Probably Vire," Doc replied. "The town is about fifteen miles north of Ger. It's pretty large, so I assume they wandered down from there."

"What made them head south?" asked Andre.

Doc shrugged the shoulder of his remaining arm. "Maybe they spotted a refugee and gave chase. Or maybe they wandered in that direction. There's no way of knowing."

"As long as they're not heading west, that's all I care about." Andre huffed. "What do you make of the fact that some of the flesh eaters wore clothes?"

Doc thought for a moment. "What type of clothes?"

"What type is there?"

"Were the clothes older in style or contemporary?"

Andre's eyebrows crinkled. "What does it matter?"

"If the clothes were old, it might indicate that the flesh eaters were wearing them when they exited the portal. If the clothes were contemporary, that means they've recently been turned."

"Shit," Andre mumbled. "I didn't notice. Bait, did you?"

"Yes. They wore modern clothes."

"Wait a minute, Doc." Andre sounded flustered. "Are you implying the flesh eaters can turn people into one of those things by biting them?"

"It's a possibility we can't rule out."

Jason unconsciously reached up and felt his shoulder where the flesh eater had bitten him two days ago. He noticed the others staring at him suspiciously.

"That doesn't make sense," said Sasha. "Several of us have been bit and none of us have turned. Are you sure about this?"

"Not at all. But it might be a good idea to stay far away from flesh eaters from here on in."

"No argument here." Andre gave Jason another wary look.

Doc cocked his head to one side in disagreement. "I'm more concerned about what we'll find in Flers or Falaise."

"What do you mean?" asked Sasha. "They weren't even heading in that direction."

"Caen is forty miles north of Flers and only twenty-four miles north of Falaise. Given what we ran into in Ger, we should consider the possibility that we'll come across another, even larger swarm tomorrow. I don't even want to think about what's waiting for us as we get closer to Paris."

None of them said anything. Jason had not thought about it before. It made sense that if the portal was in Paris then, the closer they got to the city, the greater the number of Demon Spawn they would encounter. God only knew what type of demons the portal spit out that hadn't made it this far yet.

Andre broke the awkward silence. "You're a ray of sunshine today."

As the Russian walked away, Sasha stepped over to Doc.

"Do you really think we're going to run into a lot more of these things the closer we get to Paris?"

Doc grimaced. "We've only seen a fraction of what the portal has spewed out."

Sasha turned to Jason. At first, he thought she would admonish him for coming along on this mission. Instead, her eyes showed fear. In all the time he had known Sasha, he had never seen her afraid of anything. For her to feel this way, they must be heading into some serious trouble. Then Jason detected a nuance in Sasha's aura. She knew that most of the team would die in Paris and had become resigned to that. He sensed that she didn't fear for her safety but his. Sasha not wanting him to come along had nothing to do with his being too young. She cared too much to allow something to happen to him. Jason felt guilty that he had misjudged Sasha's motives but was not ready to let her off the hook, especially after the dressing down she gave him in public. Maybe Sasha did have some affection for him; however, the way she treated him resembled an older sister taking care of her younger sibling. When she started to act like his girlfriend rather than his babysitter, then he could forgive her.

However, knowing Sasha did care, if only a little, made the prospect of going into harm's way seem not as grim as before.

CHAPTER FOURTEEN

SASHA MADE HER rounds around the farmhouse, checking on the rest of her team manning the perimeter. She kept her pace slow, enjoying the surroundings. She had not noticed how peaceful the setting was when they had first arrived. Now, with everyone asleep or quietly standing guard, she couldn't ignore the serenity of the countryside. A gibbous moon sat high, its soft light shining down on the fields and forest in the distance. Stars dotted the cloudless sky, more than she could recall seeing in her life. One streak stretched from one horizon to the next in a long ribbon of white. She now realized why ancient astronomers referred to that density of stars as the Milky Way.

The silence struck her most. Even a small city such as Mont St. Michel maintained a certain bustle at night that she had never really noticed before. Out here, the only noises came from nature, mostly crickets. A rustling near the edge of the overgrown field caught her attention. She paused for several minutes to watch a family of deer forage for food among the grass, two adults and three fawn. The animals didn't even run when they spotted her, no longer fearing man as a natural predator. After several minutes, the family moved deeper into the grass. Only then did Sasha continue her rounds.

If any good came out of the portal, it was that nature had reclaimed the land. Sasha suddenly remembered a geology professor back in college who always compared the world to a living organism and referred to humans as parasites feeding off it. He used to say that, like any living organism, the earth would one day purge itself so it could survive. She had always laughed off his lectures as the ramblings of an eco-nut. Now she believed him. A part of her wondered if the opening of the portals wasn't inevitable, nature's way of saving itself from what man had been doing to the planet. Sasha knew her professor would say yes, that is, if he was still alive. However, considering that Demon Spawn were now the dominant species, she couldn't help thinking that the cure may be worse than the disease.

Sasha slowed as she approached the driveway leading to the farm. She couldn't see Petra anywhere. She whistled once, short and loud. Petra's head appeared out of a ditch along the side of the road. Upon seeing Sasha, she waved and crawled out. Sasha walked over to her.

"Paranoid?" she asked.

"Just being cautious," replied Petra. "Better safe than sorry."

"I hear ya. I assume you haven't seen anything?"

"Some deer and a few rabbits, which is fine by me. I've been enjoying the quiet."

"It's beautiful." Sasha removed her canteen from her belt and unscrewed the top. "I could get used to living like this."

"It's very romantic."

"Are you coming on to me?" Sasha laughed and took a drink of water.

"You should be out here with Jason."

The statement caught Sasha by surprise. She spit out the water and wiped her hand across her lips. "Why do you say that?"

"Because he's in love with you. And it's obvious you feel the same way about him."

"That's not true," Sasha lied.

Petra chuckled. "You can stop the pretense. We've all seen the way you watch out for him when we're on a mission."

"I do that because he's young."

"Philippe is young, too, yet you don't protect him the same way. Besides, I can see it in your eyes whenever you look at him."

Sasha sighed. Had she really been that obvious? "I do love him."

"So why haven't you told him?"

"Because he's sixteen and I'm twenty-three. He should be with a girl his own age."

"They're all dead."

Sasha was aghast.

Petra chuckled again. "I know that sounds cruel, but it's true. Everything changed when the portals opened, even the social norms we all lived by."

"What will people think?"

"Who cares what they think? We live with death hanging over our heads every single day. God only knows how much time any of us have left, so why waste it?"

Petra's right, thought Sasha. Everything had changed over the past several months, and it seemed ridiculous to deny herself some measure of happiness. Considering how many times they had put themselves in harm's way, only luck had prevented either of them having been killed before this. She had already squandered too much time because of her own outdated sense of morality. In a few days they would be in Paris, and the odds were good that none of them would make it out alive. She needed to act now if she hoped to have any chance—

Approaching footsteps interrupted her reverie. Andre came down the driveway with the rest of his team slogging along behind him. Jason had a lock of blonde hair dangling across his face. She smiled.

"Everything good here?" the Russian asked.

Sasha nodded. "No sign of any danger."

"Let's hope it stays that way." Andre motioned to Jason. "Bait, you take over from Petra. If you see any sign of Demon

Spawn, call out and we'll come running." The teenager nodded.

Sasha stepped up to Jason. "Can we talk for a minute?"

"No time for that now," interrupted Andre. "I need you to walk the perimeter with us and show me where the others are posted. You can chat with your boyfriend later."

"He's not my boyfriend." Sasha regretted the words as soon as she spoke them. Petra shook her head in despair. Even worse, Jason showed no reaction to her outburst.

"Whatever," Andre huffed. "Let's go."

Sasha led the way to the other guard stations. As they departed, she glanced over her shoulder to see if Jason watched her leave. Her heart sank when she saw him crawling into the ditch where Petra had been, his attention focused on the farmland ahead of him rather than on her.

CHAPTER FIFTEEN

T HE GROUP LEFT the farm after sunrise and continued their trek to Flers. The first hour passed uneventfully, although Jason did not necessarily see that as a blessing. All he could think about was what Doc had said about the clothed flesh eaters possibly having been turned and the implications that had for the bite on his shoulder. He tried to ignore it. After all, if their bite could infect someone, then he should have been showing signs of becoming a flesh eater by now. So far, he had been feeling better. Even so, every twinge in his shoulder now gave him cause for concern.

About two miles outside of Flers, Andre brought the group to a halt. Jason sidestepped his horse out of line to see why. Something stood by the side of the road one hundred feet ahead of them. At first, it appeared to be a flesh eater. This demon had the same type of leathery skin, although it was not emaciated like the rest. Its head was bowed, which at this distance appeared misshapen. It stood motionless and seemed oblivious to their presence.

Slava rode up beside Andre and unslung his FAMAS. As he aimed the automatic weapon, Andre reached out and lowered the barrel.

"What's wrong?"

"The shot will attract too much attention. Besides, I want to know what it's up to." Andre shifted in his saddle. "Bait, get up here."

Jason moved his horse alongside the Russian. "What's up?"

"Do you get one of your sixth senses about that thing?"

Jason closed his eyes and concentrated. He could not detect any aura coming from it.

"I want you to check it out. If it moves, take it down with your crossbow. Slava, go with him to provide back-up. Don't use your weapon unless you have to."

The two moved forward, cautiously approaching the flesh eater. Jason placed an arrow in his crossbow. Slava held the automatic weapon in his lap, ready to fire if necessary. The horses grew skittish as they approached, and Jason had to rein in his and spur it along. When they got to within ten feet of the flesh eater, they paused. Despite their being so close, it remained still. Jason saw that the awkward appearance of its head resulted from the top portion of the skull being gone. Chunks of bone fragment littered the ground, and several strands of shredded skin dangled from the head, covering its face and neck. The brain was exposed.

"It looks like someone shot it," said Jason.

"A bullet doesn't make a wound like that. If someone had shot it, how come the brain is still intact?"

Despite their conversation, the flesh eater still had not acknowledged them. Jason hooked the crossbow onto his belt and withdrew his machete. "I'm going to go in closer. Cover me."

Slava moved his horse a few feet to the right to get a clear shot and raised his FAMAS into the high ready position. Jason inched closer, the machete pointed out and ready to stab if need be. He maneuvered his horse directly in front of the flesh eater, yet it still didn't move. Extending his foot, he nudged it in the abdomen. It bent forward. A brown, viscous liquid flowed out of the front part of the skull and splashed over Jason's leg. Jason pulled on the reigns, and the horse retreated several feet.

"Are you okay?" called Slava.

"Yeah."

Jason heard hoof steps and maneuvered his horse to see

Andre and Doc riding up. Sasha followed close behind them.

Andre stopped beside Jason. "Is everything all right?"

"Its head is filled with fluid. When it bent over, it spilled out onto my leg."

Doc withdrew a canteen of water from his saddle bag and handed it to Jason. "Wash that stuff off right away. It's probably infectious."

Andre moved his horse so he wouldn't get splattered as Jason cleaned his leg. "What do you make of it, Doc?"

"I haven't seen anything like this before. The top of its head exploded."

"Why?"

Doc shrugged. He walked his horse behind the flesh eater and leaned to one side to peer into the open skull. He winced and moved his head away. "It smells horrible. I think the liquid is pus."

"Like from an infection?" asked Slava.

"It seems that way. Whatever happened, it destroyed whatever motor function this thing had."

"An infection is killing off the flesh eaters?" Andre seemed hopeful.

"I can't say for certain without studying it further. This pus zombie doesn't seem to pose any threat."

"Pus zombie?"

"Can you think of a better term?" asked Doc.

Jason only half heard the conversation as he slowly poured the water down his pants leg, washing away the noxious fluid.

Sasha drew up alongside of him. "Are you okay?"

"Your boyfriend's fine," answered Andre. He pointed to the pus zombie. "Bait, take care of that thing. The rest of you, move out."

The others fell into line behind Andre, everyone giving the pus zombie a wide berth as they passed. Jason drew back ten feet, aimed his crossbow at its skull, and squeezed the trigger. The arrow shot into the exposed brain with a squish. The demon shot up straight, the pus sloshing over the side of its skull. It convulsed for several seconds before collapsing to the ground with a thud. Jason stared at it for a moment before racing ahead to join his place in line.

CHAPTER SIXTEEN

THE NEXT FEW hours passed without incident. After encountering the swarm of flesh eaters yesterday in Gcr, Andrc opted for caution over speed and led the group south along the D962, the major roadway that skirted town a mile to the south. Stalled cars and trucks blocked the road for as far as Jason could see. He stopped counting after he reached one hundred in the first quarter of a mile. As the group made its way between the vehicles in single file, everyone kept a watchful eye both on the road and on the town limits for any signs of Demon Spawn. Lucifer and Lilith ran on ahead, scouting for danger. As they approached the roundabout where the main road that ran south from Flers merged into the D962, the only signs of life were five rabbits munching on dandelion heads. Lucifer and Lilith gave chase, yet even the werehounds were not fast enough to catch the rabbits before they disappeared down their warren.

Twenty minutes later, the D962 merged with the east-west running D924. The group left the road and again traveled cross country. After ten miles, the field inclined toward a country road. Andre maneuvered his horse up the embankment and abruptly brought it to a halt. The others joined him, spanning out along the road. A field about five acres square spread out before them, with both flanks covered by woods. Nearly fifty pus zombies were scattered across the grass, each separated from the other by thirty to forty feet. Like the one they had run across earlier, these stood motionless. The only exception was that their heads were still intact. They reminded Jason of demonic scarecrows.

The one closest to the road lifted its head a few inches and stared at them but made no effort to move.

"They don't even care that we're here," said Jason.

"There are still too many for my liking." Andre slid the map out of his jacket pocket and unfolded it against his right leg.

"Maybe we should go around them," suggested Haneef.

"That'll take us hours out of our way." Andre refolded the map. "These woods run for several miles in either direction."

"Why don't we go through them?" asked Jason. "The one we ran across earlier didn't pose a threat."

"You want to go down there and try out your theory?" Andre's voice dripped with sarcasm.

Jason felt his chest tighten and his face flush with anger. He was sick and tired of being treated like shit. No one had a problem sending him into harm's way, yet no one would take his advice about the Demon Spawn, even though he interacted with them up close and could sense their aura. It was time to show Andre that he knew more about these things other than how to lure them out of hiding. Jason directed his horse down the other side of the embankment toward the closest pus zombie. Lucifer and Lilith trotted along beside him.

"Bait, I was joking." When Jason didn't stop, Andre glanced over at Slava and motioned toward the pus zombie. Slava unslung his FAMAS and aimed at its head.

Jason approached from the front so the pus zombie could see him. He kept the horse's gait slow and steady so as not to startle the demon. If it felt his presence, it gave no indication. As Jason approached, he began to sense an aura distinct yet slight, a psychic version of a hum. Lilith inched her way toward the pus zombie, crouching when three feet away and leaning forward, sniffing. She backed away and glanced up at Jason, uncertain about what she had smelled. Jason pulled his machete out of its sheath as he drew closer and, when directly in front of the pus zombie, prodded its shoulder with the blade. Nothing happened. He maneuvered his horse behind it. Placing his foot on its back, he gently nudged. The pus zombie swayed. Moving away ten feet, Jason positioned himself so he could keep an eye on the pus zombie and waved for the others to follow.

"The kid's got guts," said Doc.

"The damn kid's an asshole." Andre turned to the rest of the group. "Okay, people. Spread out and move out, and don't get cocky."

Jason watched as Andre descended the embankment and entered the field. The others followed hesitantly, moving off to the right and left to put distance between them. When the lead horses passed, Jason and the werehounds fell in behind Doc. He tried not to appear as smug as he felt. Andre had made look like a jerk in front of the others. Well, he showed them. Maybe now Andre would back off and the others would start showing him some respect.

The group had gone only fifty feet when Jason felt the psychic humming increase. It did not concern him because the aura was still minimal, much less than that presented by a single flesh eater. Yet he wondered why the sudden surge—

Jason heard a loud pop that sounded like a large balloon bursting. Lucifer whimpered. Jason scanned the area to find the source. He didn't notice that Doc had stopped until the two horses bumped into each other. Doc stared off to the north.

"What's wrong?"

"That one out there." Doc pointed to a pus zombie one hundred feet away. "The top of its head is gone."

"So?"

"It wasn't that way when we started to cross."

"Are you sure you're not imagining—"

Another pop sounded to their right. A pus zombie stood thirty feet away. The top of its head was gone. Chunks of skull fragment fell onto the grass and the shredded skin flaps dropped down across its face and neck. From inside the skull cavity, a white dust spread out, forming a small cloud ten feet in circumference around the shattered head.

"What is that?" asked Jason.

Doc's eyes widened. He yanked on the reigns, forcing his horse to the left, and pushing Jason's horse out of the way in the process. As he did, he cried out, "Get out of this field now! And avoid the pus zombies! They're carrying spores!"

At first, everyone stared at Doc like he had gone mad. Even Jason wondered about Doc's sanity. Then the head of a pus zombie in the center of the pack exploded six feet from Josh. The sound startled Josh's horse, which reared up and threw the American to the ground before bolting for safety. Josh lay on his back, temporarily winded, as the cloud of spores spread in his direction.

Andre spun his horse around to face the others. "Haul ass! Now!"

Ray reacted first, directing his horse toward Josh, reaching Josh as the American stumbled to his feet. Offering his hand, Ray helped Josh up into the saddle behind him. They darted away moments before the spore cloud reached their position.

Shocked into action, the others spurred on their horses. The group made a mad dash for the far end of the field, desperately trying to avoid the danger while not running into each other. One by one, the head of each pus zombie exploded, covering the field in spores. The horses panicked, making them harder to control. Luckily the animals were as desperate to avoid death as were their riders, so they maneuvered around the pus zombies.

At the far end of the group, Christophe was passing by the pus zombie that Jason had goaded when he heard Andre yelling, although at this distance he could not make out the words. The top of the pus zombie's head exploded. Christophe lowered his head so the flying gore would not hit him in the face but didn't see the white cloud of spores spreading from the shattered skull. He breathed them in and instantly began to cough. The terrified horse bolted back toward the road, throwing off Christophe. He fell to the grass with a heavy thud, his glasses bouncing to one side. Rolling onto his stomach, Christophe tried to stand but only made it to his knees. He bent over and hacked.

Jason spun his horse around and set off toward Christophe, with Doc close behind. As they drew close, Christophe looked up at them. Or more appropriately, what was once Christophe. His eyes were milky and glazed over. His skin had started to shrink around his body, already adopting a leathery texture. Christophe detected the sound of the approaching horses and snarled. Climbing to his feet, he lumbered toward Jason and Doc.

Jason raised his machete when Doc reached out and grabbed his arm. "We have to get out of here."

"I can't leave him like this."

"We can't risk sucking in those spores. Come on!"

Jason and Doc maneuvered their horses toward the tree line to the right of the field, with Lucifer and Lilith staying between them and the pus zombies. Once they reached safety, they headed north and raced after the others. Jason scanned the field to check on Sasha, and his stomach clenched.

Her horse approached a pair of pus zombies as one of their heads exploded, throwing spores directly into her path. Sasha took a deep breath, placed her hand over her nose and mouth, and closed her eyes as the horse raced through the cloud. A dusting of white covered her face and hand. Slava raced up alongside and grabbed the reigns, leading her out of danger. Once clear of the field, he yanked her horse to a stop. Sasha slid out of the saddle and fell to her knees. Slava dismounted. Grabbing a canteen of water from his backpack, he removed the cap and handed her the bottle.

"Wash that shit off before you breathe it in!"

Jason headed his horse for Sasha, terrified of what he would find. As he approached, he watched her pour water across her face while using her other hand to scrub off the spores. She took a drink, swished the water around her mouth, and spit it into the grass. Placing one finger over her right nostril, she blew the contents of her left into the grass and repeated the process on the other side. Then Sasha bent forward and began hacking.

Jason jumped off his horse and ran up to her. Slava prevented him from getting too close. Jason tried to break free but the Russian held him tight.

"Sasha!" Jason yelled. "Are you okay?"

Slowly she raised her head.

CHAPTER SEVENTEEN

WET, MATTED HAIR stuck to her forehead. Sasha's eyes watered, and snot dripped from her nose. Jason sighed with relief when he saw her green eyes staring at him rather than the murky grey of a flesh eater.

Andre rode up and tossed her another canteen of water from his rucksack. "Wash that shit off your clothes."

Sasha caught the canteen and removed the cap. Holding her breath, she slowly poured the water across her chest and arms, wiping away the last of the spores. Only when Slava gave her a thumbs up that she was clean did Sasha breathe, gasping in air. She continued to kneel in the grass, trying to calm down.

Jason was at a loss for words. "Are you okay?"

Sasha forced a smile. "I'll be fine."

"No thanks to you, Bait." Andre dismounted and stepped over to Sasha, helping the woman to her feet.

"What do you mean?" Jason felt his cheeks flush with anger.

"You led us into that field by being a cocky little ass. We almost lost Sasha and Josh." Andre walked Sasha over to her horse and helped her back into the saddle. "And Christophe is now a flesh eater."

Christophe. Jason had forgotten about him. He turned back to the field to see their former companion shambling toward the group, its arms stretched toward them, still a good fifty feet away. Andre was right. Because of him, Christophe was dead. Worse than dead.

When Jason faced forward, the others had gathered

around. He couldn't bear to face them. Nevertheless, he felt their reproaching eyes boring into him, blaming him for what had happened. The only ones not visually condemning him were Sook-kyoung and Petra because they were chasing Josh's horse. He kept his head bowed, wishing he had been the one turned into a flesh eater rather than Christophe.

After Andre helped Sasha back into her saddle, he faced Jason and crossed his arms over his chest. "You're no different than your bitch of a mother."

Jason's head shot up at the insult. "Leave my mother out of this!"

"No."

Sasha wiped the snot from her nose. "Andre, please don't do this."

The Russian waved her off with a flick of his hand. "It's time he learned the truth."

"What truth?" A knot formed in the pit of Jason's stomach.

"Everyone told your mother that her experiment was dangerous and could have unpredictable consequences. She ignored the warnings and conducted it anyway because she wanted to make a name for herself. She was reckless and narcissistic, and thanks to her we now have to deal with the portals."

"That's a lie!" Jason looked at each of his team members, hoping someone would refute what Andre had said. No one did. Jason turned to Doc, hoping for support. "Tell him it's not true."

Doc said nothing. He stared at Jason with pity in his eyes before averting his gaze. The harshness of Andre's words struck home as reality set in. In an instant, what remained of Jason's world crashed around him. He felt his chest tighten, as much from anger as from shame.

"This little stunt of yours proved you're no better than her." Andre stepped up to Jason and jabbed his finger into the teenager's chest. "You do something like that one more time and I'm sending you back to Mont St. Michel. Understand?"

Jason nodded, his movement barely perceptible.

"What?"

"Yes, sir," Jason croaked.

"Good." Andre walked back to his horse and climbed into the saddle. "Let's move out. We need to make Falaise by nightfall."

"What about him?" Slava gestured toward Christophe. "Should I put him out of his misery?"

"No. Let Bait do it. He can pick up his own mess." Andre nudged his horse's flanks and headed out.

Everyone fell in behind the Russian. No one acknowledged Jason, not even Doc. Sasha mounted her horse and called for Lucifer and Lilith to fall in beside her, which they did. Soon the only one left was Jason. He mounted his horse and moved as close to Christophe as possible while avoiding the pus zombies in case any spores remained inside their heads. Loading an arrow and raising the crossbow, he centered the crosshairs on Christophe's face. Jason's eyes momentarily locked onto Christophe's. He hoped for a sign of forgiveness, that Christophe the man didn't hold his undeserved fate against him. Instead, he saw only the lifeless grey eyes of a flesh eater. Jason wouldn't receive any absolution, nor did he deserve it. Focusing his attention on Christophe's forehead, Jason slowly squeezed the trigger. The arrow shot forward, striking Christophe directly above the nose and shattering the skull. A blue eddy of light flowed up into the sky and dissipated. The body dropped to the ground, finally at peace.

Jason turned his horse around and followed the others. Tears flowed down his cheeks.

CHAPTER EIGHTEEN

THE REST OF the journey to Falaise took place with a strained silence within the group. They confronted a jumble of emotions, not the least of which concerned the loss of Christophe. Up until now, most of them had assumed that the only Demon Spawn to have left the portal had been the soul vampires and flesh eaters, which were nightmarish enough. Running across the pus zombies had dramatically changed the dynamics of their mission. While the pus zombies were relatively benign and easy enough to avoid, their discovery meant the chances were good that other horrors awaited them before they reached Paris.

For Jason, those concerns were secondary. Right now, he struggled through his guilt and disgrace. As much as it pained him to hear it, Andre was right. He had been reckless leading the others through the field to show up Andre and impress Sasha. His arrogance cost Christophe his life and nearly killed Sasha. Up until today, he had considered himself a vital member of the team who only needed to prove himself to be accepted. He had proven himself, all right, yet not in the way he had hoped. Not only did he now question his own abilities, he feared how he would react when they came across more dangerous Demon Spawn.

Over the course of two hours, Jason had gradually fallen behind the others until half a mile separated him from the rest of the team. He kept his head bowed. Blonde hair dangled across his face as if hiding his shame. He desperately hoped someone would notice him so far behind and wave for him to catch up. No one did. That wasn't true. About an hour ago, Sasha had checked on him, although she didn't acknowledge him. Even she didn't care anymore. Several times he had thought about veering off and setting out on his own so as not to endanger the others. Maybe then they would appreciate him, though he doubted it. Every time he began to maneuver his horse away from the others, he chickened out at the last second. After a while, he gave up on the idea of leaving. The only thing worse than wandering off was the knowledge that no one would care if he did.

They reached the outskirts of Falaise an hour before dusk. Andre approached from the west, cutting through farmland to bypass the main roads into the city and avoid the center of town. Ahead of them, a tall hill dominated the surrounding area. On the western crag sat their destination—*Chateau de Falaise*, the 11th Century castle of William the Conqueror. Andre led the group along the southern slope to the eastern approaches that led up the hill to the castle. The others were already gathering around the outer gatehouse when Jason caught up with them. Andre was in the process of sending Haneef's team in to check out the castle. Jason found it telling that, for once, Andre did not ask him to be the point man. He maneuvered his horse to the edge of the hill.

Falaise spread out for several miles in every direction. Directly beneath him sat the town square, with the medieval church of St. Gervais dominating the northeast corner. The entire town seemed deserted rather than abandoned. There were not even parked cars. Jason saw no signs of Demon Spawn. In fact, he saw no life at all, which struck him as strange. Across France, wildlife had re-populated the countryside. Not here in Falaise. No deer. No squirrels. No rabbits. No birds. Nothing.

Jason started toward the castle when a noise caught his attention. He pulled back on the horse and listened. It sounded like the buzzing of an insect, only much louder. He checked the ground beneath him, at first thinking he might have disturbed a wasp's nest. Then he noticed an echo to the sound, as it if came from a distance. He closed his eyes and concentrated on the buzzing, hoping to make a mental connection with the source. Unlike with the flesh eaters, he couldn't detect anything nearby.

A loud whistle caught his attention. When Jason got back to the castle, Slava stood near the gatehouse. "Come on, Bait. The castle is clear. Andre wants us inside with the moat bridge raised before sunset."

Jason took one last look at Falaise. He no longer heard the buzzing. Shrugging, he fell in behind Slava.

CHAPTER NINETEEN

D INNER CONSISTED OF canned beans and mixed vegetables that Shane found hidden in the castle pantry, which he and Josh cooked in two large pots that they removed from the museum exhibit. This meal was nowhere near as good as the roasted chicken and scrambled eggs they enjoyed the previous night, although it didn't matter because most of the group did not feel like eating. The three team leads and Slava sat with Doc in the corner of the main hall near the fireplace, quietly chatting, while the others sat around the large dining table in the center of the hall. Except for Jason, who never showed up.

Franco shoved his plate away, slopping some of the beans onto the wooden table.

"You don't like it?" asked Josh.

"I'm not hungry." Franco's voice echoed in the spacious hall. He frowned. Leaning forward, he spoke in a hushed voice so the sound would not carry. "I've always been worried about having Bait in our group. Today confirmed it."

"That's not fair," said Neal. "He had no idea how danger-ous the pus zombies were."

"He should have known better."

"The one we ran into this morning posed no threat."

"That's because its head had already exploded."

"Let's be fair," said Petra. "None of us realized that until later."

Franco frowned and shook his head. "My point is, we're running into Demon Spawn we haven't encountered before, and Bait should have shown more caution."

"I didn't see Andre try to stop him," said Petra.

Franco's eyes narrowed and his gaze bore into the woman. "How could he. Jason ploughed ahead without thinking of others. Like his mother."

"You can't blame Jason for what his mother did," said Neal.

"I don't." Franco glared at him, forcing Neal to avert his eyes. "However, he's arrogant and overconfident, just like her. David knows that better than anyone. He watched her open up the portal."

David shrugged. "Jason is trying to be better than his mother. Give him time."

"How much time?" Franco snarled. "He's reckless. He's what you Americans call a *vaquero*. A cowboy. We're always saving his ass from the Demon Spawn and I'm getting sick of it. We lost Christophe thanks to him. How many more people have to die before he smartens up? If he doesn't fall into line soon, he'll get us all killed."

Several people around the table nodded in concurrence.

Neal kept his gaze focused on the tabletop. "He's a good kid once you get to know him."

"That's the problem," Franco replied. "He's a kid. Remember, I trained him. He has limited military skills. The only reason he's even a part of the group is because of his psychic abilities."

"I vorry about *das* sixth sense of his," said Reinhard.

"That bothers me, too," said Josh. "I like the kid, but his ability to connect with the Demon Spawn creeps me out."

"You know," said Shane, "I've always wondered about that. How do we know those things don't feel the same connection to him and are attracted to it? Jason could be leading them to us without even knowing it."

Neal spun his head toward Shane, his face flushed with anger. "You don't really believe that, do you?"

"Why not?" said Shane.

"I've wondered about that myself," added Antoine. "We always seem to attract hordes of Demon Spawn every time we go out."

"Maybe because more Demon Spawn are moving closer to Mont St. Michel," argued Neal. Antoine grimaced in disgust and drank some water.

"Maybe the reason we're seeing more Demon Spawn could be because they're drawn to him." Shane postulated. "It would also explain why so many of the flesh eaters were descending on Ger as we got there."

Before Neal could protest, Franco cut him off. "Kid, you've been hanging around Bait and Doc so much you're beginning to like the Kool Aid they're serving. Remember, Doc is as responsible as Bait's mother for the mess we're in. And now we're all on this suicide mission because Doc has this idiotic idea that he can close off the portal in Paris with that stupid device he created. We're all going to die so Bait and Doc can set things right with their consciences."

"Damn straight," said Ray.

"Here, here," added Shane.

David glared at Franco. "If this is a suicide mission, why did you agree to come along?"

Franco chuckled. "What is it you *gringos* say? 'It's better to die on your feet than live on your knees'."

David's face became crimson but he held his tongue.

Franco shook his head. "I would've felt better if we left him behind."

Petra huffed. "Thank God the decision wasn't yours to make. Andre wanted him along."

"That's not a ringing endorsement," said Antoine.

"You have a problem with Andre, too?" she asked.

"Yes, I do." Antoine leaned forward to intimidate her. "He's nothing more than a petty thug trying to be someone important. Him and that little shit Slava."

"And I suppose you're better than them?" Petra's voice

dripped with sarcasm.

Antoine chuckled. "Yes. I'm a thug, like them. I just never aspired to be a marshall."

The Moroccan's grin faded. "They're as dangerous as Bait, though for different reasons. And those two will wind up getting us all killed if we let them."

"*Ja*," agreed Reinhard.

"Then why did you both come along?" asked Petra.

"For the same reason you did," said Antoine. "To stop this nightmare and go home to our families, or what's left of them."

Ray bowed his head so no one would see the tears forming in his eyes.

"I miss my family." Sook-kyoung stared at the table. "I don't want to die, but I'm willing to risk my life if it means ending all this so I can go back to Korea."

"It's the reason we're all here," said Franco. He motioned toward the other table. "If any of those assholes do anything stupid that could get us killed, they'll have bigger problems than the Demon Spawn to contend with."

Reinhard nodded. Antoine grunted his approval.

PATHETIC, THOUGHT SASHA. Out of the entire group, only Andre and Slava ate heartily. Nothing fazed those two, not even the death of one of their team members. She knew they had been Russian street thugs before the portal opened, but always had hoped that the last several months would change them. It hadn't. Those two had no emotional attachment to anyone or anything, except for the extreme violence inherent in this post-apocalyptic world. Andre and Slava thrived on the killing and carnage, which made them far more dangerous than the Demon Spawn.

Even worse, no one seemed to care that Jason had not been seen for several hours.

Sasha had spent the last ten minutes moving around the beans on her plate, worried about Jason. Sure, he had screwed up badly with the pus zombies, yet that was still no reason to bring up the subject of his mother. Jason already felt guilty enough about her culpability in opening the portals, which was why they had all agreed to keep the truth from him. It had worked until Andre's outburst earlier in the day. Now that Jason knew the truth, it would take an even heavier toll on his emotions. She could tell by the way he had acted that the revelation depressed and distracted him, which did not bode well considering what lay ahead.

Andre cleaned off his plate and washed the beans down with water. As he spun the lid closed on his canteen, he turned to Doc. "About those pus zombies we ran into today. Do you think they're what created the newer flesh eaters?"

"It's safe to assume that."

Slava shook his head. "It doesn't make sense. How can spores infect someone?"

"It's not that unusual." Doc placed his plate on the floor. "Have you ever heard of zombie ants?"

Slava furrowed his eyebrows. "You're joking, right?"

"Not at all. There's a parasitic fungus called *Ophiocordyceps* that infects ant species. It eats away at the soft tissue of their heads and eventually infects the brain. The ants leave the nest, climb up the stem of a plant, and attach themselves to it by their mandibles. They sit there until the fungus reproduces in their heads. Then it bursts through the skull and spreads spores to infect other ants. What we saw today was just a hellish version of that."

Slava huffed. "Thanks to that asshole Bait, Christophe became infected by those spores."

Sasha started to respond. Andre spoke first. "I'm just as responsible. I should never have let you all cross that field."

Now it was Slava's turn to be incredulous. "You're defending that little bastard?"

"No. What he did was dumb. Letting you all follow him was even dumber."

"Did you have to tell him the truth about his mother?" asked Sasha.

"Don't question me on that. Bait's a good kid. He needs to get his head screwed on straight and stop wallowing in pity." Slava started to speak. Andre held up a hand and cut him off. "He's as impetuous as we were at his age. And we'd be dead today if we didn't learn from our mistakes."

Slava dropped his gaze to the floor, his pride hurt by being chastised by Andre in front of the others. "I still think the little bastard is going to get us all killed."

"The Demon Spawn will see to that. Right now, we need every advantage we have if we're going to survive this and Bait's ability to sense these things is the best advantage we have." Andre scanned the dining hall. "Where is he, anyway?"

"He went up to the roof to be alone," answered Doc.

"You mean to sulk," added Slava.

Andre shot his friend a withering glance, and Slava immediately backed down.

Sasha decided to use this moment to break away. "I'll go check on him."

"Let me," said Doc as he awkwardly pushed himself up with his one arm. "I think it's time he knows the full truth, and it'd be better if he hears it from me."

CHAPTER TWENTY

J ASON STOOD WITH his elbows resting on the wall of the castle's tower. He barely ate, picking through his bag of granola and popping an occasional raison or nut into his mouth, which he absentmindedly chewed. He directed his attention toward downtown Falaise, though with the only light coming from a full moon he really couldn't see anything except the outline of St. Gervais Church against the starlit sky. With nothing to focus on, he stared into the dark, his mind replaying the events of that day. Lilith and Lucifer lay curled up at his feet on either side of him, the former taking a nap. Lucifer pretended to sleep, although every few minutes he opened one eye to check on his master. His head suddenly shot up and his ears bent forward. He sniffed the air.

Jason heard footsteps behind him. A moment later, Doc came up beside him. "Did they send you up here you to make sure I didn't get into trouble?"

"Sasha asked me to check on you. She's afraid how you're handling this afternoon. We all are."

Jason snorted. "I doubt that. Most of them could care less if I rode off on my own."

"Yeah, some of them are assholes. You have a lot of friends down there, and they're concerned."

"Don't worry, Doc. I'm not gonna jump, though I have thought about it." *Shit, why did I say that?*

"It's natural to feel that way at your age." Doc moved up beside Jason and leaned on his one elbow, also staring out over the darkened city. "You only have Christophe's death on your hands. I'm carrying the weight of hundreds of millions of dead."

Jason didn't respond at first. He knew he had to ask the next question, even though he did not want to hear the answer. "Was my mother reckless in opening the portals?"

"Are you sure you're ready for the truth?"

"I need to know."

Doc paused for nearly a minute as he stared out across Falaise. Finally, he sighed. "Yes." The answer sliced open Jason's soul. Everything he believed about his mother, everything he had cherished about her, had suddenly been ripped away from him. Jason had come to terms with the fact that his mother's experiment had destroyed the world, finding comfort in the illusion that everything that had transpired was an accident. He now knew that this tragedy could have prevented if his mother had not forged ahead against everyone's advice to obtain her own glory. Much like he had done this morning. That realization left a void of confused thoughts and feelings.

"Why didn't you tell me sooner?" Jason asked.

"You already had enough problems dealing with what she had done. I didn't want to shatter your vision of her any further."

"Thanks." Jason meant it. "What happened?"

"Anti-matter experiments always contain an element of danger because of the consequences if the anti-matter comes into contact with matter. Your mother thought that if she could successfully generate the creation of anti-matter in several labs and sustain it, it would advance research by years. All the physicists we briefed on the project disagreed, and they tried to stop her. Lisa… your mother was so damned pigheaded…." Doc struggled to control his emotions. "Your mother was too stubborn and selfish to listen to them. She viewed the project only in terms of how it would advance her career and ignored the risks associated with it. If anyone argued against the project, she did everything she could to discredit them. Your mother spent months convincing officials at CERN that this would make them a household name and would ensure funding for the next twenty years. She finally got her way."

"Did you think she was wrong?"

"Yes."

"Then why did you go along with the experiment?"

"Because I was in…." Doc didn't complete his sentence. He turned from Falaise and leaned back against the wall. "I supported your mother. I thought the experiment would fail, that not all the labs would generate anti-matter at the same time, or in the amounts she wanted. At worst, I figured there might be a breach of one container, which the facilities are designed to handle. No one had the slightest clue that the project would open portals to another dimension. What's done is done. The best way I can assuage my guilt is to close off the gate in Paris and hopefully set things right."

Jason lowered his head. "I know what you mean."

Doc placed his hand on Jason's shoulder and squeezed gently. "I'm sorry you had to find out this way."

A long silence passed between them. Finally, Jason asked, "Is that why my father left? Because my mother was stubborn and reckless?"

"No."

"Then why?"

"Your mother loved your father as much as she loved you. She also loved her career and pursued it with a passion. After you were born, your father assumed she would spend more time at home, but she didn't. He eventually got tired of taking second place. When she took the position at CERN, he filed for a divorce, and Lisa didn't contest it." Doc thought for a moment. "You don't blame yourself for their divorce, do you?"

"That's the one thing I don't feel guilty about." Jason chuckled nervously. "Mom never talked about my dad."

Another long silence passed between them as Jason processed what Doc had told him. This marked the second time in a year his world had been torn apart, though this time he found it harder to handle the emotional sundering. He had learned enough psychology in high school to know that most kids have an idealized image of their parents, and that as children get older, they develop a more realistic concept, one that is always at odds with the earlier fantasy they had created. It's tough enough coming to terms with the fact that your mother isn't perfect. It really sucks when you find out she destroyed the world out of selfishness.

Ironically, the truth lifted a major weight from his soul. Up until now, Jason had always viewed the opening of the portals as an accident and had seen it as his mission to clear his mother's name, a burden no sixteen-year-old should bear. Now he knew that the portals had been formed because his mother had been thinking only of herself. Nothing he could do would ever change that. His mother would go down in history, if anyone lived long enough to write it, as the woman who recklessly opened portals between two dimensions, one hellish in nature. Jason no longer had to take on her guilt. He still needed to accomplish one task to set things right. Not for his mother, for himself.

Doc reached over and pushed the loose hair away from Jason's face in a fatherly gesture. "Are you okay?"

"Not really, but I will be. Once we close the portal."

CHAPTER TWENTY-ONE

THE GROUP GATHERED on horseback in the Chateau de Falaise's courtyard shortly after dawn. Jason arrived last, hanging around in back so he did not have to interact with anyone. When Sasha heard his horse, her eyes lit up. She swung hers to intercept Jason when Andre spotted him. The Russian snapped his fingers and, when he caught Jason's attention, motioned for the kid to join him. Jason flipped the reins and nudged the horse with his knees. The animal moved forward, with Lilith and Lucifer on either side. When he reached the head of the line, Andre greeted him with a friendly nod.

"Are you ready, Bait?"

"Yeah."

"Good. Lead the way, and keep your senses open for any Demon Spawn." Andre spoke to the others. "Let's head out."

Jason led the group through the outer gatehouse and along the pathway down the hill, and then headed into town. It looked like it did from the top of the hill last night. Quiet and desolate. Not even birds gathered around the bell tower of St. Gervais. Lucifer did not seem bothered by it, although Lilith kept glancing from side to side, her ears raised and on the alert for danger.

The group had passed St. Gervais when the buzzing Jason had heard yesterday started again, only this time much closer. Andre held up his hand and the others stopped. Everyone scanned the square, the surrounding buildings, and the side streets, trying to pinpoint the noise. Even though they were exposed, staying put was preferable to racing for cover and rushing into a pack of Demon Spawn.

Andre called out to the others. "Stay sharp, people."

To Jason's right, Lilith had already morphed into her demonic form and stared at the sky, growling. Jason followed her gaze and gasped.

A dozen wasps the size of horses swarmed out of the church's bell tower and descended on the group. The closest, barely thirty feet away, bore down on Doc.

"Doc, behind you!" Jason yelled.

Upon seeing the wasp, Doc snatched up the saddle bag with the anti-matter device and leaned into his horse, hoping to present a smaller target. His horse panicked and bolted, throwing him. Doc huddled over to protect the device and landed on his back, knocking the wind out of him. As his horse raced across the square toward a side street, Petra set out after it. The wasp landed on Doc, positioning itself so its stinger hovered over the human's head.

Lilith and Lucifer lunged at the wasp, each grabbing a wing and yanking the giant insect off its victim. The wasp thrashed around, shredding its wings between the two sets of canine teeth. Spinning its lower body, it rammed its stinger into Lucifer. The tip broke off on the werehound's scales. Lucifer jumped out of the way. His jaws were still clamped tight on the wasp's left ring, ripping it off. The insect flailed about until the other wing came off in Lilith's mouth. Righting itself, it crawled toward the church.

Jason spoke to David, who was alongside of him. "Take my horse."

When David grabbed the reigns, Jason slid out of the saddle, unsheathed his machete, and ran over to Doc.

"GET INSIDE THE church!" yelled Andre.

The Russian had spun his horse around to warn the others

and didn't see the wasp swooping down on him. It buzzed past his head, knocking him out of the saddle.

SLAVA RAISED HIS FAMAS and fired a three-round burst into the insect attacking his friend. The bullets thudded into its abdomen. They seemed to have no effect other than to cause it to buzz angrily. Slava switched his weapon to full-automatic mode. He noticed something flying at him from the right. A wasp was bearing down on him less than thirty feet away. Raising the weapon at the new target, he squeezed the trigger, releasing the last seven rounds. The wasp's head exploded, yet momentum kept the body going. The dead insect slammed into Slava, knocking over him and his horse.

"FOLLOW ME!" YELLED Franco. Spinning his horse to the right, he headed around the side of the church toward the north transept. The others fell in behind him. Franco jabbed his heels into the horse's belly, urging it to run faster. He hoped they would make it to safety before the wasps got them.

EVERYONE FOLLOWED FRANCO except Sasha. She stayed in the center of the square, unholstered her minigun from her leg mount, and fired up the weapon. The whir of its motor drowned out the buzzing around her.

"Haneef, fall back on me!"

Haneef maneuvered his horse alongside her so the two gunmen faced in opposite directions. Each fired a five-second burst into the approaching wasps, the barrage of bullets shredding four of them.

Two of the remaining wasps landed in the square, one only a few feet from Slava. The other crawled toward Jason and Doc. A third flew off after Petra. The rest veered off and went after the group trying to get into St. Gervais.

"Haneef, protect the others! I'll take care of these bastards!"

Bullshit, she thought. *There are too damn many of them. I can't save everyone.*

THE WASP CREPT onto Jason, pushing him down onto Doc. Its abdomen extended up and out, ready to plunge its stinger. Jason thrust his machete up into the raised abdomen and twisted the blade, gouging a hole in the insect. A yellowish-green viscous fluid flowed from the wound and dripped onto his hand. The wasp tried to attack but, with the blade embedded in it, the stinger only moved a few feet, stopping inches from Jason's head. Jason shoved in the blade up to its hilt and twisted it from left to right. The wasp's buzzing intensified.

Seeing their master in danger, Lucifer and Lilith rushed to his defense. Lilith clasped the wasp by a wing and Lucifer by one of its opposite legs, yanking the demon insect off Jason. Lilith plunged her stinger into the wasp's thorax, injecting it with paralyzing venom. The insect went limp.

Jason lifted the semi-conscious doctor to his feet, threw the saddle bag with the device over his shoulder, and the two limped toward St. Gervais Church.

RAY WAS LAST in line heading for the church when a wasp dived at him, driving its stinger into his back. Because he carried one of Haneef's spare ammo packs, he felt nothing more than a heavy shove against his shoulder blades that nearly dismounted him. The wasp pulled back for another attack. Haneef rode up and fired his minigun, shredding the wasp in mid-air and splattering Ray in yellowish-green blood and body parts.

Franco reached the church first. Sliding out of his saddle, he raced up and pushed against the door. It would not budge.

"Open the damn door!" screamed Sook-kyoung.

"I can't. It's locked."

Another burst from Haneef's gun killed a wasp that dropped to the ground between Shane and Josh. Both men had all they could do to keep their horses from bolting.

"Let me try." Antoine dismounted and, as he approached, he unslung his FAMAS. Franco jumped aside. Antoine fired two three-round bursts into the lock and kicked it. The wood shattered and the doors swung open.

Everyone rushed inside.

The other two wasps followed. One erupted into bits from a concentrated burst of fire from Haneef's minigun. The other barged its way through the open doors and into the transept.

ANDRE STRUGGLED UNDERNEATH the wasp. He kicked at its head and kept his hands pressed against its abdomen, trying to prevent from being stung. The stinger lunged at him. He tightened his elbows. As the abdomen curled up under the insect, it pushed Andre along the pavement.

The wasp shifted its position. Its legs grabbed hold of Andre's torso so he couldn't move and attacked again. The Russian twisted his body as far as he could to the right. The stinger missed his head and struck his shoulder, slicing through skin and shattering his clavicle. Excruciating pain shot through his body, although nowhere near as bad as when the wasp pumped venom into him. A burning sensation seared through his veins and skin, as though someone had injected him with acid.

Andre screamed as the upper left part of his body went numb.

SLAVA LAY ON the ground, dazed from his fall. However, his friend's agonized scream snapped him back to reality. Rolling to one side, he saw the wasp with its stinger lodged in Andre's shoulder.

"No!"

Seeing his FAMAS inches away, Slava crawled onto his knees and picked it up. He aimed between the insect's eyes and squeezed the trigger.

Nothing happened.

Shit, I used up my ammo killing that other wasp.

Popping out the empty magazine, Slava reached into his ammo pouch, removed a full magazine, and slammed into the weapon.

PETRA CAUGHT UP with Doc's horse before it raced down the side street between the castle and the municipal building. Grabbing the reins, she brought it to a halt. Once the horse had calmed down, she spun it around and sped across the square toward the church.

Hearing a loud buzz, Petra raised her head and stared into the angry eyes of a wasp flying straight for her.

SASHA QUICKLY SIZED up the situation. Haneef had taken care of the wasps attacking the rest of the group. The werehounds were ripping apart the insect that had attacked Jason. Andre was in trouble, but she couldn't use the minigun to help him without killing him in the process. That left the wasp bearing down on Petra.

She had only seconds before it got too close to Petra for her to fire. Aiming for the space between the young woman and the insect, Sasha let loose a three-second burst. The wasp flew into the stream of bullets and blew apart. What remained of its carcass was propelled to one side by the blast, cartwheeling out of Petra's way. Ducking her head, Petra raced through the rain of blood and body parts and headed for St. Gervais.

INSIDE THE CHURCH, pandemonium broke out. The wasp landed on the one of the statues by the transept arch and spun around, sizing up its next victim. It never got a chance to attack. Eleven weapons opened fire at once, bombarding the insect in a fusillade of bullets. It thrashed around, unable to fly because of its shredded wings. Falling from the statue, it crawled around the floor in a circle, desperate to escape. Renato pulled his machete from its sheath and ran forward, driving the blade into the wasp's head. The insect stopped moving.

PAIN GAVE WAY to a numbness that spread through Andre's shoulder and down his chest. On gut reaction, he used his good arm to cradle the damaged left shoulder. Not that it mattered. He knew he was about to die.

The wasp jerked its abdomen down again. This time its stinger struck the top of Andre's skull. He convulsed once from the blow, and then venom spurted into his brain. His mind blanked out. Andre was only vaguely aware of being lifted off the ground before he lapsed into a coma.

SLAVA HAD PULLED back the bolt on his FAMAS when he saw the wasp drive its stinger into Andre's head. Tears welled up in his eyes.

Dear God, don't let him die this way.

Clutching Andre's body between its legs, the wasp took off and headed away from the square. Slava raised the automatic weapon and emptied the magazine, missing because of his blurred vision. The wasp dropped low and skimmed across the square before disappearing down a side street.

Slava sat in the center of the square on his knees, sobbing like a child.

SASHA SURVEYED THE situation. Petra reached the church with the stray horse. Jason and Doc were still limping across the square and would be safe in a few minutes. The two were-hounds joined them, protecting their master.

No more wasps were left except the crippled one slowly crawling back toward the church. Riding over behind it, Sasha aimed the minigun and squeezed the trigger. She held it down for a good ten seconds, as much to kill the Demon Spawn as to purge her own anger. When she was done, it was unrecognizable.

Sasha glanced over at Slava and silently wept with him.

CHAPTER TWENTY-TWO

THE SURVIVORS STOOD in a circle at the front of the nave to be as far away as possible from the dead wasp sprawled across the north transept floor. Lilith and Lucifer, now back in their dog-like forms, sniffed and pawed at the carcass. The horses rested in the south transept, with Petra tending to them. Jason leaned against the wall, replaying in his mind the death struggle he had gone through. Doc sat on the pew nearest the group, sipping water from a canteen while Neal checked his vital signs. Still trying to recover from the loss of his friend, Slava sat at the far end of the pew, occasionally wiping tears from his eyes. Haneef positioned himself by the exit, his minigun reloaded and drawn, scanning the outside for any more insects that might be around.

Sasha broke the silence. "Neal, how's Doc?"

"He's winded from the fall and his back muscles are badly bruised. Thankfully he didn't hit his head, so there's no concussion."

"Is he well enough to travel?"

"He should be after a few hours rest."

Doc wiped the canteen across his face, mixing the condensation with his sweat. "I'll be fine. Give me a few minutes to catch my breath and then we can move out."

"To where?" asked Antoine.

Sasha crinkled her eyebrows. "What do you mean?"

"Are we continuing to Paris or heading home?"

"There's nothing to discuss," said David. "It's too dangerous to continue."

"It's just as dangerous to go back," Franco replied. "Remember, there's a swarm of flesh eaters between us and Mont St. Michel, way too many for us to handle."

"So?" David tried to drum up support from the others. "They were heading south, so we'll go north."

"Suppose there's an even bigger swarm to the north?" Ray chimed in.

"Now you're guessing."

Most of the group began to debate amongst themselves, each expressing his or her opinion of why they should proceed ahead or go back. It soon devolved into a series of arguments that became more vocal as tempers flared. Jason listened with a growing sense of disgust. He stepped away from the wall and rejoined the group. "We're going to Paris."

"You're not serious?" asked Reinhard.

"I am."

"How many more people do you vant to get killed?"

Jason glared at Reinhard. The German stood straight, towering six inches above Jason and holding his ground. For a moment, Jason considered taking a swing at him.

Sasha broke the standoff. "Jason, Reinhard is an asshole, but he's right. We've only been on the road two days and we've already lost two of our group. God knows what other Demon Spawn are waiting for us between here and Paris. If we continue, more of us are going to die."

Jason softened his anger when he answered her, although his tone remained firm. "We knew there'd be risks when we set out."

Sasha pointed to the wasp lying on the transept tiles. "We're not ready for this."

"And do you think Mont St. Michel is? Do you think they can defend against these wasps, or the pus zombies, or whatever else is out here? They're depending on us."

"Who's 'they'?" Josh snorted. "Jacques and the other elitists who never leave the abbey?"

"No." Jason snapped. "I'm talking about the refugees outside of town. What do you think is going to happen to them once the flesh eaters reach Mont St. Michel? If you don't care about them, what about us? How long would we survive a siege from the Demon Spawn? I don't want to go back and wait around to die."

Sasha moved closer to Jason and spoke softly. "Are you sure you're not pushing for this because of your mother?"

The question did not anger him as it usually would have. He had moved beyond that. "My mother destroyed the world because of her own recklessness. Nothing I can do will alter the past or how history views her. I realize that now." Jason looked at each of the others. "However, we have a chance to close the portals and take this world back. Not to make amends for anything my mother did, but because it's the right thing to do. That should be reason enough to push on."

"You realize what you're getting us into?" asked Doc. He meant it as an honest question. There was no anger or recrimination in his voice.

"I have no idea what we're getting into. It'll probably be a lot worse than what we've encountered so far. Are you…" Jason scanned the others standing around him. "…any of you, willing to go back to camp and tell the others we didn't try because it was too hard?"

No one answered. Jason turned to Slava. "What would Andre have done?"

The Russian sniffed. "He would have told us to nut up and move out."

"I'm with you," Sasha said to Jason. She reached out and gave his arm a squeeze.

Jason smiled at her and turned to Haneef. "What about you?"

Haneef shrugged. "It's Allah's will."

"Doc?"

"What choice do I have?" he said affably. "I'm the only one

117

who knows how to use the device."

With the team leads in consent, the others chimed in their agreement, except for Reinhard. Jason walked over to him, having to look up to meet his gaze. "And you?"

A grin of respect pierced his lips. "A German never backs down from a good fight. Count me in."

"Thank you."

Antoine crossed his arms across his chest. "With Andre gone, who's going to lead us?"

Shit, I hadn't thought about that. Jason hesitated only a moment before responding. "Slava will."

The Russian's head shot up. "No way."

"Why not? You're Andre's second in command."

"I am… was his friend. I'm a follower, not a leader."

Jason sighed. "Sasha, I don't think anyone will take offense if you're in charge."

Sasha raised her minigun. "Haneef and I have enough to do lugging these things around. Doc should be the one to take command."

Doc shook his head. He stood up, using his arm to support his shaky legs. "Face it, Jason. You're the only one here dedicated to this mission. You're also the only one qualified to lead us. If you won't do it, then we should head home."

Jason expected someone to object. He wanted someone to object. That would give him a reason to refuse. Instead, to his shock, they all sought guidance from him. Somehow this whole mission had now fallen on his shoulders. If he declined, the others would vote to return to Mont St. Michel and they would never close the portal. Whatever happened then would be on his conscious. If they continued, he would be responsible for everyone, and he knew that some of them, if not most, would never make it out alive. In either case, he would have blood on his hands. The question was how much.

Jason made his decision. "Saddle up. We move out in ten minutes. Who has the spare map?"

Slava reached into his inner jacket pocket. "I do."

"You keep it and stay close to me." Jason faced the door. "Sasha, Haneef. You're my back-ups in case something happens to me. Let's go over our strategy for the next leg of the mission."

CHAPTER TWENTY-THREE

JASON LEFT ST. Gervais through the north transept and reined in his horse at the top of the stairs. Lilith and Lucifer flanked him. Haneef and Sasha stepped out after him and stood on either side of the church doors. Placing their backs against the façade, they unslung their miniguns and held them in the firing position. When the two gunners nodded that they were ready, Jason proceeded down the stairs and into the street. Lilith and Lucifer stayed by him.

He glanced up at the bell tower where the nest originated, searching for movement. The thought occurred to him that they should have checked out the tower from the inside in case the wasp that took away Andre had doubled back. What good would it do? He had watched Andre take a stinger to the head, which must have scrambled the Russian's brains. They wouldn't be able to do anything for him, and taking the time to search the tower would only delay their getting back on the road. Besides, he didn't really want to know what was up there.

Jason and the werehounds traveled two hundred feet down the street, making as much noise as possible to attract the wasps. The rustling of wings fluttered across the square. His horse jumped back, almost throwing him from the mount. It even startled the werehounds. Jason spun around in the direction of the noise, expecting to see the surviving wasp bearing down on him. Instead, the commotion came from a flock of birds that had been resting in the shade of the water fountain and had taken flight. Only then did Jason notice that he had been holding his breath, and that his bowels and kidneys were straining not to release.

Some leader I am.

Jason scanned the roads for flesh eaters or other Demon Spawn. Once certain no dangers lurked nearby, he stopped his horse and waved the others on. One by one they exited the church. Petra and Sook-kyoung brought out Sasha and Haneef's horses and helped them into the saddle. Once the group gathered, the three teams formed up in single file, only this time each team kept fifty feet between themselves.

Jason stayed ahead of the others, reconnoitering the area. He set off to the right down Rue Gonfroy Fitz Rou, only pausing when he reached Rue Champ St. Michel. When his team had caught up and could cover him, he set off down Rue Champ St. Michel and headed for the edge of town. His team stayed one hundred feet behind him. It took less than an hour for them to cross Falaise. They exited the city into the woods, which they followed into open farmland before heading northeast for the N13, the main highway running between Caen and Paris. He planned to cross the N13 a few miles east of Lisieux and head east until they reached the Seine. After that, they would follow the river to Paris. By using this route rather than the main roads, Jason figured the team would encounter fewer Demon Spawn.

At least that is what Jason hoped.

CHAPTER TWENTY-FOUR

T HE REST OF the day passed without incident, which Jason was grateful for. The group had stopped around one o'clock for lunch, rested for an hour, and set off again. With luck, they would cross the N13 by dusk and set up camp for the night near the Seine.

As they approached the N13 halfway between L'Hotellerie and Thiberville, he noticed something out of place a quarter of a mile ahead of him. Much of the surrounding countryside on this side of the highway had been scorched black. Several wrecked vehicles stretched eastward for half a mile, ending near a pile of debris that stood in their path. Something stuck up from the road, towering sixty feet in the air. He assumed it was metal by the way it reflected the sunlight. Another large object sat on the embankment in the center of a scorched area, the tip also reflecting the sun.

Jason stopped his horse and called for the others to join him, waiting until they had gathered around.

"I want to check out what's up ahead. Sasha, your team is with me. The rest of you stay here and keep your eyes open. If you see any danger, fire off a few shots to get our attention and we'll fall back on you."

As the others formed a defensive circle in the field, Jason and Sasha's team approached the highway. They formed a line abreast, Sasha, Reinhard, and Antoine on Jason's right, the Gainesville Mafia on his left. Lucifer and Lilith raced ahead to scout for danger. Jason kept his eyes focused on the highway, scanning it for any signs of Demon Spawn. When they approached to within one hundred feet, he shifted his attention to the object resting on the embankment. It was charred and twisted. At first, he didn't recognize it. As they drew closer, though, he realized it was the port wing of a passenger aircraft. The engine had been torn off, leaving only the mount still attached. The wing itself, except for the tip, had been seared black by fire, most likely from the fuel tanks igniting.

They maneuvered their horses up the embankment and onto the N13.

"Oh, dear God," Sasha gasped. Jason thought it was an understatement.

The team stood in the middle of a crash site. It began six hundred feet to their right with two crushed cars in the westbound lanes and the remains of an eighteen-wheeler in the eastbound. The top of the trailer had been sheared off. Scorched earth began at the truck and curved to the left, finally ending where the port wing sat charred on the embankment. Beginning after the eighteen-wheeler, the pavement in the westbound lane was dug up as if something huge had dug its way across the surface. Chunks of metal, debris, and luggage littered the highway. Jason could make out a set of wrecked landing gear. The destroyed section of highway ended at the object that jutted up. At this distance, Jason could see it was the severed tail of the passenger liner that had been up ended. The blue stripes of an Air France jet, weathered from exposure to the sun and the elements, were still visible.

A breeze blew in from the west, bringing with it the smell of death. The others unslung their weapons and prepared to defend themselves. Jason knew the smell didn't belong to flesh eaters because he couldn't sense their presence. Nor did Lucifer or Lilith react. Besides, rather than their sickeningly sweet stench, this smelled like charred meat although less pungent, as if it had been diluted with time. He immediately knew where the odor came from.

"Stand down," he ordered. "We're not in any danger."

"How can you be so sure?" asked Antoine.

Jason didn't reply. Spurring on his horse, he headed left around the tail section. The others followed with their weapons still at the ready.

Reaching the opposite embankment, Jason's fears were confirmed. The main body of the airliner sat on the embankment, its nose pointing toward the field beyond, the metal and interior cabin scorched from the flames. A line of crumbled bodies stretched between the tail section and fuselage, with a mass of charred human remains bunched around the latter, survivors who had tried to escape while on fire and burned to death before they made it very far. Half a dozen other bodies spread out from the wreck, their bodies only partially charred. Jason didn't even want to think about the horrors that remained inside the aircraft.

The front doors of the aircraft were open and the emergency chutes deployed, so at least a few people had made it out alive.

The wind blew again, wafting over the wreckage and filling their nostrils with the stench of charred meat. Bill leaned to one side and vomited his lunch onto the highway.

Sasha grew pale. "Wh-what happened?"

Josh moved up beside Jason to get a closer look. "The plane must have been taking off from Charles de Gaulle Airport when the EMP hit. The pilot tried to land on the highway rather than crash into a field. He might have made it if it wasn't for the stalled vehicles. At least it happened quickly."

"We've seen worse," Antoine added matter-of-factly.

"How can you say that?" snapped Sasha. "Those people burned to death."

"They were the lucky ones," said Jason. "Did you notice the bodies that were only partially charred? The rest of their bodies didn't decay. They were stripped clean."

"By flesh eaters?" Reinhard's voice croaked.

"Probably."

Antoine chuckled. "Now the flesh eaters are into barbecue."

Sasha glared at the Moroccan, spun her horse around, and headed back to the others.

"What do we do now?" asked Shane.

"They're dead, and we can't do anything for them." Jason nudged his horse so he faced Shane. "Go back and tell the others we'll cross here as planned. Warn them it's gruesome so no one freaks out. The rest of us will wait here."

Shane nodded and road off after Sasha.

Jason looked at the rest of the team. "Spread out and keep about a hundred feet between you. Let me know if you see anything moving. Once the others have passed, fall back into line."

They acknowledged him and rode off to take up guard positions. Jason moved eastward down the highway, finding a spot where the pavement seemed easy enough to cross. The werehounds fell in behind him. He would stay here and usher the others through the wreckage.

Though outwardly calm, Jason's nerves were on edge. Not because of the carnage they had come across. In that respect, Antoine was correct. They had all seen worse. As they got closer to Paris, they came across an increasingly greater level of destruction and even more ferocious Demon Spawn. He had no idea what would be waiting for them when they reached the city. And as had been proven back in Falaise, his ability to sense the flesh eaters and soul vampires didn't extend to all Demon Spawn. Although he would never admit it to the others, he feared what they would find waiting for them.

He also feared that he didn't know how well he could lead them once they entered the city.

CHAPTER TWENTY-FIVE

THE GROUP STOPPED for the night five miles northeast of Thiberville. Jason ordered them to set up camp several hundred feet into the woods, that way they could build a fire that would not be seen. As always, each team took a four-hour guard shift along the perimeter, with Haneef's team drawing the first watch. When dinner ended, Jason made his way over to Doc, with Lucifer and Lilith in tow. Doc was rolling out his sleeping bag as Jason sat down on a rotted log. Blonde hair fell across his face. Jason tried to blow it away. It kept falling back, so he pushed it aside with his hand. The werehounds curled up on either side of him.

"Do you have a minute? I'm curious about something."

"What's up?"

"Why didn't I detect those wasps this morning before they attacked? I always know when flesh eaters or soul vampires are around, and I even felt a faint aura from the pus zombies, but I had no idea these particular Demon Spawn were in the area until we heard their buzzing." Jason leaned closer and glanced over his shoulder, making sure no one could hear him. "You don't think I'm losing my ability to sense these things, do you?"

Doc paused. "I've been thinking about that. The common link between the Demon Spawn we've encountered previously is human souls. Every time we've killed a flesh eater, we've seen the soul escape. And since pus zombies were once human, I assume their souls are probably still present inside the body. And of course, the soul vampires feed off them. That's where I think your psychic link is with—the souls. The wasps, on the other hand, were just monsters. It makes sense you wouldn't have a link with them."

"Great." Jason sat back and sighed. "So, I could wind up leading us all into a trap."

"No more than any of us would. At least now we know that you're not able to detect every Demon Spawn we'll encounter, so we won't get caught off guard again."

"That's not much comfort."

Doc chuckled and went back to spreading out his sleeping bag.

"How are you feeling?" asked Jason.

"My back and shoulders hurt from the fall. And when I hit the ground, the device slammed into my sternum. I think I may have bruised a rib. It's going to hurt a lot more in the morning."

"Do you feel well enough to go on?"

"Yeah."

"Good." Jason felt an honest concern for the Doc's well-being, so he broached the next subject carefully. "I need you to do something for me."

"What's that?"

"I need you to teach me and some of the others how the device works."

Doc was crestfallen. "Are you planning on sending me back?"

"No. But the incident with the wasps got me thinking. You're the only one who knows how to use that thing. If the Demon Spawn take you out, this mission fails. I figure the more of us who know how to deploy it, the greater our chances of success."

Doc thought about that for a few seconds. "Fair enough."

Once finished laying out his sleeping bag, Doc grabbed the saddle bag with the device and placed it in front of him. As he talked, he unlatched the flap and pulled it back.

"The design is quite simple. It has to be, otherwise I never would have been able to put it together without machine tools."

Doc reached into the bag with his good hand and removed the device. It had the shape of a football, only twice as large. The outside cladding was stainless steel. A one-inch rim ran up and down the length of the device and allowed the two halves to be joined with more than a dozen bolts. Jason sat forward and stared. It was the first time he had seen it. Doc handed it to him. Jason gingerly took it, intuitively knowing the destructive power it possessed.

"Usually anti-matter is created in a gaseous state, which is highly unstable. A year ago, your mother and I found a way to turn anti-matter into a solid. Theoretically, anti-matter in a solid state will still react violently if exposed to matter. We created six samples of solid anti-matter and stored them in these containers at CERN, which were left behind during the evacuation. That was the reason why Jacques sent Gruber's team to CERN months ago—to retrieve those samples."

"Why didn't you or Jacques tell anyone?"

"We didn't want to get anyone's hopes up. If those samples were destroyed, then this entire mission would have been scrapped."

Jason nodded. "Are all six samples in here?"

"No, this is just one of them. I left the others safely stored back in the infirmary. If for some reason this fails, I wanted to have back up." Doc pointed to the device. "The design is very simple. A chunk of solidified anti-matter sits at the center of the device in a vacuum inside a thick glass sphere. The anti-matter is held in place in the center of the vacuum by magnets surrounding the sphere."

"How do you detonate it?"

"All you have to do is throw it into the portal."

Jason furrowed his eyebrows. "That's it?"

Doc nodded. "I got the idea after what happened to my arm. The portal in Paris is an exit portal, so nothing from this world will be able to pass through without being destroyed. That means all you have to do is throw the device into it. The casing, nesting, and tube should disintegrate instantly. Once the anti-matter is exposed, it should generate an explosion that, with luck, will snuff out the portal."

"Wouldn't it widen the portal?"

"I don't think so." Doc thought for a moment. "Have you ever seen a fire crew put out an oil refinery blaze?"

"No."

"They lower explosives into the fire, place it near the top of the burning well, and ignite it. The blast creates a vacuum that only lasts for a few milliseconds, just enough time to starve the flames and extinguish the fire. This works on the same principle. In theory, the explosion of the anti-matter should be enough to blast the portal shut."

"In theory?" asked Jason.

Some of Doc's confidence deflated. "Yeah."

"And if you're wrong?"

"Then we died trying."

That last thought did not impress Jason very much.

He started to ask Doc what made him think they could get close enough to the portal to deploy the device when Lucifer's head shot up. His ears bent back and his lips curled. A growl escaped from deep in his throat. A moment later, Jason winced as the presence of numerous Demon Spawn overwhelmed his senses.

A blood-curdling screech cut through the darkness. A moment later, Haneef's minigun sprang to life, its staccato firing echoing amongst the trees, followed by a chorus of screeches.

Jason jumped to his feet and grabbed his crossbow. "Soul vampires!"

CHAPTER TWENTY-SIX

JASON RACED OFF toward the sound of the gunfire. The two werehounds morphed into their demonic forms and began to run after him. Jason spun around. "Stay here and guard Doc."

Lilith immediately circled back around and crouched down by Doc, ready to spring to the attack. Lucifer inched forward, wanting to stay with his master. His ears were flattened and his eyes pleaded. Jason didn't have time for this.

"I said stay. Keep Doc safe."

Lucifer whimpered once before going back and taking his place opposite Lilith.

By now, additional weapons fire could be heard throughout camp as the rest of the group sprang into defense. The gunfire came from the north where Haneef had been on guard. So far, no other firing had occurred. Jason wondered if that meant that the attack was a head-on assault coming from only one direction, which seemed unlikely considering the soul vampires were superior hunters. He assumed that either the attack on the flanks had not taken place yet, or that in their excitement the rest of the group had forgotten to circle the wagons.

LUCIFER AND LILITH faced south, their ears arched forward. A second later, Doc heard the rustling of soul vampires racing through the undergrowth toward him. He stumbled to his feet and clutched the saddle bag tight against his chest. The two werehounds placed themselves between him and the approaching demons.

Two soul vampires emerged from the darkness. The closest one lunged, aiming for Doc. Doc flinched, ready to be taken down. Lucifer jumped and slammed into the soul vampire in mid-leap, his jaws snapping shut around its neck. The two hit the ground. Lucifer pinned the demon on its back, his front paws on its chest and his jaws still clenched around its throat. With a ferocious twist of his head, the werehound ripped out the soul vampire's throat. Its screech drowned out into a blood-soaked gurgle and its body convulsed for a few seconds before going limp. Lucifer slapped the eyeless head with a paw, making sure it was dead.

The second soul vampire darted toward Lilith. She bolted forward to confront it. At the last second, the demon broke left and circled around her. Lilith tried to stop, sliding several feet along the fallen leaves and twigs before regaining her footing. The soul vampire cut back to the right. For a moment, Doc thought it would come after him. Instead, it ran past him toward the center of camp.

OUTSIDE THE GLARE of the campfire, Sasha lifted her minigun. Antoine stood behind her, holding the ammo pack in place while she slid her arms through the straps. Jason rushed over to them.

"Where are the others?" he asked.

"Most went north to help Haneef." Sasha rested the straps on her shoulder and fastened the harness around her waist. "I sent some of my people to watch the flanks."

"What about to the south?"

"We're going to take care of—"

The sounds of one of the werehounds and a soul vampire engaging in a struggle cut off Sasha. Growls and screeches accompanied the scuffling. The three looked toward where Doc sat.

In the fringes of the fire light, Jason saw a soul vampire

rushing through the woods toward them. He raised his crossbow, aiming at the moving target. Antoine saw it, too, and shoved Sasha out of the way. She fell to the dirt, the weight of the gun pinning her down. The soul vampire lunged, passing over Sasha and hitting Antoine instead, knocking him over.

RESTING ON HIS knees, Doc struggled to remove his Glock from its holster when he heard something approaching. His eyes locked on the shadow. Lucifer lifted his head from the soul vampire's carcass and growled. Doc exhaled with relief when he saw that the approaching figure was Reinhard.

"Are you okay?" he asked. "I'm fine."

Doc staggered to his feet and Lucifer saddled up beside him.

"Vere is Bait?"

Doc gestured behind him. "He went to check out the gunfire."

Reinhard relaxed. "I'll stand guard here. Go see if anyone needs you."

Doc nodded and headed back into camp with Lucifer staying close to his side.

HANEEF STOOD IN the center of the line, firing short controlled bursts as a horde of soul vampires swarmed them. The Gainesville Mafia, Renato, and Philippe stood to his right, with Neal, David, and Franco to his left. They had already taken down ten of the demons in less than a minute, and at least another half dozen came crashing through the woods toward them.

One soul vampire leaped out of the dark toward Haneef. He pressed the trigger and swung the barrel toward it. The hail of gunfire tore it apart, throwing the shredded carcass backward until it collided with another approaching demon. The second one stumbled and fell to the ground. Before it could get back up, Haneef lowered the minigun and decimated it with a twenty-round burst.

Behind them, Petra cried out for help.

AS THE ATTACK unfolded, Petra, Sook-kyoung, and Ray grabbed their weapons and moved off to protect the left flank. Using the trees as cover, they scanned the area ahead of them for signs of movement. Petra noticed that every few seconds Ray would check behind them, making sure nothing was sneaking up from the rear. She had begun to breathe easier when the horses off to her left stirred. At first, they merely stamped their feet. After a few seconds, the commotion grew into a panic. They whinnied and bit at the bridles that tied them to the trees. She knew it could mean only one thing.

Petra called out to Sook-kyoung. "The vampires are attacking the horses."

Before Sook-kyoung could stop her, Petra broke rank.

She found a single soul vampire attacking the last horse in the herd. Every time it got close, the horse kicked at it with its hind legs, smashing its hoofs into the demon's face and chest. The soul vampire judged its attack and, after one kick when the horse's legs were descending, it leapt onto the animal's back and plunged its fangs into its neck. The horse bucked, trying to throw off the demon.

Petra switched her FAMAS to single shot mode and aimed, centering the sights on the soul vampire's head. She pulled the trigger. Because of the horse's bucking, the bullet hit the demon's neck. It released its bite on the horse and spun around, seeing Petra standing only ten feet away. She steadied her aim for another shot when the demon lunged. Petra raised the assault rifle across her face. The soul vampire crashed into her, propelling them both to the ground. It plunged its head toward her neck and closed its jaws around the weapon's barrel. Petra locked her elbows, trying to keep the demon at arms' length. She knew from the pain in her muscles that she would not be able to hold it away for long.

"Somebody help me!" she yelled.

SASHA TRIED TO get her footing in the dirt when she heard something on four legs run up to her. She expected to see a soul vampire going for her throat. Instead, Lilith crossed in front of the woman and stood to her left, her head darting around in search of danger. A second later, a hand wrapped itself under her shoulder and lifted her off the ground.

"Did you get bit?" asked Doc.

"No. Antoine pushed me out of the way in time."

Fear suddenly gripped her. Spinning around, she desperately searched for Jason.

JASON DROPPED HIS crossbow and unsheathed his machete as he ran over to help Antoine, although the Moroccan didn't need help. Even though he was on the ground with the soul vampire crouched on top of him, Antoine had his left hand around its neck, holding the demon in place while he pounded his right fist into its face. With each punch, the soul vampire became more disoriented. After the fifth blow, it wrenched itself free from Antoine's grip and tried to escape, running only a few yards before tumbling onto its side. Antoine jumped to his feet and chased after it. He kicked the soul vampire in the abdomen. The demon mewled and curled up in a fetal position. Antoine continued savaging the demon until, on the seventh kick, it convulsed violently. A pathetic moan escaped from its jaws, followed by a trickle of blood. The soul vampire's head dropped to one side.

Stepping over, Jason raised the machete and brought it down across the demon's neck. The head bounced in the dirt before coming to a stop a few inches from the lifeless body.

"Are you hurt?" asked Jason.

"It takes more than a Demon Spawn to bring me down." Antoine coughed up a wad of phlegm and spit it onto the demon's severed head.

Jason smiled at the bravado. Then he heard Petra cry out in agony.

PETRA SMELLED THE stench of acid coming from the soul vampire's mouth. She shifted her body to the right and her arms to the left, which turned its head to one side. The soul vampire vomited. The FAMAS lodged in its throat diverted much of the spew, but not enough. One stream shot down her left arm and splattered her face. The burning was immediate and intense. She felt the layers of skin shear off and screamed as the acid ate through her muscles. Christ, she even felt it melting her teeth. Petra released her grip on the FAMAS. The soul vampire flicked its head to the right, tossing the weapon into the woods. It turned back and snarled, its jaws open wide, ready to feed. *Thank God*, she thought. *Please put me out of my misery.*

She was only vaguely aware of someone rushing up, and then the soul vampire was no longer on top of her. Blood dripped across her face, providing some relieve from the agony. It was the last sensation she remembered.

"GO HELP PETRA," said Ray. "I'll be fine."

Sook-kyoung headed toward where they had tied up the horses. She found Petra pinned to the ground by one of the demons. It had vomited acid bile on her. Even over the woman's screams, Sook-kyoung could hear the sizzling as it ate away at Petra's flesh. The soul vampire ripped the automatic weapon out of Petra's hands. Sook-kyoung ran up and launched a drop kick into the demon's face. Her foot connected with its mouth, knocking it off Petra. Broken fangs and blood dripped onto the wounded woman's face. The soul vampire rolled into a crouching position. It snarled at Sook-kyoung, preparing to pounce. Sook-kyoung took up a defensive stance. When it lunged, she jumped and spun her body to the right, using her left leg to drive a roundhouse kick to the demon's head. It stumbled off to the right and landed face first in the dirt, dazed. Sook-kyoung rushed over, raised her right leg, and brought the heel down on the back of its neck with a loud crack. The soul vampire went limp.

Sook-kyoung raced over to Petra and knelt beside her. When she leaned over and tilted Petra's face to the side to get a better view, her dinner rose up in her throat. The left side of Petra's cheek had been burned away, exposing the jaw underneath. Her arm had suffered third degree burns, and her flightsuit was seared into the flesh in several places. The skin and muscles on her hand were gone, leaving only a few meaty clumps covering the knuckles and thumb.

"Doc!" Sook-kyoung screamed. "I need you now!"

HANEEF HEARD SOOK-KYOUNG'S cry for help. His group had gunned down the last soul vampire nearly a minute ago, and now the woods were quiet except for the panicked neighing of the horses and the shouts and screams from the others. He closed his eyes and said a prayer to Allah for whichever of their comrades had fallen.

"Is everyone okay?"

Each of those in the line applied in the affirmative, except for Renato. Haneef snapped his fingers to get the Italian's attention, pointed to him, and raised his eyebrows. Renato smiled and gave him a nod indicating he was fine.

Stepping away from the others, Haneef headed toward the mass of mutilated soul vampires.

"Where are you going?" asked Josh.

"You guys stay here and keep me covered. I want to get a body count."

JASON AND DOC were already heading toward the sound of the scream when Sook-kyoung called to them. Jason could tell by her voice that something bad had happened. The two quickened their pace. They found Sook-kyoung kneeling beside Petra. The latter didn't move. Even in the dim light this far from the campfire, Jason could tell she had been hurt badly. The panic in Sook-kyoung's eyes confirmed Jason's worst fears.

"One of the vampires spit acid vomit on her." She spoke rapidly, running her words together. "You have to do something for her."

"Let me see." Doc knelt beside Petra and placed his index and middle finger against her carotid artery.

"Is she…?" Jason let his question fall off.

"She's unconscious. Give me your canteen."

Jason unscrewed the top and handed it over. Doc held it above Petra's face and poured it out in small amounts, washing away the residual acid. As he cleaned her up, he glanced to Sook-kyoung. "My medkit is attached to my saddle. Please get it for me."

"W-will she be all right?" Sook-kyoung stammered.

"Not if I don't get my medkit."

Sook-kyoung nodded and ran off.

Sasha and Antoine arrived at the scene. When Sasha saw Petra's face she gasped. Even Antoine closed his eyes and bowed his head.

"Go find Neal and bring him here," Doc ordered Sasha.

She hesitated a second before darting off into the dark.

Petra opened her eyes. They wandered for several seconds, glazed and unfocused. Finally, she recognized Doc and forced a wan smile that seemed grotesque through the seared off skin from her cheek. "Hey, Doc," she rasped.

Doc took her right hand and squeezed, trying to offer comfort. "How are you feeling, Petra?"

"Tired." She shrugged and winced. "And my left arm hurts."

"You'll be fine. Just lay there and stay calm."

Sook-kyoung came up with the medkit and unlatched the top. Doc reached in and pulled out a small vial filled with a colorless liquid and a hypodermic needle. He handed them to the Korean. "Fill the needle with eight milligrams."

Sook-kyoung took them. "What is it?"

"Morphine."

Jason knelt on the other side of Petra. He spoke quietly so no one else could hear. "Is she going to make it?"

Doc shook his head.

CHAPTER TWENTY-SEVEN

NEAL CAME RUNNING up. Jason stood and walked over to Sook-kyoung and Antoinc. Sasha followed him.

"Were there any other casualties?" Jason asked Sook-kyoung.

She stared at Petra lying on the ground.

"Sook-kyoung!"

She snapped her attention to Jason. "What?"

"Were there any other casualties?"

"Not on the left flank."

"Good. Go check on Ray and stay with him until I figure out what we're going to do."

"Yes, sir." Sook-kyoung raced off.

Sir? Jason would have laughed if he could have found anything humorous about the situation. He stepped over to Antoine.

"I don't want to be surprised again. Take up position to the south in case there are any more of those things lurking around."

The Moroccan nodded and walked off.

Slava appeared out of the darkness and approached the campfire. "Who screamed?"

"Petra," said Jason. "One of the soul vampires vomited on her."

"How bad?"

"Most of her left arm and half her face are burned."

"Shit."

"Did you guys suffer any casualties?"

The Russian shook his head. "Only three soul vampires attacked us, and we took them out easily enough. It sounded like all the fighting came from the north."

Jason had not heard from Haneef's team yet. He was about to send Slava to check when he saw Haneef and Josh approaching.

"How did you make out?" asked Jason.

"No one was hurt. I used all my ammo, though." Haneef unstrapped his backpack as he spoke and slid it off his shoulders.

"How many came after you?"

"Twenty-three."

"Christ," said Slava. "That means almost thirty of them attacked us."

"We've never seen them travel in such numbers before," added Sasha.

"They didn't sneak up on us like they usually do." Haneef rotated his shoulders to work out the kinks. "They started their charge about three hundred feet out. I heard them before I saw them. Thank Allah, otherwise we would have been overrun."

"Why are they behaving this way?" Jason asked almost to himself.

"Because they're starving." The answer came from Doc. Only then did Jason realize the doctor had joined them, leaving Neal to dress Petra's wounds. "They abandoned their pack mentality and went feral, putting aside cooperation and stealth out of desperation for food. One of them even went after the horses, which we've never seen them do before. I bet they haven't eaten in weeks."

"Which means…?" Slava's question trailed off.

Sasha answered. "There's no more food in the area."

"Which means there are no humans in the area," added Jason.

No one wanted to openly speculate what that meant for their chances of survival.

Jason changed the subject. "What's going to happen to Petra?"

"She's not going to make it." Doc lowered his gaze.

"Are you sure?"

"If I could get her proper medical care, she might have a chance."

"Then we have to head back to Mont St. Michel," demanded Sasha.

"That won't do any good. It's a three-day journey, and the ride would kill her. Besides, her wounds are so bad that within forty-eight hours they'll become infected. Within a week her body will go septic and she'll die."

"Don't you have any antibiotics to give her?" Sasha pleaded.

"Not enough to stave off the infection that she's going to develop."

"Is she in pain now?" asked Jason.

"Not that much. The burns happened so quickly that most of the nerve endings in her arm and face were destroyed. She's uncomfortable, although not as much as she should be under the circumstances. The morphine I gave her is to help her sleep."

Jason swallowed hard, already knowing the answer to his question. "What do you recommend?"

Doc hesitated. "You're not going to like my answer."

"No!" cried Sasha. "We're not going to kill her."

"She's dead already," Doc replied with as much humanity as he could muster. "Once the infection sets in and spreads, she's going to be in unbearable pain. Sooner or later we're going to have to end her suffering."

"Besides," added Slava. "If we take her along, she'll slow us down and make us vulnerable to whatever else is waiting out there."

Sasha turned to Jason, her eyes pleading. "You can't let them do this."

When Jason glanced over at Petra, his heart sank. She had been mortally wounded trying to protect the animals she loved so much. Lucifer and Lilith sat facing her, whimpering. Even they knew she would not make it. He remembered a month ago when they had to shoot one of the horses that had developed an intestinal blockage they couldn't remove. Petra cried for hours. Now he had to make the same decision about her, with the difference being that Petra was human and not an animal.

"Slava, make a stretcher that we can drag behind one of the horses. We're taking her with us in the morning."

"Are you sure?" the Russian asked.

"Consider what you're doing," added Doc. "You're not helping her any."

"I know. But I'm not going to put her down here in the woods like a dog. Tomorrow night we'll find an abandoned farmhouse and let her die in bed with some dignity."

Slava nodded. "I'll get right on it."

As the Russian ran off to make the stretcher, Jason looked at Sasha, hoping she approved. He noticed she had a tear in her eyes.

Doc placed his hand on Jason's shoulder and squeezed. "Your mother would be proud of you."

Screw my mother, Jason sneered inwardly. *Petra is going to die because of the world she created.*

CHAPTER TWENTY-EIGHT

AFTER THE ATTACK by the soul vampires, no one risked more than a few minutes sleep. Jason waited until half an hour after dawn before setting out to ensure they had plenty of daylight to see by in case any more Demon Spawn lurked in the area. A low overcast hung in the sky, which kept the sun from beating down on them. At least that would make Petra a little more comfortable.

Petra's horse followed thirty feet back, pulling behind it the stretcher Josh and Shane had rigged together for her and tethered to the saddle. Doc rode on one side of Petra's horse and Neal on the other, the latter holding the reins in his hands so the animal couldn't run away. The stretcher bumped and jostled along the uneven terrain. The trip would have been unbearable for Petra if Doc had not given her a second dose of morphine.

Jason promised himself that he would make sure she died peacefully and with dignity.

They had ridden for nearly two hours when Sasha rode up alongside of Jason. "We're not heading to Les Andelys like we originally planned, are we?"

"No, we're not." Jason's eyes narrowed. "How did you know that?"

"Because Les Andelys is to the north, and we've been heading into the sun all morning. Why the change in plans?"

"I was studying the map last night and I think I've found a better route." Jason pulled the map out of his jacket pocket and passed it to Sasha, who opened it up to the surrounding region.

The Seine River made a long S turn to the southwest, then to the northeast, and then southwest, a diversion of six miles. Les Andelys sat at the tip of the northeast bend. "The bridge crossing the Seine at that point would put us right in the center of the city. If we run into any Demon Spawn, we'd have no place to run."

"So where are we heading?"

"Villers sur Le Roule." Jason leaned over and stretched out his hand, pointing to a small village near the end of the second southwest loop where the Seine straightened out and continued running east. "There's plenty of open farmland south of the village, so we can pick up the river there. Less than a mile east of that is a bridge outside of Gaillon."

"Gaillon?" Sasha studied the map. "Jason, that town is five times the side of Les Andelys.

"There's several hundred feet of farmland and warehouses between the town and the riverbank. If we run into Demon Spawn, we have more room to maneuver."

"That's risky." Sasha handed back the map. "You should have consulted us."

Jason felt his chest tighten and his face flush. "Why?"

Sasha stared at him, unable to respond, which made Jason even more furious.

"Everyone, including you, asked me to lead the group. Now you're questioning me. Would you have expected Andre to clear his decisions with the rest of you?"

Sasha remained silent, but Jason already knew the answer. "You don't trust my judgment because I'm only sixteen."

"I didn't say that," snapped Sasha. The tone of her voice expressed more hurt than anger.

"If you didn't think I was qualified to lead this group, you should have taken over command. You didn't, and now I'm in charge. So, deal with it." Jason whipped the reins to get his horse to move faster. "Fall back with your team. And stay alert."

Sasha stared at him, a pained expression on her face. *Good*, thought Jason. *Now you know what it feels like.*

He left Sasha behind and didn't bother to look back.

SEVERAL HOURS LATER, the group traveled through the woods south of Villers sur Le Roule. The Seine River should be only a quarter of a mile in front of them. Jason kept his eyes on the tree line, hoping to catch a glimpse of it. He heard galloping behind him, hoping it was Sasha coming up to apologize for her behavior. This time Doc joined him.

"Is Petra okay?"

"I guess," Doc answered, distracted. "Something's wrong."

"What?"

"Have you noticed how hot it's suddenly gotten?"

It had not registered with Jason until now. He had assumed it was the late morning temperature rise, except that the sun remained behind the clouds and they were in the woods where it should be cooler. It now became apparent that the closer they got to the Seine, the warmer it became.

"And listen," added Doc.

At first Jason didn't hear anything, but after a few seconds he heard what Doc was referring to. He had not noticed it at first because it blended with the surroundings. From ahead of them came a low, steady rumble like the sound of a furnace, only louder. He assumed either Villers sur Le Roule or the forest might be on fire, yet he saw no indications of black smoke. The sky was clear except for the clouds.

The group broke through the tree line into open ground. The Seine lay two hundred feet ahead of them, or more precisely, what used to be the Seine. In place of water, a river of lava flowed between the two banks, a reddish-orange mass that moved past them heading west. All the vegetation and structures within fifty feet of the banks had been burned away.

A lava bubble exploded with a pop, spewing a finger of molten rock across the ground where it sizzled against the scorched earth. Lilith whined and raced back to the rear of the group.

Slava moved up on Jason's left. "What the…?"

"Any theories about this?" Jason asked Doc.

Doc shook his head. "Beats me."

"What do we do now?" asked Slava.

"We stick to the plan," Jason answered. "We'll follow the river east and see if there's any place to cross. Tell everyone to keep at least one hundred feet between themselves and the lava."

As Slava went to back to pass along the orders, Jason and Doc headed east. Less than a mile ahead of them sat the outskirts of Gaillon.

CHAPTER TWENTY-NINE

THE GROUP APPROACHED the split in the road outside of Gaillon. Jason opted for the southern route that led to the warehouse district rather than the one that ran along the river, wanting to put as much distance as possible between his people and the lava. Gaillon was a quarter of a mile to the south opposite overgrown farmland. Everyone remained on high alert, with their weapons unslung and prepared for anything that might lunge at them from the buildings to their left or the tall grass to their right. Lucifer and Lilith stayed close to their master. Jason closed his eyes and concentrated on his surroundings, trying to detect the presence of any Demon Spawn. Nothing stirred, not even wildlife.

Passing underneath the elevated road that led to the bridge, Jason veered left and led the group up the ramp leading to the highway. Cars and trucks sat at various angles across the two lanes, having been left where they stalled following the EMP. He raised his hand and ordered the others to stop. "Stay here. I want to check the bridge and make sure it's safe to cross."

Sasha moved out of line to join him, but Jason pointed to Haneef. "You're with me."

Sasha brought her horse to a stop, a pained expression on her. She spun the horse around so she didn't have to face Jason.

Jason and Haneef continued ahead, maneuvering around the abandoned vehicles. The heat became stifling the closer they got to the bridge. Sweat poured down Jason's face and soaked the back of his flightsuit. Even the horses were uncomfortable and strained to go back, pulling against their harness and snorting in protest. The two riders found it difficult to keep them moving forward. As they approached the span, Jason realized their attempt at crossing here would be futile. The heat from the lava had melted the asphalt and exposed the steel structure. Even the metal frame had suffered damage, the intense heat warping and twisting the girders in the center.

Haneef frowned. "My friend, even Allah isn't going to be able to get us across here."

"Damn it."

"What now?"

"We continue going east. Hopefully we'll find a place to cross before we reach Paris."

The two started to head back. Jason paused and stared down into the lava where something had caught his attention. He studied the surface for thirty seconds, hoping to see it again. There was nothing there except the lava flowing west.

Haneef noticed Jason had stopped. "Is everything all right?"

"I thought I saw something." Jason spurred on his horse. He convinced himself that he had imagined it, that last night's encounter with the soul vampires had made him jittery and he was now seeing demons where they didn't exist.

Still, he could have sworn he saw the top of a head and a pair of eyes staring at him from the center of the lava flow.

CHAPTER THIRTY

THE GROUP CONTINUED east along the riverbank. The sun had begun its slow descent in the west and in two hours it would be dusk. They would need to find a place soon to set up camp. After last night, Jason didn't want to be out in the open once the sun had gone down.

Half a mile ahead of them sat another town. Jason consulted the map. It was Notre Dame de la Garenne. A few miles beyond that was Le Goulet. According to the map, Le Goulet was a small village with no major structures other than a scattering of homes. Jason figured that would be a good place to rest, and hopefully there would be no Demon Spawn around to worry about. They could set themselves up in one of the houses, which would be easily defendable. Plus, it would provide a decent place to put Petra to rest.

As they made their way past the outskirts of Notre Dame de la Garenne and into the village, a sense of unease settled over Jason. It was not the usual sixth sense he felt whenever he detected the aura of flesh eaters or soul vampires. This felt more like a premonition that something lurked nearby, watching them. Unslinging his crossbow, he pulled back the bolt and dropped an arrow into the slot. Out of the corner of his eye, he saw Slava staring at him. The Russian moved ahead and slid his FAMAS off his shoulder.

"What do you see?"

"I don't see anything," answered Jason. His eyes scanned the buildings and streets in front of him. "I feel it."

"Your sixth sense?"

"No. More like a gut feeling that something dangerous is nearby."

"That's good enough for me."

"Drop back and warn the others to be careful. And let's pick up the pace. I want to clear this town as quickly as possible."

"You got it." Slava backtracked to warn the others and immediately yanked the animal to a stop. His eyes grew wide. His lips trembled. "Mother of God."

Jason spun his horse around and cursed under his breath.

At first, Jason thought a stream of lava had overflown the banks behind Haneef's team. Then the lava stream pulled itself upright and took humanoid shape. It stood thirty feet tall, with legs and arms as thick as trees. A bulbous outcrop on top of the torso served as the thing's head. Its fiery orange eyes fixed on Philippe, the last person in line on Haneef's team. Before Jason could react, the magma monster lumbered onto the bank only a few yards from Philippe. Each movement of its molten legs sounded like the sloshing of waves colliding with a seawall. Philippe heard the noise, but by the time he saw the magma monster it was too late. Its arm swung out, slapping the Frenchman and his horse. Both burst into flames as they were tossed to one side. The two thrashed around as fire consumed them, the terrified neighing of the horse mixing with Philippe's agonized death cries.

Since Sasha's team brought up the rear, she had time to fall back. Once the team reached the outskirts of the town, they headed inland and disappeared behind a warehouse. Renato went to help Philippe, an act of courage that cost him his life. The magma monster saw the Italian and moved toward him, leaving burning footsteps in its wake.

"Renato!" Jason shouted. "Get out of there!"

Renato tried to run. However, his horse panicked at the approaching menace and spun around in a circle. The magma monster lumbered forward and reached out a fiery hand, snatching Renato from his saddle. Globs of lava dripped onto the horse. The terrified animal bolted, bucking and neighing as it disappeared down a side street. Renato screamed as his cloths and skin ignited. The flames climbed up his torso, searing his face black. The Italian's eyes exploded in their sockets, and his tongue shriveled in his mouth. His anguished cries became stifled when he breathed in, the intense heat burning out his vocal cords and searing his lungs. The creature gazed curiously at the corpse in its hand. Arching its arm back, it flung Renato's charcoaled remains into the center of the lava flow.

Jason called out, "Everyone move inland and head for the other side of town! We'll meet up there!"

Slava kicked his horse in the side and led the way, with the others following him off the embankment and into town. Doc and Neal dragged Petra's horse between them, the frantic ride bouncing her around on the stretcher. As the others escaped, Jason hung back, serving as a decoy to keep the creature distracted so it didn't go after the others. Beside him, the two werehounds hung close, too terrified to morph into their demonic forms. Lucifer crouched forward on his front paws, growling and barking at the approaching Demon Spawn. Lilith glanced up at Jason as if pleading him to run. The magma monster was less than fifty feet away.

"Hang tight, girl."

Jason heard the familiar clatter of a minigun. Sasha had backtracked and now stood seventy-five feet behind the creature, still mounted on her horse, the minigun blazing. Hundreds of rounds tore into it with no affect. A few shells passed through the Demon Spawn, exiting out its chest as chunks of molten metal. The magma monster turned to face the nuisance. Upon seeing Sasha, it plodded toward her. Rather than retreat, she stood her ground, pumping a useless fusillade of gunfire into it. Jason became frantic. He yelled for Sasha to run, but she couldn't her him. Or she was too stubborn to listen. He wanted to go to her rescue, yet his horse wouldn't budge. Jason watched in horror as the magma monster drew nearer to Sasha. If she didn't move within the next few seconds, it would be close enough to strike her down.

Something flashed out of one of the side streets and slammed into the creature's torso, exploding with a white flash of light. The creature bellowed, an ungodly cry that sounded like the roar of an anguished blast furnace. The area around the impact zone turned grey and hard. A second and third object shot out of the same side street in rapid succession, one striking the creature's abdomen, the other its head. Both exploded with the same white light, and both created the same grey, hardened area. The magma monster wailed and held its hands up to its side, trying to deflect the objects. It slogged its way back toward the Seine. As it re-entered the lava flow, a fourth object struck it in the center of its back. The magma monster howled one final time before disappearing beneath the surface.

With the danger gone, Jason finally got his horse to move. He set off after Sasha, pausing when he got to the side street from where the projectiles had come. Seven figures stood at the intersection. They all wore leather greatcoats. Six were men, three of whom carried rocket launchers. The other three carried satchel bags and AK-47s, the latter of which they kept trained on him and Sasha. The three men with the rocket launchers moved toward the lava flow, keeping their weapons ready in case the magma monster returned.

The seventh person was a young girl about Jason's age. She had long brunette hair tied in a ponytail that hung down to her waist. An AK-47 dangled from her left hand, pointed at the ground. Though she had the poise and bearing of a fighter, her face was soft, having lost none of its teenage charm. She approached Jason and grinned, her cheeks puffing out. She walked up to his horse and extended her right hand.

"I'm Jeanette," she said with a French accent. "As you Americans say, it looks like we showed up in the nick of time."

CHAPTER THIRTY-ONE

J ASON SLID OFF his horse and stood for a moment, dumb-struck. He could not be quite sure if it was because his life had been saved thanks to this group of strangers who appeared out of nowhere, or because they were led by an attractive teenage girl. He pushed the loose hair back behind his ears as he stepped forward. Lucifer and Lilith started to follow, so he motioned for them to stay. Jeanette offered her hand and Jason took it. His palm tingled when he touched her. The girl's skin felt especially warm and silky. He gave it a single weak pump.

Way to go. Jason felt his face flush. *This girl defeated a magma monster. No handshake of yours is going to hurt her.*

Trying to dig himself out of his embarrassment, Jason of-fered up the only smartass response he could come up with. "Better in the nick of time than too late."

Damn, what a lame answer. A part of Jason hoped the magma monster would come back out of the Seine and drag him away.

Jeanette smiled. When she did, her green eyes glowed. "And do you have a name?"

"Jason."

Off to his right, Sasha cleared her throat. She stood a few feet away holding the horse's reins in her hand. He detected the jealousy underneath the forced grin. "Oh, and this is Sasha, one of my team leaders."

One of the men carrying an AK-47 stepped up beside Jeanette and spoke in French. Jeanette responded and began to walk away. "Come with us."

"Is everything okay?" asked Sasha.

"Yes, Francois is suggesting we get out of her before the magma monster comes back."

"Where are we going?" Jason asked.

"We're taking you back to our place. It's not far from here and it's well defended. You're welcome to stay the night."

Jason perked up. "I'd like that."

Jeanette beamed.

Sasha huffed.

The three men carrying rocket launchers waited until the others were clear before following.

Jason caught up with Jeanette, leading his horse behind him. "I have to round up the rest of my group."

"My people are doing that now. They'll meet us on the other side of town."

"Thanks for helping out back there. We were lucky you came along when you did."

"It was more than luck. We were on patrol when we saw your group walking along the embankment. It's a shame we arrived too late to save your friends."

In the excitement of meeting Jeanette, Jason had forgotten about Philippe and Renato. He closed his eyes and said a silent prayer for his fallen comrades.

Sasha moved up along the other side of Jeanette. "I pumped a couple of hundred rounds into that thing with no effect. How did you stop it with regular rocket shells?"

"Oh, there's nothing regular about them. The shells contain liquid nitrogen. It freezes the skin. It's the only weapon effective against that thing."

"Where did you find liquid nitrogen out here?" asked Jason.

"We didn't find it out here," Jeanette chuckled. "We confiscated it on one of our foraging raids into Paris."

Jason stopped short. "You've been to Paris?"

"Several times." Jeanette glanced over her shoulder. "Why?"

"Because that's where we're heading."

The girl's face became grim. "We need to have a long talk first."

Jason let the conversation drop. A few minutes later, they reached the southern outskirts of Notre Dame de la Garenne. The rest of his team milled around in a circle. Four men stood nearby with their weapons cradled in their arms. Jeanette swiped her hand across her neck and the four men relaxed, slinging the weapons over their shoulder.

Doc knelt by Petra, giving her a shot from a hypodermic. When he saw Jason and Sasha approaching, he said, "Thank God. I thought that thing had gotten you."

"We're fine. How's Petra?"

"She got jostled around as we raced through town. She's been moaning for the past ten minutes, so I gave her another shot of morphine."

"What happened to her?" asked Jeanette.

"Last night we were attacked by thirty soul vampires," answered Doc. "One of them spewed acid on her."

Jeanette mouthed the question "thirty?" to Jason. He nodded.

"You'll be safe tonight," she said. "Our camp is not far from here. You'll be able to get a good night's rest, and we'll find a bed to make your friend comfortable."

"Thanks."

"My pleasure." Jeanette flashed him a flirtatious smile. "Let's move out. I want to make it back to camp before night fall."

★   ★   ★

THE GROUP CONTINUED south for another hour, crossing through fields and farmland covered in high grass. Off in the distance were three deserted villages, the buildings dark and silent against the encroaching dusk. The only sound came from birds chirping their final song of the day and the crunching of the dried underbrush beneath their feet.

Jason was apprehensive. Not because of their newfound friends. So far, no one on Jeanette's team had given him any reason to make him fear for his people's safety. No, his concern came from their security methods. For the past ten minutes, they had followed a well-worn path through the grass that even flesh eaters could follow like an arrow leading directly to food. If Jeanette's travel patterns were so predictable, he wondered how secure her camp could be.

There were a lot of things Jason wondered about, and not just Jeanette. Who were these people? How did they get here? Most importantly, how did they survive this long? His teams had only been out here for a few days and already had run into more Demon Spawn then they had seen in the past six months and had lost three of their number with one severely wounded. Yet these people not only seemed to have survived, they had adapted and taken the fight back to the Demon Spawn. And they claimed to have traveled frequently into Paris. He would have to find out as much as he could about Jeanette's group.

As they exited the overgrown grass, Jeanette and the others spread out in a line abreast. She stopped and waited for Jason. Two hundred feet ahead of them sat a wooded area. At first nothing seemed unusual. Once his eyes adjusted to the fading light, he noticed three dark shadows within the tree line. Jeanette removed a hand-held radio from her belt, keyed the microphone, and spoke in French. Someone responded, also in French. Only then did Jason realize that the shadows belonged to well-camouflaged Humvees. He probably would not have noticed them if a guard had not climbed out of the vehicle on the left and waved them on. A beam of light emanated from the woods, beginning as a sliver and growing wider. It took a second for Jason to realize that the light came from inside an underground bunker, the door of which was opening.

Jeanette smiled at Jason. "Welcome to the Enclave."

CHAPTER THIRTY-TWO

FROM WHAT JASON could see of the bunker entrance, the exterior walls were at least three feet thick. A flight of cement stairs descended to a landing before turning right.

"What is this place?" asked Jason.

"It's an underground bunker from World War II. The Nazis used it to hide supplies from Allied bombing."

The group paused by the entrance. The blast door looked new, and a string of fluorescent lights hung from the ceiling above the stairs. "This is in pretty good shape for a bunker that's over seventy years old."

"Reno purchased it from the state ten years ago and has fixed it up."

"Who's Reno?"

"Claude Reno, the leader of the Enclave. He's a...." Jeanette thought about the right word. "I think you Americans call them 'preparationists'?"

"You mean prepper?"

"*Oui*. The locales laughed at him when he began renovating this bunker for Armageddon."

Jason grinned. "No one's laughing now."

Jeanette nodded. She motioned to the guard who stood outside the Humvee and issued an order in French. The guard responded and keyed his radio.

"Renaud is calling up two of my people to carry your friend's stretcher." Jeanette explained. "She can have my room where she'll be comfortable."

"Thanks." It suddenly dawned on Jason. "How do the

microphones work? I thought everything electronic was wiped out by the EMP?"

"They were. Reno had placed several radios in a steel container that shielded them from the pulse. If it wasn't for him, we would never have survived out here this long."

The sound of footsteps caught their attention. A man ascended the stairs. He appeared to be in his early fifties, with a well-shaped physique, graying hair, and a five-o'clock shadow. His brown eyes were serious and intense. As he approached, his face broke into a smile.

"I assume these are our guests?"

"*Oui.* This is Jason, the leader of their group. Jason, this is Reno."

The man extended a calloused hand and gave Jason's a firm pump. "Welcome, my friends. Our place is yours, so make yourselves at home. I only ask that you store the miniguns and automatic weapons in our armory. You'll get them back when you leave. You can keep your side arms and machetes, if you like."

"Thanks," said Jason. "What about the horses?"

"We have a corral nearby where we keep livestock. We'll put them in there. It's constantly guarded, so they'll be safe."

Lilith saddled up beside Jason and whined. He scratched behind her ears. "May I bring Lilith and Lucifer with me?"

Reno studied the two animals, his eyebrows furrowed. "They're werehounds?"

"Yes, although they're more like pets. They go everywhere with me."

Reno glanced over at Jeanette, who nodded her approval.

"They're welcome." Reno spoke loud enough so the rest of the group could hear. "We don't have much space, so we'll set you up in the community room. It'll be cramped, but you'll be able to get a safe night's sleep. Follow me."

With that, Reno spun around and went back into the bunker. Jeanette placed her hand on Jason's shoulder and ushered him inside. The others followed.

CHAPTER THIRTY-THREE

D INNER WAS A pleasant treat, and not because all of Jason's people could eat together at one sitting without having to post a guard. Because the Enclave maintained livestock and a garden, tonight's menu consisted of steak, carrots, and green beans. Being a special occasion, Reno also brought out several bottles of red wine. All three teams devoured their meals like they hadn't eaten in months. Jeanette even provided Lucifer and Lilith with their own choice cuts, which endeared her to the werehounds.

Jason, Doc, Sasha, Haneef, and Slava sat at the table with Reno and Jeanette. Everyone from Jason's side told their stories, except for Sasha. She sat sullenly through the meal, casting an occasional glare at Jeanette. After Jason finished relating the details of their journey up to the encounter with the magma monster, he sat back and waited for Reno's reaction.

"You're lucky you made it this far," said Reno.

"How so?" asked Doc.

"Several months ago, this area was uninhabitable because of the demons." Reno refilled his wine glass. "I bought this bunker and renovated it because I wanted a safe haven for me and my brother's family when the crisis hit. I always figured it would be social unrest brought about by economic collapse or political crisis, or maybe the disruption of the power grid due to a solar flare. Who would have guessed I would be defending my family from demons from another dimension?

"Anyway, after the EMP took down most of Europe, Charles and his family moved in and we settled down to ride out the chaos until things blew over. They never did. Once the TV and radio stations went off the air, Charles and I ventured out once a week to check on the situation. You can't imagine the nightmare that took place outside this bunker. Most of those who tried to escape from Paris stuck to the main roads, making them easy prey for the soul suckers. Not many Parisians lived through those first few weeks. Some of the locals tried to escape using back roads, although most of them didn't fare much better than the city folk. Once the food supply dwindled, the soul suckers moved on. For those who survived, things got better for a little while.

"That's when the gangs arrived." Reno drank some more wine. "They weren't trying to survive. They just enjoyed raping and killing, like the *Boche* from World War II. That's why I began letting others join our group, mostly locals who had stayed behind and some stragglers whom I felt I could trust. It was as much to save them as to bolster our own numbers against the gangs. At one point, close to fifty of us lived here, which turned out to be a Godsend."

"Why?" asked Sasha.

"Because then the other demons arrived. We lost five of our people the first time we encountered those magma monsters in the Seine, like the one you ran onto earlier today."

"There's more than one?" asked Haneef.

Reno nodded. "We've seen as many as three at one time. They never stray more than a few hundred feet from the lava flow. The flesh eaters weren't too bad. They're slow and stupid, and don't pose much of a threat if you can avoid them. Except for those things whose heads exploded and spread spores. Have you run into them yet?"

"Outside of Falaise," said Jason. The image of Christophe came back to him, and so did the guilt. "We lost one of our people to them."

"That's how my father died." Jeanette's eyes watered up. "He had gone to check on one standing in a field when its head burst, infecting him."

"We call them pus zombies because of the fluid in their skulls," said Doc.

"What an appropriately disgusting name for them." Reno took another sip of wine. "Since the number of people living here had increased so dramatically, we had to send out scavenging parties to bolster our supplies. Almost every time we did, we had to battle the demons. Over time, our ranks dwindled to twenty-nine. Eventually, the demons moved west in search of food and the frequency of the attacks decreased. Other than the magma monsters, we haven't seen any of the demons in almost two months."

Jason performed a quick mental calculation. At the Demon Spawn's rate of advance, they should reach Mont St. Michel in less than six weeks.

"What happened to the gangs?" asked Sasha.

"The demons got most of them." Reno finished his glass. "And they deserved what happened to them, if you ask me."

"Jeanette told us how you protected the hand-held radios from the EMP," said Doc. "Did you also protect a long-range radio?"

"I did."

"Do you have any news about the rest of the world?"

"Yes, although none of it is good." Reno sighed. "The same thing happened with the experiments being conducted in Russia, China, Japan, and the United States. As far as I can tell, the electronic blackout extends across Europe from Great Britain to beyond the Ural Mountains. Most of China and all of Japan are out of communication. Second-hand reports from the U.S. military in Okinawa say the Asian mainland is in chaos and that in Japan rioting and cannibalism are rampant. The east coast of the United States was taken down by the EMP. Apparently everything west of the Rockies is functioning normally, although their resources are stretched to the limit as survivors make their way west. The only regions not affected by the EMP are Latin America and Africa. The Middle East remained untouched for a while, at least until six months ago when Israel and Iran got into a nuclear exchange. Tel Aviv, Tehran, Damascus, Amman, Cairo, Riyadh, Baghdad, and Kuwait City were obliterated. There were even unconfirmed reports that the Iranians nuked Mecca because the Saudis backed Israel. Most of the region is contaminated by fallout. No one has heard from the area in months and what little news comes from the region is all from Sudan."

Haneef bowed his head and muttered a silent prayer.

The rest of the group sat in stunned silence. No one knew what to say. There was nothing to say. Even in the depths of worldwide despair, mankind could not put aside its petty differences for the common good.

Jason broke the silence. "Jeanette says your people have been to Paris since the portal opened."

Reno nodded. "In the beginning, we sent in several parties to scavenge for supplies. We stopped that about three months ago because the number of demons infesting the city became too great."

"Then you know where the portal is located?"

Reno nodded again. "It's inside Notre Dame Cathedral. Why do you want to know?"

"We're going to close it."

Reno appeared stunned. "How do you plan on doing that?"

"I've created a device with solidified anti-matter," answered Doc. "If I can insert it into the portal, I think I can collapse it."

"'Think'?"

A glimmer of doubt shattered Doc's confidence. "We won't know until we try."

"We'd like your help," Jason said.

Reno leaned back in his chair and rested his elbows on the arms. "What do you need?"

"Your people have been to Paris and know what to expect," Jason said. "We'd like to have some of them accompany us."

"What you ask for isn't easy."

Jason spoke quickly. "I know you don't have a lot of people left—"

"That's not the problem," interrupted Reno. "I haven't sent teams into Paris for almost three months because it's too dangerous."

"It's our only chance of closing the portal."

Jeanette leaned forward. Her voice was soft and soothing. "Jason, you have no idea how dangerous Paris has become. The demons you encountered so far are nothing compared to what you'll find in Paris. Most of the ones that come out of the portal don't venture beyond the city. Paris is full of monsters."

Jason felt his hopes sink. "You won't help us?"

"I didn't say that," said Reno. "I have to give it some consideration. You realize that there's a good chance none of you will come back from this trip? If I send any of my people with you, I'm condemning them to certain death."

"I know that. But we have to try." Jason paused. "I hope you agree with me."

"Let me discuss it with the others. I'll give you my answer in the morning." Reno stood up from his chair, signifying an end to the conversation. "Until then, please enjoy our hospitality."

"We will. Thank you."

Reno motioned for Jeanette to follow and the two disappeared into the kitchen.

When they were out of earshot, Sasha asked, "Do you think he'll help us?"

"I hope so."

"You heard them," said Slava. "Paris is crawling with Demon Spawn. What if they decide not to help?"

Jason thought for a moment, although he already knew the answer. "Then we continue on to Paris without them."

CHAPTER THIRTY-FOUR

LUCIFER ROLLED ONTO his back, grateful for the tummy rub from Jeanette. As she gently scratched her fingers up and down his stomach, he twisted from side to side, his tongue drooping out of his mouth in canine ecstasy. Lilith was more cautious. She circled the group from a distance, her gaze switching from Jeanette to Jason and back. When Jason urged her to go ahead, Lilith inched forward, her neck stretched and her ears flat against her head. Much to Lucifer's chagrin, Jeanette stopped scratching and gingerly reached out, palm down, to Lilith. The werehound sniffed Jeanette's hand for several seconds before licking it once. Jeanette moved her hand toward Lilith's head. The werehound flinched, yet let the young girl proceed. All resistance crumbled when Jeanette began scratching behind Lilith's ears.

"These are really demon dogs?" asked Jeanette.

"We call them werehounds, but yeah. Lilith changes into something that is a cross between a porcupine and a scorpion, and Lucifer morphs into this scaly spiky thing I can't even describe."

She looked between the two werehounds. "Which one is Lucifer?"

"The one on his back with the forlorn eyes because you stopped petting him."

Jeanette reached out with her free hand and began scratching Lucifer's stomach again. He whined with joy and rolled around under her touch. "You say they're fierce fighters?"

"I've seen Lilith and Lucifer rip apart flesh eaters like they were rabbits. They can even take down soul vampires."

"Where did you find them?"

Jason chuckled. "Actually, they found me. About five months ago, we were out on a search and destroy mission when we stumbled across them outside of Calais. They were in animal form and none of us knew the wiser. They followed us back to Mont St. Michel, so I adopted them as pets. They accompanied me every time I left camp. I didn't realize they were werehounds until three weeks later. On one run, we were ambushed by half a dozen soul vampires. We probably would have lost several of our people if these guys hadn't changed into their demonic form and tore into them, at least the ones going after me. I don't know what scared me more. Almost being killed or watching them morph."

"I'm surprised you were allowed to keep them."

"They had never threatened anyone, so Jacques, our leader, agreed to let them stay as long as they posed no danger. Andre pitched a fit. Thankfully, he lost that one."

"Who's Andre?"

An image of the wasp stinging Andre in the head and flying off with him crossed Jason's mind. He quickly forced it out. "He was a friend."

"Oh." Jeanette knew enough to drop the subject. "I've never seen werehounds before."

"Neither have I. These are the only ones I know of."

"They're not like any of the other demons. These guys are gentle."

"Bishop Fiorello theorizes that the portals are gateways into Hell and the flesh eaters are humans condemned to Hell for their sins. If so, that's probably what happened to Lucifer and Lilith."

"What type of sin can a dog commit?"

Jason shrugged. "I don't know. Maybe chasing Jesus' cat or shitting on God's front lawn."

Jeanette threw her head back and laughed. Not a girly

laugh, but a guffaw. Her face lit up when she did. Jason took it all in. The dimples on her cheeks. The bounce of her hair. The way her chest arched out. He couldn't remember the last time he, or anyone else in Mont St. Michel, had laughed like that. *My God*, he thought. *How could someone living so close to one of the portals still enjoy life so much?*

As Jeanette caught her breath, her mood suddenly became serious. "Do you believe in God?"

The question caught Jason off guard. "Do you?"

"Not anymore. I mean, if God did exist, how could he allow the portals to happen?"

"I don't know. Maybe we're being punished."

"You do believe?"

"I guess so. I never believed in God before. My mother w…." Jason stopped himself, not wanting to admit to Jeanette that his mother created the portals and that maybe the world was being punished because of her actions. "My mother wasn't religious and never raised me as such."

As if trying to pick up the mood, Lilith stepped up to Jeanette and licked her face. The young girl squealed and held the werehound close, hugging her neck. They fell over backward, with Lilith landing on top of Jeanette.

Jason jumped up. "Are you okay?"

"Yes," Jeanette giggled. "Get her off me. She's heavy."

Lilith responded by licking even harder, her tail wagging so hard it slapped against her legs. Now Lucifer rolled over and joined in, lapping Jeanette's other cheek. Jason only half-heartedly tried to pull them off. When he yanked on Lilith's thighs, the werehound shifted her weight, knocking him over. Jason tumbled on top of Jeanette, and she quickly wrapped an arm around his waist. Their laughter cut through the underground bunker. The laughter also sliced into Sasha's heart.

She stood by the door leading into the room where Jason and Jeanette were playing with the werehounds, hidden by the wall as she peered around the jamb. She had been searching for Jason so she could thank him for coming to her rescue that afternoon. That was only a pretense, though. She had decided to tell Jason how she truly felt about him. Petra's suggestion a few nights previous that the rules about dating had died along with everything else in society had made sense. However, a special urgency was created that afternoon with the arrival of Jeanette. That little flirt infuriated Sasha, though nowhere near as much as the way Jason fawned all over her. Sasha realized that if she didn't make a move soon, someone like Jeanette would steal him away.

As Sasha neared the room, she knew it may already be too late. Jason had never laughed that way around her. It sounded content, a rare quantity in this demonic new world. Her worst fears were confirmed when she peered around the doorway and saw the two of them rolling around on the floor, Jeanette's arm clutched around Jason, the two werehounds jumping into the fray with their tails wagging. It reminded her of back home in the days before the portals, of the good times with her family, and of a life that she would never get back. She could tell by the gleam in Jason's eyes and the way he smiled that he felt a genuine affection toward Jeanette. Sasha had seen him look at her that way on dozens of occasions, and each time she had scorned his advances. What hurt most was that it easily could have been her on the floor in Jason's arms. She and Jeanette were so much alike—two beautiful, tough, strong-willed young women who had so much to offer. The only difference was that Sasha had squandered her one chance at happiness in life while Jeanette embraced it. The emptiness in Sasha's heart felt like a void. Her chest restricted and it seemed as if the life had been sucked out of her.

Sasha quietly made her way down the hall, leaving the sounds of other people's joy behind her. She contemplated heading back to the community room to rest, although she knew she would never sleep the way she felt. Instead, she made her way to Jeanette's room to check on Petra.

Doc stood by the bed, his fingers pressed against Petra's carotid artery.

"How is she?"

The expression on his face told her the answer. "An infection has set in. She's running a fever and her pulse is elevated."

"How long…?" Sasha could not bring herself to finish the question.

"Three days, maybe four. She's very strong. This time that'll work against her."

"Is she in pain?"

"She would be if I hadn't shot her up with morphine. I don't have enough to keep her drugged until the end. Jason is going to have to make a decision soon."

"Good luck with that," Sasha mumbled.

"What?"

"Nothing." Sasha stepped over to the bed and took Petra's hand. She could feel the fever through her friend's fingers. "Can I stay with her for a while?"

"I don't see why not." Doc started to leave and paused at the door. "Call me if she comes around."

"I will."

Sasha waited until Doc had left. When he did, she placed her head against Petra's chest and cried.

CHAPTER THIRTY-FIVE

ANDRE KEPT SLIPPING into and out of a state of semi-awareness. He couldn't even call it consciousness because, during those fleeting moments when he emerged from his stupor, all he knew for certain was that he was alive. Everything else seemed to have been wiped from his mind. Andre couldn't feel his body and none of his limbs responded when he attempted to move them. He had no idea how long he had been out or how long he had been here. He didn't even know where "here" was. Earlier he had been able to open his eyes by sheer force of will, yet the effort exhausted him so much he passed out. Not that it did much good, though. He could barely make out his surroundings because of the dim light.

In his more lucid moments, Andre recalled the attack by the giant wasps, of being knocked from his horse and struggling with one of the insects, and of having it drive its stinger into his skull. After that, his body became paralyzed and his memory faded. He had a fuzzy recollection of being carried away by the wasp and of the insect perched on his chest, with something stabbing his stomach. At least he thought of it as stabbing. He had felt no pain, just an intense pressure pushing against his abdomen. Andre felt the same sensation again, only this time pushing outward. Thank God his nerves had been numbed by the wasp's toxin otherwise he knew he would be in agony.

Andre tried moving his arms and legs to no avail. None of his limbs would respond. Instead, he concentrated on opening his eyes. After several seconds of straining, the lids parted enough to allow him to take in his surroundings. Soft white light filtered in from above, probably from the moon. His eyes scanned the area. Wherever he was, it was small, only a few yards square with stone walls and wooden beams. He focused on something large and dark directly in front of him. He recoiled in terror, or at least his mind did, fearing it might be the wasp. The object sat still and silent. After a few moments, he recognized the shadow in front of him as a huge bell. As Andre slowly put the pieces together, he realized that the wasp must have brought him back to the bell tower of St. Gervais.

But why?

The pushing sensation against his abdomen grew more intense. Andre tried to look down. His body did not respond. Summoning all his effort, he forced his head to lower until his chin rested on his chest. The skin around his abdomen had extended to five times its normal size, and it bulged as something moved beneath the surface. A stinger ripped through the skin and tore a six-inch-long gap up his chest. A wasp the size of a football pushed its way through. The hole widened, and more insects exited, nearly a dozen in total. They crawled over his body, down his legs, and across his chest. One scurried across his face. Andre screamed in terror, but only internally since his vocal cords were paralyzed. Panicking, he wanted to shake them off, yet his body refused to move. Andre watched as the wasps maneuvered around his torn-open abandon and formed a circle around the hole. One by one, they dug their heads into his body and began tearing off chunks of flesh with their mandibles.

Andre lost what little rationality remained as he descended into insanity. In his psyche, he began laughing maniacally.

JASON WOKE UP with a start. Terror gripped him, and his heart beat frantically. Instinctively, he brushed at the wasps devouring his body, stopping only when he realized nothing was there.

Slowly the fear subsided, although his heart still pounded and every nerve in his body seemed on fire. *Thank God*, he thought. *It was only a nightmare.*

Unlike a dream, however, these images stayed with him and became more intense. Even though safe inside the bunker, Jason felt the terror and desperation welling up inside of him. He realized that what he experienced was much worse than a nightmare. He had seen a vision of Andre's death.

"Are you okay?"

The question came from Sasha, who was in the sleeping bag beside him. She lay on her side resting on one elbow. Her eyes expressed tenderness and concern.

"I'm fine," he snapped, not knowing how to deal with what he had experienced.

"Are you sure? You cried out a second ago."

Jason noticed that most of the others were also awake and staring at him. He spoke loud enough for everyone to hear. "Everything's okay. I had a really bad dream."

One by one the others rolled over and went back to sleep.

"I'm here if you need me," said Sasha as she slid back into her sleeping bag, though this time she made sure to face him.

Jason lowered his head back onto his pillow and pretended to sleep. He attempted to push the vision from his mind, yet it remained etched in his memory. He doubted he would be able to doze off after this.

One nagging thought competed with the nightmarish images in his mind. By not killing Andre as the wasp carried him away, he had inadvertently condemned his friend to a fate more horrible than death.

Jason vowed he would not make that mistake again.

CHAPTER THIRTY-SIX

BREAKFAST WAS AS enticing as dinner the previous evening, with bacon and eggs plus assorted fruit. The newcomers ate heartily, none of them having seen a spread like this for months. Jason pushed the food around on his plate, occasionally sampling something, his mind still bothered by last night's vision. The image of the baby wasps ripping through Andre's stomach had become imbedded in his mind as if it had happened to him. In a way it had, since he had channeled the Russian's last terror-filled moments. Jason did not even want to imagine how unnerving the episode would have been if he also had been able to channel the pain Andre endured.

Jason realized that he sat by himself. Everyone from his group had broken off in their own cliques and chatted while they ate, or were seated with the Enclavers, making new friends. The only ones paying any attention to him were Sasha and Doc, who sat along with Neal two tables over. Sasha mouthed, "Are you all right?" Jason forced a smile and nodded.

At that moment, Reno entered the dining hall. Jeanette was a few steps behind him. On seeing Jason, they approached the table and sat opposite him. Doc and Sasha joined them. From across the hall, Slava and Haneef excused themselves and approached. Reno waited until they had all gathered around the table. "I consulted with some of the others last night about your request to provide an escort into Paris."

"And?" asked Jason.

"We all agree that we can't afford to send any of our people with you."

Jason made no attempt to hide his disappointment. "I'm sorry to hear that."

"To be honest, we're not sure your plan will work. There's more Demon Spawn in Paris than you can imagine, including demons you haven't encountered yet that make the undead and soul suckers seem tame. Even if you make it to Notre Dame, we're not convinced your device will succeed in closing the portal."

"Understandable." *I'm not even sure if it'll work*, thought Jason.

"We've lost too many people already on our raids into Paris. It's why we don't go there anymore. However, we will provide you with support. There's a fortified warehouse outside of Nanterre, near where the red line for the Paris Metro ends. It served as a layover when we used the subway system to enter the city."

"Why the subway?" asked Slava.

"It's the safest way to enter Paris. There are fewer Demon Spawn underground than on the streets." Reno paused. "I'll send along a team of four who will stay behind at the warehouse and mind your horses. They'll wait forty-eight hours. If you're not back by then, they will have orders to leave your horses and return to the Enclave."

"Aren't you worried about letting so few people travel the countryside alone?" Sasha asked.

"Not many Demon Spawn have wandered this area for the past few months. It's a risk, but an acceptable one. It's all we can offer."

"We'll take it," said Jason. "Thank you."

Jeanette cleared her throat. Reno ignored her. The girl reached over and nudged her uncle on the shoulder.

He sighed. "Are you certain about this?"

"Yes."

Reno sighed. "While we can't condone sending a team in

with you, Jeanette has volunteered to lead you to Notre Dame. She went to school in Paris for a year and accompanied several of the raiding parties when we used to send them."

"We can't allow that," said Doc. "She's much too young."

Jeanette bristled at the insult. "I'm just as old as Jason, and you let him lead you."

"That's different," Doc argued.

"How?"

"Because…." Doc didn't have an answer. He turned to Sasha. "Help me out."

Sasha didn't respond. Jason thought she was confused, as if uncertain how to respond. Not that it mattered. This was his group and he decided to end the argument.

"Jeanette is going with us. Without her, we don't stand a chance of making it to Notre Dame alive." He glanced up at Jeanette. "*Merci.*"

"*Mon plasir,*" she flirted.

Reno reached out his hand and placed it over Jason's, the touch surprisingly gentle. "Please take care of my niece. She's impetuous, just like the rest of her family."

"I will." The words were promise enough. Reno gave Jason's hand a squeeze.

"When do we leave?" asked Slava.

"Tomorrow morning." Reno removed his hand. "It's fifty miles to Nanterre, so you'll spend the first night in Bouafle and proceed to the warehouse the following day. Jeanette will lead you into Paris on day three."

"Sounds good."

"We'll give you enough food and water for seven days. Right now, I suggest you all rest. You will need all your strength when you reach Paris."

Reno stood and, with a nod to Jason and the others, left the dining hall. Jeanette paused long enough to flash Jason a flirtatious smile and then joined her uncle.

With less than twenty-four hours until they departed, that gave Jason plenty of time to do what he had to.

CHAPTER THIRTY-SEVEN

THE REST OF the day passed quicker than expected, mostly because there were so many tasks to complete before their departure, which thankfully kept everyone from thinking about the dangers they faced. The teams spent most of the day cleaning their weapons and stocking up on food and water for the journey. Sasha and Haneef checked their miniguns and reviewed their ammo supply. Each of them already had used one full backpack of ammunition, and they were still two days from Paris. Jason had admonished them to conserve their ammo until they reached Notre Dame, though in reality he knew that would be a lot easier said than done.

Jason and Jeanette spent the day going over their plans for entering Paris. Once in Nanterre, the group would set out on foot through the Metro. They would follow the red line underneath the suburbs into the city and make their way to the station closest to Notre Dame Cathedral, which was a distance of a few blocks. Then they would surface, make a dash for the cathedral, and close the portal. The plan seemed simple enough, although Jason couldn't help remembering a quote his high school history teacher had told him that came from some German general: "No battle plan survives first contact with the enemy."

For Jason, the most difficult part of the day occurred when he went outside to check on the horses. Sook-kyoung and four young kids from the Enclave, three girls and a boy, were feeding and grooming them. He thought of Petra and how, if she were not on her death bed, she would be out here taking care of the animals she loved so much.

Everyone settled down right after dinner, and most of them dozed off quickly despite their anxiety about tomorrow. Jason lay in his sleeping bag for over an hour. When he was certain the others were asleep, he got up and quietly slipped out of the dining hall. Making his way down to the lower levels of the bunker, he found Jeanette's private room and stepped inside.

Petra lay on the cot. No one attended to her. Jason knelt beside her. The putrid odor of decayed tissue wafted up from underneath the sheets, signifying that the infection had spread. He was tempted to see for himself but refrained, not wanting to take from Petra the last shred of dignity she had left. Instead, he pushed aside the sheet along the left side of the cot until he exposed Petra's arm. Wrapping his fingers around her hand, he squeezed gently. He wanted to reassure Petra that someone cared for her, wanted to offer her a moment of comfort, even if she didn't consciously realize it. Jason felt the fever radiating from Petra's palm. Thankfully, Doc had been keeping her sedated with morphine otherwise the pain she experienced from the infection would be unbearable. They could have shot her back at the camp site, or overdosed her on narcotics, which would have ended her misery sooner, but that would have meant leaving her body in the woods. Jason would not allow that. He owed Petra a better departure from this world.

Standing up, Jason moved to the end of the cot. Bending over, he stroked her hair several times, pushing the loose strands off her face and wiping away the sweat. Placing one hand behind her head, he lifted it up and, with his other hand, removed the pillow.

"Please forgive me."

Jason placed the pillow over Petra's face and held it in place with both hands. Her body twitched as the flow of oxygen to her lungs stopped. She gasped for breath beneath the material. Jason pushed down tighter, hoping to end her torment quickly. Petra's body gave one final twitch and went limp. Placing the pillow back under Petra's head, Jason stroked her hair one final time, pushing the strands back into place and making her look as presentable in death as possible. He wanted to shed a tear over his friend, but none flowed.

"You're in a better place now."

CHAPTER THIRTY-EIGHT

E VERYONE TRAVELING TO Paris gathered in the dining hall two hours before sunrise. The Enclave provided a hot meal, although no one ate much. Everyone engaged in idol small talk as they came to terms with what they would face over the next few days. Doc entered the dining hall halfway through the meal to announce that Petra had died in her sleep. The news sent a bad vibe throughout the group. Although everyone had expected it, and was glad that the young woman no longer suffered, her death created an ominous undertone for the coming journey. When Doc joined Jason at the table, he offered a nod of approval, silently acknowledging that Jason had done the right thing.

Ninety minutes later, the group mounted their horses. Reno and the rest of the Enclave leaders stood at a respectful distance. When they were ready to depart, Reno came forward and offered Jason his hand.

"Please keep Jeanette safe."

Jason gave the hand a firm pump. "You have my word on it."

"Good luck, my friend. You'll need it."

Reno stepped aside and motioned to open the corral gate. Jason swung his horse around and headed out, with Jeanette close behind. The others fell in line, Jason's team first and then Haneef's and Sasha's. Other members of the Enclave had gathered around the fence to wish them well. Jason assumed most of them also came to say goodbye.

The group broke through the woods into an open field.

The sun had crested the horizon, bathing them in the first light of dawn. A morning mist hung low to the ground. Birds chirped in the nearby trees and, a few yards ahead of them, a rabbit darted from its warren and raced across the grass. It was a beautiful morning, like the one's Jason remembered when his mother would take him to the countryside for long weekends.

Too bad it would probably be his last.

BOOK THREE

CHAPTER THIRTY-NINE

ONCE CLEAR OF the bunker, the group formed up in its usual traveling formation. Jeanette rode on Jason's right, leading the way, while Lilith and Lucifer plodded along on his left. Slava trailed behind, keeping close to Doc and the saddle bag containing the anti-matter device. They were flanked on either side by two of the Enclavers, Jean and Emile. The other two Enclavers brought up the rear.

The group rode through farmland and forest for almost an hour before eventually emerging onto the A13, the main highway that led to Paris. Jeanette led her horse up the embankment and headed east. They continued along the A13 for over an hour. Jason waited for Jeanette to lead them back into open country, which she never did. Finally, he moved up alongside of her.

"How long are we going to stay on the highway?"

"Until we reach Chambourcy. Then we'll pick up the A14 into Nanterre. It's the quickest way. It'll get us there in less than two days."

"Isn't that dangerous? What about the Demon Spawn?"

"We haven't seen any demons out here for the past two months, so we'll be safe." Her voice trailed off. "I wish I could say the same for when we reach Paris."

Jason paused, not certain if he wanted to ask to the next question. "What exactly will we find in the city?"

"Hell on earth."

"Isn't that a bit melodramatic?"

"It's a fact." Jeanette looked over at him. For the first time,

Jason saw fear in her eyes. "The portal is spewing demons. It's impossible to move around the city now without running into hundreds of them. It's why we stopped going there."

"What type of Demon Spawn?"

"Mostly the undead and soul suckers."

"Your uncle said we'd run into other demons there. What type?"

"I don't know. No one ever got closer than a thousand yards to Notre Dame, and that was at night. The sole survivor of that raid reported seeing other demons around the cathedral, some about the same size as the lava monsters, but couldn't make out what they were in the dark."

"Survivor?"

Jeanette nodded. "Five of our people made it near Notre Dame. Only one got out of the city alive."

Shit, thought Jason. *What have I gotten us into?*

JEANETTE WAS RIGHT about the journey being faster along the A13, despite all the abandoned vehicles. The closer they got to Paris, the more cars and trucks lay scattered along the highway. At first, they made Jason nervous because he expected the Demon Spawn to come out of hiding and attack. However, they encountered only wildlife for the first five miles, and none of the Enclavers seemed concerned. Lucifer and Lilith were at ease, racing about and sniffing each vehicle, and occasionally chasing a squirrel or rabbit. Soon even Jason relaxed.

Outside of Buchelay, three figures sprawled across the highway. At first, Jason thought they were flesh eaters. As they drew closer, he saw they were skeletons. The exposed bones had been picked clean of flesh and bleached white by the sun. Each wore soiled, weathered clothes in various states of disrepair. The pavement beneath each had been stained dark from where the corpses had rotted away.

"What happened here?" asked Jason.

"They're the remains of those overrun by demons. Their numbers increase the closer we get to Paris." Jeanette seemed confused. "You haven't seen them before?"

Jason shook his head. "By the time the Demon Spawn made it to Normandy, everyone was already dead or had evacuated the region."

"I'm sorry. I didn't know." Jeanette waved Jean over. "Go back and warn the others that they'll be seeing a lot more of this the closer we get to Paris. I don't want anyone freaking out on us."

"Yes, ma'am." Jean spun his horse around and rode back to the others.

"Will it be like this in Paris?" asked Jason.

"Worse," replied Jeanette. "In Paris, the dead outnumber the demons."

CHAPTER FORTY

THE GROUP ARRIVED on the outskirts of Bouafle an hour before sunset. The town sat to the south, silent and desolate. To the north, farmland stretched to the horizon. Jeanette led the way off the A13 and down the embankment toward a copse of trees north of the eastern end of town. Nestled within the trees sat a two-story farmhouse. Everyone dismounted. As the Enclavers gathered up the horses and brought them around back, Jeanette led the others inside.

The Enclave had stocked the farmhouse with enough canned goods to last a group of twenty almost a month. As the others relaxed, Josh and Shane prepared a dinner of beef stew and vegetables, both from cans. Everyone slowly opened up and the dinner conversation was amiable, a welcome switch after the long, quiet journey. By the time they had finished eating, most of the members were laughing. Jason hated to bring up the subject of their mission.

Jason stood. "Okay, people. Tomorrow we'll be entering the outskirts of Paris. Jeanette warned me that the city is swarming with Demon Spawn, more than we've ever encountered before."

The mood became solemn.

"She also told me that there are Demon Spawn in Paris we haven't encountered yet."

"What type?" Slava asked.

"We don't know," answered Jeanette. "My people who went to Notre Dame couldn't get close enough to see them clearly, and most of them died getting that small bit of information."

Jason could feel the trepidation spread through his people. "Jeanette says we should be safe on the trip to Nanterre and shouldn't run into any Demon Spawn until we get out of the subway. However, it's been two months since any of her people have come this far, so the situation may have changed. In any case, I want us all to be on our guard tomorrow. What's our ammo situation like?"

Haneef shrugged. "I used up a full pack between the wasps and the soul vampires the other night."

Sasha bowed her head. "I used up a full pack in Falaise, and another half pack fighting the magma monster."

Shit. "What about the rest of you?"

"I haven't used that much," said Antoine. "Five magazines, six at most."

"Same here," added Reinhard.

Ray raised his hand. "Ditto."

Most of the others responded the same way until the conversation got to Josh. He pointed to the rest of the Gainesville Mafia. "We're down to less than a hundred rounds each."

"How did that happen?" Jason blurted out.

"We used up a lot defending the camp from the soul vampire attack the other night," Josh answered defensively.

Double shit.

Jeanette broke in. "We have some ammunition hidden away in the basement. Most of it is for our AK-47s. There might be some 5.56 mm rounds for your weapons. You're welcome to it. Unfortunately, we don't have any ammo for the miniguns. We also have a dozen flashlights. We'll need them if we hope to make it through the subway without getting lost."

"Thanks," said Jason. "From here on in, try to conserve as much ammunition as possible until we get to Notre Dame Cathedral. We're going to need everything we have if we hope to fight our way inside and close the portal."

"What happens if we run into Demon Spawn?" asked

Sook-kyoung.

"We'll avoid them if we can," answered Jason.

"Easier said than done," said Reinhard.

"And we still have to deal with all the Demon Spawn left behind once the gate is closed," said Antoine. "Assuming we're successful."

Jason could feel pessimism gripping the group. That would get them killed quicker than anything else. He sought Doc's guidance.

"Hopefully the closing of the portal will disorient the Demon Spawn long enough for us to make our way back to the subway." Doc offered the explanation as a lame hope.

Jason knew the others saw through it, although he still appreciated the gesture. "Any questions?"

There were none. "Good. We'll post guards around the perimeter. Same shifts as we've done in the past. For those of you not standing guard, get a good night's sleep. It'll be the last rest you get until we leave Paris."

CHAPTER FORTY-ONE

JASON MADE HIS rounds, checking on those standing guard. Jeanette had offered her Enclavers for each of the watch shifts. Jason appreciated the gesture more than Jeanette would ever know. It eased some of the pressure on his people who had been picking up the slack after having lost so many in the group. More importantly, it propped up his people's morale, even if only slightly. For the first time since leaving Mont St. Michel, his group felt as though they were not alone in their endeavor, that there were other survivors who supported them. His people realized that what they were undertaking would have benefits far beyond their own small group. The surge in confidence had bolstered their wavering determination. Jason hoped his people could maintain that cohesion until they completed their mission.

Jason made his way back to the farmhouse. He broke into a grin when he saw Jeanette sitting on the front steps.

"Couldn't sleep?" Jason asked as he walked up.

"Not really. I wanted to talk to you without the others around." She patted the step beside her.

"What did you want to talk about?" asked Jason as he sat beside her.

"Do you really think you can close the portal and put an end to all of this?"

"Doc says the device will work, and Jacques has enough faith in him to send us here to accomplish it."

"I asked if *you* think it's possible."

Jason started to reply with some bullshit bravado but

paused, knowing Jeanette would see right through that. He owed her the truth. "I don't know. I'd like to think we could. But if what you say is true, there are several hundred Demon Spawn between us and the portal. That doesn't put the odds in our favor."

Jeanette stared down at the steps. "Then why bother?"

"What else can we do? If we stay holed up in Mont St. Michel, we'll die anyway. The Demon Spawn are moving in our direction. In a few weeks they'll reach the city. Once they do, we have no chance of defeating them. If I'm going to die, I want to at least die trying to stop this."

Jeanette sat silent.

"Your uncle made it clear he thinks we'll fail."

"I'm afraid he's right."

"If you think we have no chance of success, why did you agree to come along?"

"Because you're the only ones who've had the guts to try." Jeanette's gaze met his. "Everyone we've come across these past eight months has been escaping from the Demon Spawn. And it's not just here in Europe. No one has tried to shut down the portals. The Russians, Chinese, Japanese, and Americans have all run away and gone into hiding, hoping to wait out the apocalypse. Not you. You're taking the fight back to them. I haven't seen bravery like that in a long time, not even from my uncle. I want to be a part of it, no matter what happens."

Jason stared into Jeanette's eyes, only this time he didn't see fear or resignation. He saw admiration. She looked at him the way no other girl ever had, not even Sasha. It made him feel good. It made him feel like a man rather than a scared teenager.

He bent forward and lowered his head toward Jeanette. She closed her eyes and leaned into him. Their lips met. Jason had never felt anything so wonderful. Her mouth was soft and warm. When she kissed him, his heart soared. The tip of Jeanette's tongue ran across his lip. Sliding his left hand around her waist, Jason pulled her close.

Jeanette broke the kiss and placed her hand on Jason's chest, preventing him from drawing her near, though not pushing him away. "I can't."

"I'm sorry." Jason felt more disappointment than anger. He removed his arm from around her waist and slid several inches across the step. "I thought you wanted me to—"

"I did," Jeanette said quickly. "I mean, I do. Not now."

"I don't understand."

She brushed the blonde hair off his face and cupped his cheeks in each hand, staring deep into his eyes. He saw the same admiration he had a few seconds before, this time mixed with affection. "I care for you, but I can't get too close to you right now."

"If not now, when? We could all be dead in two days."

"That's the point." Jeanette smiled at him. "In two days, we'll be in Paris fighting for our lives. You have to stay focused on getting us to the portal and closing it, not worrying about whether your girlfriend is okay."

"I can manage that."

"Trust me on this. Put me out of your mind for the next few days. The others need you to get them to Notre Dame. Once we've succeeded, we can pick up where we left off." Jeanette kissed him on the forehead and then stood up and headed back into the house.

Jason watched her leave. He knew she was right, although that didn't change how he felt about her. When she reached the front door, he called out. "Hey."

She paused and glanced over her shoulder.

"You're teasing me to make me fight better?" Jason said it good-naturedly.

Jeanette flashed him a coquettish smile. "No. I'm giving you a reason to live."

CHAPTER FORTY-TWO

J ASON STOOD AT the entrance to the subway near Nanterre Station. Red and orange tinted the underside of the clouds, and the first rays of the sun painted the sky along the eastern horizon a light blue. As the night burned away, the others caught their first glimpse of the station. Hundreds of skeletal remains littered the platform and tracks, many with limbs separated from their bodies and most twisted at ungodly angles. Their clothes were tattered, with the remnants stained from blood and gore. Suitcases and backpacks were mixed in among the dead. The human debris field started at the end of the platform nearest the subway entrance and fanned out from there, with corpses spreading away as far as he could see. These people must have been waiting for a train to take them away when a swarm of Demon Spawn burst from the tunnel and descended on the platform. Jason tried not to imagine the carnage that must have taken place here. He knew they would more than likely experience it for themselves soon enough.

Lilith moved up alongside of Jason, leaned into his leg, and whimpered. He scratched behind her ear. "It's okay, girl."

Jason focused his attention on the tunnel. The darkness inside was complete and all consuming.

He faced the group. They had traveled all day yesterday without incident, arriving at the warehouse a half a mile from the tunnel entrance early in the afternoon. Jason had ordered an early start this morning, wanting to make sure they arrived at Notre Dame with plenty of daylight left. Leaving the horses with the four Enclavers, the rest set out on foot for Nanterre

Station an hour before dawn. They had already geared up and were ready to go. Only three of the flashlights they found in the warehouse were heavy-duty systems with wide beams; Jason carried one, and Ray and Neal carried the other two, providing light for Haneef and Sasha, respectively. The other hand-held flashlights were distributed among the rest of the group, each being taped to the barrels of their weapons. They all stood around the platform waiting on Jason. No sense delaying the inevitable.

"I'm not going to bore you with a pep talk because we all know what we're facing and how important this mission is," said Jason. "Just remember, once the shit hits the fan and we encounter the Demon Spawn, we're all expendable. If anyone gets lost or falls behind, the rest of us go ahead without them. If anyone gets trapped by the Demon Spawn, they're on their own. Our only concern is getting to Notre Dame and closing the portal. The only thing we have to protect at all costs is the device." Jason pointed to the saddle bag draped over Doc's shoulder. "That's the only thing we go back for."

"And Doc," said Sasha. "He's the only one who knows how to use it."

"Even Doc is expendable."

Doc's eyebrows raised in shock.

"The device works by throwing it into the portal," Jason continued. "As long as one of us gets close enough to toss it in, we've succeeded. After that, those who are left will fight their way out. If you get separated, make your way back here. We'll wait one full day for stragglers and then head back to the Enclave.

"This is it, people. Let's make the world proud."

Facing the tunnel, Jason took a deep breath and slowly exhaled to steady his nerves. Jeanette stepped forward and slipped her hand around his, giving it a loving squeeze. Neither of them saw the pained expression on Sasha's face.

Releasing Jeanette's hand, Jason headed off into the subway, with her right beside him. Lucifer and Lilith took up their usual positions on either flank. The others followed.

In seconds, they were swallowed up by the darkness.

CHAPTER FORTY-THREE

T HE HEAVY-DUTY FLASHLIGHTS had limited affect against the dark inside the subway. Shining it to the right and left, the beam danced across the walls. When aiming straight ahead, it penetrated only one hundred feet before dissipating. Jason tried not to think about the possibility that Demon Spawn could be lying in wait ahead of them and his group wouldn't know it until the demons were practically upon them.

Only vermin populated the tunnel. Every few seconds, a beam of light would fall across a rat, which would scurry off and disappear into the shadows.

"That's a good sign," said Jeanette.

"What is?" asked Jason.

"The rats. Animals usually run when demons are around."

"How far do we have to go?"

"It's a little over eight miles to Notre Dame. We're now on the commuter line. We'll follow this for a few miles, then switch over to the Yellow Line which will take us right to the cathedral." Jeanette looked over at him, her smile radiant even in the back glow of the flashlight. "As you Americans say, a piece of cake."

They walked for less than an hour before arriving at the first station. Jason ran his beam along the length of the platform, searching for the exit. He spotted movement in the shadows at the opposite end of the platform. Every weapon and flashlight immediately focused on the source—a pack of wild dogs. Jason counted six, mostly larger breeds. They were crowded around a deer, feasting on the carcass. The pack raised up, their mouths covered in blood and gore. A German Sheppard, the presumed pack leader, stepped toward the new prey, its lips curled back to reveal its fangs. The others spread out around it.

Before anyone could react, Lucifer and Lilith bounded onto the platform and morphed into their demonic forms. The pack stopped. Their ears flattened against their heads and their tails wrapped under their legs. Lucifer crouched and growled. The Sheppard yelped and bolted for the nearest stairwell, with the rest of the canines close behind it. Within seconds, the pack disappeared onto the main level, the only sign of their presence being the clacking of their nails on the tiles as they raced to safety.

Only then did Jason realize that his bladder strained not to relieve itself.

The two werehounds morphed back into their dog-like forms. Lucifer stayed on the platform, keeping guard in case the pack backtracked. Lilith wandered over to Jason and was rewarded with a scratch behind the ears.

Franco moved up beside Jeanette. "Why didn't you didn't warn us the wild dogs?"

"They've never been a threat before. The city is full of them, pets abandoned by their owners after the portal opened. We used to come across them all the time. Back then, they ran when they saw us."

"I wonder what changed?" asked Jason.

"They've probably exhausted their food supply," offered Doc.

"If that's the case, things must be pretty bad topside," added Jeanette.

The group continued. Lilith stayed between Jason and Jeanette. Lucifer waited until the group had cleared the station and re-entered the tunnel before following, though he paused every few seconds to check his rear him and make sure the pack didn't double back on them.

After walking another few hundred feet, Jeanette paused and raised her hand for the others to stop.

"What's wrong?" asked Jason.

"There's a train up ahead on the westbound side of the tracks. We usually check it before proceeding to make sure nothing has made a home there."

"You think that's likely?"

Jeanette grinned. "Do you want to take the chance?"

"Shane and Josh, you're with us. The rest of you wait here until we're sure it's safe."

Lucifer and Lilith attempted to follow. Jason stopped them. "Protect the others."

Lilith walked back, taking up position beside Sasha. Lucifer tilted his head and blinked his brown, pouty eyes.

"Do as I say, boy."

The werehound whimpered once and sat on his haunches.

As they approached the train, their flashlight beams reflected off the metal surface of the lead car. Except for layer of dirt and some rust around the door, it seemed normal. Jason closed his eyes and felt for any Demon Spawn. He could not sense any auras. He inwardly breathed a sigh of relief, although he knew his sense was only reliable with a limited number of demon species.

Jeanette stopped by the front door and removed a flare from her leather jacket. "What's that for?" asked Jason.

"There are several trains like this that stopped when the EMP hit. We checked them out on our first trip down here. We left all the interior doors open and only closed the outer ones. That way it's easier to tell if something's inside." Jeanette walked over to the car and crawled up onto the small metal platform. When she tried opening the door, it would not move. Placing the flare under her arm, she used both hands, yet the door would not budge.

"Let me try." Shane slung his FAMAS over his shoulder. He stepped over to the train, helped Jeanette down from the platform, and took her place. Grabbing the handle in both hands, he pushed as hard as he could until the door slid open.

A large, dark grey mass fell swarmed out of the train. Shane tumbled off the platform, landing on his back between the twin rails. The grey mass landed on top of him. It dispersed upon impact as several hundred rats scattered in every direction, their combined squeals still not as loud as Shane's screaming. Within seconds, the horde of rodents had disappeared into the shadows. The only movement came from Shane crawling backwards on his hands and feet. When he bumped into Josh, he yelped with fear.

"It's okay," said Josh, patting his friend on the shoulder. "It's only rats."

"*Only* rats!?!"

"There's nothing to be afraid of."

"Bullshit." Shane stood up and shook his body as if throwing an imaginary swarm of rodents off him. "You know, I hate rats."

Josh smiled. "You're kidding?"

"What do you mean?"

"You have no problem fighting flesh eaters and soul vampires, but you're scared of one little rat?"

"One rat? There were hundreds of those little bastards in there."

Jeanette giggled.

Shane glared at her. "It's not funny. Those things are creepy."

She broke out into a full laugh. Josh also guffawed, taking great pleasure at his friend's expense.

"Screw you guys."

Jason couldn't hold back any longer and laughed along with the others.

By the time the rest of the group came running up to see what had happened, even Shane snickered at the ridiculousness of the situation.

CHAPTER FORTY-FOUR

A FTER EXPLAINING THE joke to the others, and after tossing a few flares into the once-rat-infested subway cars to make sure they were clear of Demon Spawn, the group continued down the tunnel. Forty minutes later, they entered Charles de Gaulle *Etoile*. Like at Nanterre, skeletons littered the platforms and tracks. Piles of bones stood in front of each exit where those who had tried to escape were butchered in their tracks. No matter where Jason shined his light, he saw the remains of the dead. Because of the lack of ventilation, even after so many months the stench of death was overpowering, a mixture of decay, body fluids, and brimstone mixed with stale air.

Jason felt his eyes water. Bile rose up in his throat.

Jeanette paused and waited for the others to catch up. A chorus of mumbles emanated from the group. Slava glanced over his shoulder and ordered, "Stow it."

"We'll transfer over to the Yellow Line from here," Jeanette said to Jason.

"Why not continue along this one?"

"Last time we were down here, a water main had broken between this station and the next. The tunnel was flooded. It doesn't matter, though. The Yellow Line will also take us to Chatelet Station. From there we can pick up the Purple Line to Cite Station right in front of Notre Dame. Let's go."

Jason helped Jeanette onto the platform and then climbed up himself. Antoine and Reinhard assisted Sasha and Haneef, who were hampered by their miniguns and backpacks.

Jason shined his flashlight down the pedestrian tunnel.

More skeletons lay on the floor. "Jeanette and I will go first. Sasha, you're with us. Haneef, bring up the rear. And everyone, stay alert. God knows what we'll run across down here."

The three set out for the next station, with Lucifer and Lilith in tow. The rest of the group followed at six-foot intervals. Haneef exited the station last, walking backwards down the tunnel so he could keep an eye on their rear, and checking behind him every few seconds so he didn't trip over the dead.

They moved slowly because the pedestrian tunnels were small and interconnected, creating numerous blind spots where Demon Spawn could hide. At each corner, Jason knelt and aimed his crossbow as Jeanette lit a flare and tossed it down the tunnel's length. Sasha stood close by, her finger hovering over the trigger of the minigun, ready to step in if they encountered anything. Only when they were certain a tunnel was clear would they move on to the next. Seven minutes later, they entered the Charles de Gaulle *Etoile*'s Yellow Line station. Here the dead were even more numerous, completely covering both the inbound and outbound platforms and spilling onto the tracks. Sasha gasped. Jason reached out and held her hand, giving it a reassuring squeeze. Her fingers closed tight around his. Jason didn't notice. He let go of Sasha's hand and moved beside Jeanette.

"Which way?"

She pointed to the subway tunnel off to their left.

The group moved out.

THE NEXT THREE stations they passed through—George V, Franklin D. Roosevelt, and Champs Elysees Clemencau—were as cluttered with dead as the last. Thankfully, they encountered no Demon Spawn or wild dogs, just rats that hurried away as they passed.

A hundred yards beyond Champs Elysees Clemencau, Jeanette paused again. "Ahead of us are two subway cars stalled side by side and blocking the track. We've opened all the interior doors and closed the outer ones. We'll use the same procedure as before—open the door, toss in a few flares to make sure nothing is inside, and pass through."

"We wouldn't want to run into any rats," teased Josh.

Shane raised his hand and extended his middle finger.

"Knock it off," ordered Jason. Then, to Jeanette, "Lead the way."

Everything appeared in order as they approached the two trains. Still, Jason had a bad feeling. It wasn't the same sixth sense he got when flesh eaters or soul vampires were nearby. Yet that didn't stop the cold chill running down his spine. Nor did it help that even Lucifer and Lilith seemed on edge.

The train on the left, the one closest to them, sat twenty-five yards ahead of the one on the right. When they reached it, Jeanette climbed onto the small metal platform. The door opened with no difficulty. She removed a flare from her pocket, struck the end, and tossed it as far as she could. It passed through the open door at the far end and hit the floor of the next car in line, sliding across the surface before coming to a rest under one of the seats. The harsh glow lit up the interior. Nothing moved.

"It's all clear. Let's go."

Sook-kyoung climbed up first. She and Jeanette helped up Sasha and Doc. Neal started to climb on board when a scurrying sound caught their attention. Flashlights darted in every direction, searching for the source of the noise.

"What was that?" asked Bill.

"Rats?" Shane had a hopeful tone to his voice.

"That was too damn big to be a rat," answered Antoine.

"There!" yelled Reinhard, pointing down the tunnel.

All flashlights shined in the direction they had come from, illuminating the demon.

All Jason could say was, "Jesus Christ."

CHAPTER FORTY-FIVE

A CENTIPEDE TWENTY feet long and two feet in diameter emerged from the shadows and scurried toward them. Everyone raised their weapons and took aim, pausing when another twenty centipedes appeared out of the dark, crawling along the walls and ceilings.

Sasha tried to make her way back to the tunnel. Jeanette stopped her. "There's too many. Move!"

Before Sasha could protest, Sook-kyoung grabbed her by the arm and led her down the car. Jeanette pulled Neal up and shoved him and Doc after the two women. The others switched their automatic weapons onto different targets and fired three-round bursts, blasting several of the insects from the wall and ceiling. For each one killed, more came out of the darkness, circling to attack.

Haneef raised his minigun. Jason pushed down the barrel. "Save your ammo for Notre Dame."

"We'll never stop them with small arms."

Jason knew his friend was right. Shane had climbed onto the subway car, with Josh waiting to be next. The centipedes were closing in, more than thirty of them by now. They did not have enough time to get everyone aboard. The second train was twenty-five yards away.

"Come with me." Jason set off for the second train. Lucifer and Lilith ran beside him. Slava, Haneef, Antoine, Reinhard, Ray, and David brought up the rear.

FRANCO CLIMBED UP into the subway car after Josh and Shane and turned to help Bill. Bill had one foot on the platform when a centipede closed in behind him. It wrapped its mandibles around his left leg and clamped shut. The twin forcipules behind its head closed around his thigh and punctured the skin. Bill screamed from pain and fear. When the insect injected paralyzing venom, he lost all sensation in his leg. The centipede darted back, yanking Bill off the platform and onto the tracks.

Franco withdrew his machete and jumped off to save Bill.

JASON RAN UP to the second subway train and jumped onto the platform. His heart pounded, both from the adrenaline rush of the attack and not knowing what was on the other side of the door. "Slava, cover me."

The Russian took up a firing position by the platform, his FAMAS trained at the car. Jason grabbed the handle and slid the door aside.

The car was empty.

"Haul ass!"

DAVID BROUGHT UP the rear of the line heading for the second subway train. He spun around to check on the centipedes. One was less than five feet away. He raised his FAMAS and emptied the remainder of his magazine, pumping six rounds into the insect and tearing apart its head. The rest of the body curled into a lifeless ball. David spun around and sprinted toward the others. A centipede darted out from underneath the adjacent subway car and swerved into his path. He jumped over the insect and twisted his foot on landing, tumbling onto the tracks.

The centipede curled around and lunged at him.

FRANCO RAN AROUND to the centipede's side and raised the

machete over his head. Swinging with all his might, he brought the blade down on the insect's abdomen behind the first set of maxillipeds, slicing the head from its body. The mandibles still dug into Bill's leg.

A centipede fell off the ceiling directly behind Franco and thrust its head forward to grab his right leg. A burst of gunfire ripped into its flank, throwing the carcass down the tunnel. Franco saw Jeanette kneeling on the platform, smoke billowing from the muzzle of her AK-47.

"Hurry up," she yelled. "And don't look behind you."

Franco didn't listen and wished that he had. Three centipedes were bearing down on him less than ten feet distant. He grabbed Bill by his belt and dragged him toward the car.

DAVID SWUNG HIS FAMAS like a baseball bat, slamming the stock into the centipede's head. The blow stunned the insect. Rolling to his feet, he dropped the automatic weapon and pulled his machete from its sheath. Holding it above his head in both hands, he drove the blade into the insect's head. The centipede convulsed. David shoved the blade in deeper and twisted. With one final, violent shake, the insect went limp.

He placed his foot on the insect's head and twisted to pull out his machete when he heard movement to his right. From the beam of the flashlight mounted on his abandoned weapon, he saw another centipede emerge from underneath the adjacent subway car. Leaving his machete, David limped after Jason and the others.

FRANCO LIFTED BILL and dumped him on the platform, keeping his head low so that Jeanette could get a clear shot at the centipedes chasing him. She stopped firing and dragged Bill inside. Franco climbed up. Spinning around, he grabbed the door handle. A centipede crawled across the platform and curved its upper body inside the car. He slammed the door on the insect, trapping it. Its head swung to the left, the mandibles snapping at Franco's legs. The Spaniard stepped back, his weight still pressed against the door.

"I need some help here!"

Jeanette ran up. She aimed her AK-47 and pulled the trigger but heard a metallic click. She was out of ammunition. Popping out the empty magazine, she grabbed a full one from off her belt.

A second centipede crawled over the first, shoving its way through the opening. Reloading and pulling back the slide, Jeanette aimed and fired. The bullets ripped through the two insects. The door slammed shut as a third centipede attempted to crawl in. Its mandibles clacked against the glass, trying to get at Franco.

"Are you all right?" Jeanette asked.

"Just scared." Franco struggled to regain his breath.

Jeanette focused her attention to Bill. The centipede's severed head was still attached to his leg. She pulled out her bayonet.

"How are you doing?"

"My left leg is numb," Bill gasped. "Will I be okay?"

"You should be. First, we got to get out of here."

The mandibles were locked. With no time to be delicate, and with Bill's leg numb anyway, Jeanette dug the tip of the bayonet underneath the left side of the appendage and twisted. Blood pooled around the wound. Using the blade for leverage, she popped out the mandible. The severed head dropped to the metal floor, leaving two holes the size of golf balls in Bill's leg. Blood stained his green flightsuit. They could worry about patching it later.

Franco helped Bill to his feet and draped the American's left arm over his shoulder. "Let's get out of here."

The three set off after Sasha and the others.

HANEEF CLIMBED ABOARD the subway car last after having helped Lucifer and Lilith on board. "Where's David?"

Jason looked down the tunnel. He saw David's automatic weapon on the tracks, the beam at an awkward angle. "The centipedes must have gotten him."

"May Allah be with him."

Jason closed the door and locked it.

SASHA FOLLOWED SOOK-KYOUNG down the subway car. Every few seconds she gazed over her shoulder to see if the others were there. She saw only Doc and Neal. Her heart sank.

She slammed into Sook-kyoung, who stood in the center of the aisle. "Why did you stop?"

"Because of that."

A large object blocked their path. Globular in shape, it extended up to the ceiling and out to the walls. It was milky-white, with the texture of silk. A curtain of cobwebs covered the space behind it. Sook-kyoung reached out to feel it.

"Don't do tha—" warned Sasha. The minute the Korean's hand touched the object, a crack ran down its surface. Spiders pushed through the opening and swarmed into the subway car. Each had the appearance of a tarantula, with brown-and-black mottled fur. Only these were the size of cats.

CHAPTER FORTY-SIX

JASON HAD ALMOST reached the end of the first subway car when he heard David banging on the window. "Let me in!"

Jason raced back, knowing deep down he would never make it in time. He reached the door and flipped the lock. Before he could open it, a centipede lifted itself up and plunged its mandibles into David's arm. He fell onto the tracks. Two other centipedes swirled around him and pounced, one biting his leg and the other his neck. David's scream drowned out into a gurgle. Closing his eyes and saying a silent prayer for the man who had protected him since CERN, Jason locked the door again and set off after the others.

SASHA GRABBED SOOK-KYOUNG'S shoulder and shoved her to the rear. She aimed the minigun at the sac and squeezed the trigger. The bullets blasted it apart, allowing more spiders to swarm out. Some crawled up the walls and across the ceiling, while even more scurried down the aisle. Sasha fell back, aiming at those that were closest. The roar within the confines of the car was deafening. She squinted to see through the glare of the barrels and the cloud of gunpowder smoke. Several stray rounds ricocheted off the metal walls and bounced around inside. Swinging the minigun back and forth, Sasha tried to kill as many of the arachnids as possible. There were too many to get them all.

Doc ran up to Sook-kyoung. "What's wrong?"

"Spiders!" she croaked. "Hundreds of them!"

Sasha's gun stopped spitting bullets. There were no more rounds left in her backpack. At least sixty spiders still crawled across the floor and walls.

"I'm out," she said.

"What do we do now?" asked Neal.

"We make a run for it."

JASON ENTERED THE second car when he heard Sasha's minigun come to life in the adjacent train. To his left he saw the flashes of muzzle fire through the dirty windows but could not make out what was attacking her. Not that it mattered. He had to get out of the train before he could help her and Jeanette.

SASHA RAN DOWN the subway car, pushing through the swarm of spiders. One of the arachnids launched itself off the wall and landed on the ammo pack. It couldn't maintain its grip and slid off.

Sook-kyoung shouldered her FAMAS and withdrew her machete. She leaned her head back so Doc and Neal could hear. "Keep close to me. Yell if you get into trouble."

Sook-kyoung set off after Sasha. A spider jumped from the floor toward her. She slashed out with the machete, cutting it in half. Two more dropped off the ceiling. One landed on Doc's back, the other the saddle bag carrying the anti-matter device. Doc yelped. Neal knocked away the first one. The second raced across the bag and onto Doc's arm. Neal swatted it onto the floor and kicked it aside.

As they passed through the remains of the sac, a spider leapt off the back of one of the seats and landed on Neal's left arm. Its fangs dug into his skin, injecting him with venom to paralyze the muscles and enzymes to liquefy them. Neal stopped running and tried to pry off the arachnid. Sook-kyoung ran back to Neal and spun him so the spider faced her. She placed the machete against Neal's arm and ran the blade down the length, slicing away the arachnid.

"God," Neal squeezed below the wound. "It feels like it's on fire."

Sook-kyoung pushed Neal ahead of her. "Don't stop if you want to live."

BY THE TIME Jason reached the end of the subway train and jumped out into the tunnel, the others were waiting for him. They had also heard the battle going on inside the adjacent train and looked nervously at each other. Lucifer and Lilith perked up when they saw him. His group was at the entrance to Concorde Station and were exposed.

"What's going on with Sasha?" asked Haneef.

"Did any of you think of helping her?" snapped Jason.

"You told us not to go back for anyone," explained Franco.

"Without Jeanette, we don't know how to get out of here. And Doc's trapped in there with the device." Jason moved toward the other subway train. "Ray, you're with me. The rest of you stay here and make sure those centipedes don't overrun us."

Jason and Ray rushed to the end of the adjacent train, opened the door, and disappeared inside.

The others stepped into the station about thirty feet, their flashlights and weapons aimed at the tracks beneath the two trains, waiting for the centipedes to catch up with them.

JOSH AND SHANE rushed into the car with the shattered sac and stopped. Sensing their presence, several of the spiders crawled in their direction.

"You know, I hate spiders almost as much as I hate rats."

"Then now might be a good time to haul ass, buddy." Josh

sprinted down the car. He ploughed ahead like his old days on the football field, running as fast as he could. He kept his eyes on the spiders in front of him. Several lunged. He dodged each one, ducking and weaving as best he could in the confines of the aisle. One landed on his arm, but he brushed it off before it could bite. Shane followed, opting for the more frantic approach, flailing his arms wildly as he ran. Three spiders jumped at him, each belted away before they could land. Shane didn't care how ridiculous he looked as long as he made it out alive.

INSIDE THE SUBWAY station, Reinhard detected a heavy scent of uric acid. He had no idea what generated it, although he figured it couldn't be anything good. Stepping to his left, he shined his flashlight on the subway platform, slowly spanning its length. He didn't see anything.

Lilith whimpered. The werehound sat beside Reinhard, her ears folded down and her eyes wide with fear. Lucifer stepped backwards, away from the opposite end of the station. Reinhard shown his flashlight in that direction and felt his bladder empty into his flightsuit.

"You've gotta be freaking kidding."

CHAPTER FORTY-SEVEN

HANEEF SAW WHAT had caused the German's outburst. All he could say was, "Allah is definitely not with us today."

A tarantula the size of an armored car lumbered out of the tunnel at the opposite end of the station. Its eyes glowed in the glare of the flashlights. It inched in their direction.

"I think that's a good enough reason to expend ammunition," said Haneef.

"I'm not arguing." Reinhard stepped aside to give him a better shot.

Haneef aimed his minigun and squeezed the trigger.

JASON AND RAY had climbed into the subway car when Sasha collided into them. She cried out and pushed him away until she realized who it was. She gave him a hug. He knew by her panicked expression that something bad was going down.

"Are you all right?" he asked.

"No."

Sook-kyoung pushed past them and headed for the exit, practically shoving Ray into the seats as she ran by.

"What's going on?" Ray called after her.

"The train is infested with oversized spiders," panted Sasha, trying to get her breath.

Doc ran past, with Neal in tow. "We have to get out of here."

"Where are the others?" Jason asked.

"Behind us." Sasha ran off.

Jason peered down the subway car. He didn't see anyone else.

HANEEF STOOD IN the center of the station, directing a steady stream of gunfire into the tarantula. The first hundred rounds bounced off its exoskeleton. He wondered if they would be able to stop this particular Demon Spawn and began searching for an escape route. The concentrated stream of fire soon took its toll. The arachnid stopped and shook. It started to move away when its thorax erupted, exploding chunks of gore and yellowish-green blood across the platform. The massive legs collapsed and the shattered carcass collapsed onto the tracks.

Haneef relaxed his arms, letting the minigun dangle by his side, and breathed a sigh of relief. Every muscle in his body felt drained.

"I didn't think you were going to stop that thing," said Antoine.

"Neither did I." Haneef noticed that the two werehounds still seemed spooked, both staring at the opposite end of the station. Lilith whimpered again. Reinhard raised his flashlight and stepped to the right, shining the beam past the carcass. From deeper down the tunnel, two more giant tarantulas approached, each the same size as the first.

The others sought guidance from Haneef. He sighed. He had used up more than half of his backpack taking down the first tarantula and didn't have enough left to defeat these two.

A scurrying noise came from behind them. A centipede emerged from underneath one of the subway cars. It paused as its antennae swirled in the air, searching for prey.

Haneef used his head to motion toward the subway cars. "Reinhard, Slava, guard my back. The rest of you, get out of here now."

Haneef summoned every ounce of energy he could muster, lifted the minigun, and maneuvered to get a better shot at the approaching tarantulas.

JASON HEARD THE roar of Haneef's minigun. "Shit!"

The sound of running feet caught his attention and he directed his flashlight down the car to see Josh and Shane approaching. Jason stood in the aisle to block their path. "Where's Jeanette and the others?"

"They were supposed to be right behind us," Josh wheezed. "I heard a commotion at the door. I think the centipedes got them. Sorry."

Shane pointed toward the station. "What's going on out there?"

Jason didn't know, and that bothered him. Haneef wouldn't be using up so much ammunition on a minor threat. And they still had the centipedes to contend with. Doc and, more importantly the anti-matter device, were safe. As much as he hated to admit it, Jeanette and the others would be here by now if they had made it past the insects. He had to do what was good for the group, not his heart.

He pushed Josh and Shane down the aisle. "Let's get out of here while we still can."

Before following the others out, Jason paused long enough to peer down the subway car one last time.

JEANETTE LED THE way. They moved slowly because Franco supported Bill and it was difficult to maneuver down the aisle. What worried her was that she could see the centipedes racing along the windows on the exterior of the car and hear their legs darting across the metal roof. The insects would more than likely be waiting for them when they exited.

Jeanette stopped when she entered the car with the spider sac and tried to take in the situation. "We've got a problem."

"What no—?" Franco's words trailed off when he saw the

spiders spreading out along the walls and ceiling.

"Leave me here," said Bill. "I'm slowing you down."

"I'm not abandoning anyone." Jeanette slung the AK-47 over her shoulder. Reaching into her jacket, she pulled out the last three flares, lighting them one at a time. Their glow filled the car, driving the spiders toward the other end. "Are you ready?"

"Go for it," moaned Bill.

Jeanette lobbed one of the flares down the car and into the sac. The remains burst into flames, rapidly burning through the silk. The spiders nearest the fire scattered, leaving a clear path.

"Let's go!"

Jeanette ran down the aisle, holding one flare in each hand. Franco and Bill limped along behind her. Whenever she saw a spider that seemed ready to attack, she shoved a flare toward it, forcing it to retreat.

They had almost made it the entire length of the car when Bill's leg became tangled up in a segment of unburned sac, tripping him to the floor and out of Franco's arm. The Spaniard bent down to help him back up when several spiders swarmed over Bill. Bill flayed at them. Franco tried to sweep away as many as he could, but the arachnids were too numerous. They had already covered Bill's chest and legs, their fangs biting deep and injecting him with paralyzing venom until his movements became sluggish. A few spiders went after Franco.

Realizing his efforts were futile, Franco jumped up and ran backwards three feet, unslinging his FAMAS in the process. He paused long enough to take careful aim and release a three-round burst into Bill's head, shattering the skull and putting his friend out of his misery. Then he spun around and raced off after Jeanette.

BY THE TIME Jason and Ray reached the exit door to the subway car, the battle between humans and insects was in full swing, and the humans were losing.

Haneef had taken down the second tarantula. Like with the first, he had to concentrate his minigun on its thorax until the rounds burst through the hard exoskeleton, but that had used up most of his remaining ammunition. He figured he had less than two thousand rounds left, nowhere near enough to kill the last tarantula. It crawled over the carcasses of the other two, exposing its belly. Hoping for the best, Haneef aimed his weapon and fired.

Everyone else shot or hacked away at the centipedes swarming out of the tunnel and into the station. Reinhard and Slava stood back-to-back, machetes drawn, striking at five insects circling their feet, slashing chunks out of them and keeping them from closing in. Josh and Shane were running across the tracks, avoiding as many centipedes as possible and shooting those that got too close. Sasha was only a few paces ahead of them, being slowed by the weight of the minigun. Sook-kyoung stayed with her. When one centipede came too close, she gave it a side kick with her boot and sent the insect tumbling away. Even Lucifer and Lilith joined in. Having morphed into their demonic forms, they pounced on every centipede that got near them, tearing them apart with their fangs.

Jason searched around for Doc. Antoine had grabbed him by the arm and rushed him over to the platform, which the insects had not yet made their way to. Neal followed, making sure nothing snuck up on Doc from behind. When the three climbed up off the tracks, Jason called out and got the Moroccan's attention.

"What?" Antoine yelled back.

Jason pointed up. "Get Doc out of here. Head for the street."

"What about you?"

"We'll be right behind you."

Antoine obeyed and led Doc and Neal down the pedestrian

tunnel.

"All set?" asked Jason.

Ray shook his head. "No."

"Good. Let's go."

The two jumped down onto the tracks as a centipede ran between them. They ignored it and started running. Several centipedes were on the ceiling above him and were angling toward the platform. They had only seconds before they would be overwhelmed.

THE ROAR OF Haneef's minigun died out as it expended the last of its ammunition. The tarantula still lumbered forward. There was nothing more he could do now. Taking a few steps back, he headed for the platform.

SASHA MADE IT to the platform but didn't have the energy to lift herself onto it.

Sook-kyoung hopped up beside her. "Come on."

"I can't. I'm exhausted."

"Enough of this bullshit." Sook-kyoung knelt and grabbed Sasha's hand. She couldn't pull her up because of the added weight of the minigun.

Something grabbed Sasha around the waist. She screamed. Josh had his hands clasped around her waist and lifted her. Shane jumped up and took her other hand. Together, the three hoisted Sasha onto the platform. Josh and Shane joined them moments before a pair of centipedes swarmed around where they had stood.

JASON AND RAY made it to the platform seconds later, practically diving onto it to avoid the insects. Lucifer and Lilith followed their master. Slava and Reinhard hacked their way close enough that the others could lift them to safety. Beneath them, dozens of centipedes darted back and forth across the tracks, and another dozen raced toward them along the ceiling.

"Is this it?" asked Haneef.

"I'm afraid so," replied Jason.

Jason started to lead the others to the pedestrian tunnel when he heard Jeanette's voice calling to him. Jeanette and Franco stood in the doorway of the subway car. Her eyes shifted down at the mass of centipedes and back up to him.

"Hang on a second," Jason yelled.

"That's about all the time we have." Jeanette pointed toward the opposite end of the station. The tarantula was less than fifty feet away.

"Sasha, Haneef. Get out of here while you can. Take Lucifer and Lilith with you. The rest of you, reload and prepare to lay down cover fire into the centipedes on my mark."

It took only three seconds for everyone to do as told. When everyone had reloaded their weapons, Jason yelled, "Now!"

Slava, Reinhard, Josh, Shane, and Ray each fired a single shot into the area just beneath the subway car, killing some of the centipedes and scattering those nearby. They rolled back their fire to clear a path to the platform, stopping only when each one ran out of ammunition. Jeanette and Franco jumped from the train and ran before the other insects could give chase. Jason reached out and, when Jeanette got close, grabbed her hand and yanked her up onto the platform. The two fell over backwards on top of each other.

Franco was one yard from the platform when the tarantula suddenly jumped, covering the last thirty feet and crushing Franco to the tracks. The others moved backward to get away, all except Reinhard who reloaded. The tarantula sunk its fangs into Franco's abdomen and injected paralyzing venom. The Spaniard's body instantly slackened. Before Reinhard could take the shot that would end his friend's suffering, three of the centipedes crawled up onto the platform and rushed him.

Reinhard squeezed the trigger on his FAMAS and swung it from left to right, spraying the insects and knocking them back onto the tracks.

Jason jumped up and helped Jeanette to her feet, and then pushed her toward the pedestrian tunnel. "Come on!"

None of the others needed to be told twice. They followed Jason down the tunnel, Reinhard being the last to leave. As he exited, a dozen centipedes swarmed the platform where they had stood a moment ago.

Running as fast as he could in the dark confines of the pedestrian tunnel, Jason hoped he had taken the same route as the others. He couldn't afford to get separated with a third of his team having been killed and a swarm of pissed off insects chasing them. After a few minutes, he heard a commotion up ahead and saw sunlight pouring down a stairwell that led to the street. For a moment, he had to close his eyes against the brightness. He had never been so glad to see the sun before. Taking Jeanette by the hand, he ran up the stairs, taking the steps two at a time.

The others stood huddled around the top step, blocking his path. "Move!" he yelled. "The bugs are right behind us."

Sasha's eyes dulled by defeat. "We can't."

Jason shoved his way past the others and immediately understood her desperation. Rather than taking the exit up to the street, somehow Antoine had gotten onto the underground pedestrian walkway that crossed underneath the street and brought them up in Place de la Concorde. They now stood in the middle of the center island near the Luxor Obelisk.

At least a thousand flesh eaters filled the square around them.

CHAPTER FORTY-EIGHT

E VERY FLESH EATER in Place de la Concorde turned toward the group and began their slow advance.

"We're screwed." Doc dropped to his knees, physically and emotionally drained.

"No, we're not." Jason yanked the doctor to his feet and shook him. The adrenaline pumping through his veins suppressed his fear. Jason prayed it didn't wear off until they were out of this mess. "There's a lot of them, but they're slow. We can maneuver between them."

"To where?" asked Slava.

Jason didn't have the answer. He looked to Jeanette.

She pointed east. "The Louvre is half a mile in that direction, just past the Tuileries Garden. We should be safe there."

"Half a mile?" Sasha moaned. "I'll never make it. I'm exhausted."

"Then stay here and die."

Sasha stiffened at the comment. However, it had the desired effect on her and the rest of the group. "Don't fight them. Use your machetes to defend yourself. Only use your weapons if necessary. Let's go."

Jason and Jeanette led the way, with Lucifer and Lilith on either flank. The flesh eaters were spaced out enough that it was easy for the group to avoid them. Only a few got close enough to grab at members of the group and were dispatched with a slash from a machete or knocked down by the blow from an automatic weapon to the face.

The first real danger came when they crossed the street and

tried to race between the two buildings on the sidewalk. Here the path narrowed to only a few yards, making it impossible to run around the flesh eaters. The werehounds raced ahead, knocking over the two demons in Jason's path. Everyone else hacked or shoved their way through. A female flesh eater grabbed Sasha by the arm as she ran past, pulling her to the ground. Coming up from behind, Josh tackled it out of the way. Shane helped Sasha to her feet and they ran off after the others.

Passing through a set of arched walls, the group entered the Tuileries Garden. Flesh eaters swarmed either side of the octagonal pool at the entrance. Jason headed for the pool and vaulted over the edge. As the group waded across, three flesh eaters gathered near the opposite side.

Lucifer and Lilith bound ahead, morphing into their demonic forms. They tore apart the outer two flesh eaters. Jason paused long enough to place an arrow in his crossbow and fire. It struck the third between the eyes, dropping it to the ground. The three blue eddies of lifeforce were dissipated by the group as they climbed out of the pool and rushed into the Tuileries Garden.

The garden stretched ahead of them for half a mile. The group easily avoided the flesh eaters for the first hundred yards. However, those at the far end began bunching up, waiting to swarm the humans. Before they reached the gathering pack, Jeanette grabbed Jason by the arm and pulled him to the left. The group veered down one of the side paths, and then swung right onto a smaller one that paralleled the main path, avoiding the danger. A minute later, they broke out into the open grassy area in front of the Louvre. The museum was a thousand feet away.

Jason sprinted ahead with the greatest of effort. Each breath was belabored as his lungs strained from exhaustion. His legs began to cramp up, the muscles straining against the physical exertion. He didn't know how much longer he could go on. If he stopped to rest, even for a few seconds, he'd be dead. He pushed on, demanding that his body respond.

The others were just as tired. Doc stopped in the middle of the grass, gasping and wheezing as he tried to catch his breath. Neal grabbed him by the arm and pushed him along, almost knocking Doc over. Sasha and Haneef had fallen back to the end of the group, unable to keep up because of the weight of the miniguns. Haneef paused, disconnected the ammo belt from his weapon, and slid the empty pack off his shoulders. He bolted off as a pair of flesh eaters reached out for him.

By the time the group reached the traffic circle in front of the museum, everyone had slowed to a brisk walk. Sensing their vulnerability, the flesh eaters closed in. Now the fighting became hand-to-hand. Bayonets gouged out eyes. Machetes hacked away at necks and heads. Automatic weapon stocks smashed against demon faces. The dash to safety had devolved into a slugfest. Everyone would take down the closest flesh eater to them and then sprint ahead a few feet out of harm's way, only to tire quickly and pause, giving the flesh eaters a chance to catch up. Jason scanned the area. There were fewer flesh eaters here than in the garden, but they were steadily closing in. Josh and Shane reloaded their assault rifles. Taking aim at the flesh eaters between them and the museum, the pair took careful shots, bringing down those blocking their path. It gave the group the burst of optimism it needed. As one, they surged forward, rushing into the path cleared by their comrades and heading toward the Louvre.

Jeanette swung right and headed for a service door along the museum's southwest façade. She tried the knob. It was locked. Reinhard ushered her aside and fired several rounds into the knob. The door popped open. Jason pushed it aside and rushed in, fearful of what he might find, although it couldn't be any worse than the fate that awaited them outside. He audibly sighed with relief when he saw no Demon Spawn in sight.

The closest flesh eater had closed to within ten feet away when the last of the group entered and Jason slammed shut the door. "Find something to block this!"

Antoine and Reinhard were already pushing a heavy display case filled with ancient Mediterranean artifacts across the floor. Josh and Ray helped. They moved the case in front of the door as the flesh eaters pounded on the outside. The group jumped back, hoping that the barricade would hold. It did.

"How long do you think it'll keep them out?" Neal asked.

"Long enough for us to regroup and rest," said Jason. "Come on."

They staggered into the museum to find a safe place to hold up.

CHAPTER FORTY-NINE

F ORTY MINUTES LATER, as the rest of the group rested on the lower level, Jason, Jeanette, Sasha, Haneef, and Slava made their way to the southeast corner of the Louvre's roof to survey the landscape. From this vantage point, they could see the western tip of Ile de la Cite, the small island in the middle of the Seine River where Notre Dame was located. The cathedral stood on the eastern tip, although buildings blocked their view of the square out front. All they could see of the structure were the twin towers soaring above the rooftops. East of Ile de la Cite, the Seine still flowed as a river until it split to wash around the island. The northern branch flowed past the Louvre until it reached the western end of the island. There it merged with the Seine's southern branch, which now had become a stream of lava. At this point, the water evaporated with a cloud of steam and a sizzle audible even on the roof of the museum.

"Thank God for small favors," said Jason as he brushed hair out of his face.

"What are you talking about?" asked Slava.

Jason pointed toward Ile de la Cite. "The lava flow is only along the southern banks of the island. That means the bridges to the north are still intact, so we can get to the cathedral that way. Plus, the lava will give us cover to Notre Dame."

"How so?" asked Haneef.

Jason pointed to the street beneath them that ran past the Louvre. Beginning where the lava flowed into the Seine and heading west, nothing moved along either bank of the river.

Only farther to the east, where water still flowed through the Seine, did Demon Spawn roam the riverbank. "The Demon Spawn avoid the lava. We can use that to our advantage. It's only a six-hundred-foot dash along the riverbank to Port Neuf, the first bridge crossing over into Ile de la Cite. Once on the island, we cross over to the southern bank and follow it until we reach Notre Dame."

"What about magma monsters?" Sasha asked.

"They shouldn't be a problem," said Jeanette. "We've only ever seen them outside of Paris. Even if one does appear, there are enough side streets on the island for us to move inland and avoid it."

"You see." Jason forced a smile. "We lucked out."

"You call that lucky?" Slava grinned.

Haneef failed to catch the Russian's sarcasm. "I do. We're lucky we've made it this far. Allah must be giving us his undivided attention."

Jeanette leaned closer to Jason. "Maybe I should go on ahead and scout out Notre Dame. We don't want to get ambushed like we did in the subway."

"It's too dangerous," said Jason. "I can't risk sending a scout team ahead. We've lost too many people already."

"Then let me go alone."

"I'm not willing to let you take the chance. Besides, you said earlier that the last team of Enclavers to get near Notre Dame reported Demon Spawn they had never seen before. We have to go in expecting the worse." When Jeanette tried to argue, Jason held up his hand. "Besides, it'll take too long. We only have a few hours of daylight left, and I don't want to storm the cathedral at night. We'll go now and hope for the best."

No one disagreed with the logic, although none of them were happy about being reminded that the worst probably lay ahead of them.

The leaders descended back to the lower level where they had left the rest of the group. Lucifer's head popped up as they arrived. Once he saw that the approaching figures were friendly, he laid his head back down to rest.

"How is it?" asked Josh.

Jason moved to the center of the group so he didn't have to talk loudly. "The area is clear around the museum, although we couldn't see what's waiting for us at Notre Dame. We're going to head for Ile de la Cite, cross the nearest bridge, and make our way to the southern banks of the island. We'll approach Notre Dame from that direction. That's the good news."

"What's the bad?" Antoine asked.

"We used up a lot of ammo in the subway. Most of you are down to less than a hundred rounds. When we lost Franco, we lost a full pack of minigun ammunition, so we have only one backpack left." Jason gestured to Sasha. "Use it sparingly. We'll need as much ammo as we can to fight our way out of the cathedral once we plant the anti-matter device."

"If we make it that far," said Reinhard.

"Cut the crap," Jason barked.

Everyone snapped their heads toward him.

"We've made it to within half a mile of our target, so there's no reason why we can't finish the job. All we need to do is toss the device into the portal and hope that it works. If it does, then most of us stand a good chance of making it back alive. If it doesn't... well, life probably won't be worth living anyway."

As inspirational talks went, Jason knew this wasn't his finest hour. Not that it mattered. They were too close now to have second thoughts.

"Mount up, people. We move out in five minutes." Jason moved up to Neal. "How's the arm?"

"Hurts like a son of a bitch." Neal unconsciously rotated his left shoulder. "Doc fixed it up as best he could, put a bandage on it, and gave me a local for the pain. He says there's some necrotic tissue forming from the bite, but I should be fine."

"Good."

Haneef picked up his minigun from off the floor and began to strap it on. Jason walked over to him. "You might as well leave that here. You don't have ammo for it."

"I don't have another weapon."

"I know. But it'll only weigh you down." He leaned in close so only his friend could hear. "Stay to the rear. If anyone doesn't make it, grab their weapon."

Haneef stared at him. His eyes showed anger. After a moment, he realized Jason was right and he nodded his begrudging acceptance. Stripping out of the minigun, he left the weapon on the floor.

Eight minutes later, the group exited by the Louvre's southeast door and made their way to Port Neuf.

CHAPTER FIFTY

O NLY A HANDFUL of flesh eaters covered the eighty yards between the Louvre and Port Neuf and less than a dozen staggered along the bridge. The group avoided them with little difficulty. Only a few of the demons maneuvered close enough to pose a threat and were quickly disposed of. Within minutes, the group reached Ile de la Cite, crossed to the southern bank, and moved down Quai des Orfevres.

Here the temperature was forty degrees hotter because of the lava. Sweat formed around Jason's underarms and back, and beads of perspiration dripped down his face. He ignored the discomfort. He also ignored the sixth sense that welled up inside of him, growing with an intensity he had never felt before. Some of the sensations were familiar to him, those belonging to the flesh eaters. He had been able to suppress and shove them into the background of his psyche. However, two auras were so intense they threatened to overwhelm his abilities, drowning out the flesh eaters in an emotional orgy of anguish. Jason forced them down. He focused on the side streets ahead of him and the river to the south, watching for any sudden danger that might appear.

They came to Petit Pont, the last bridge before the open square in front of Notre Dame. Jason motioned for the others to stop and waved them against the nearest building where they could not be seen. He and Jeanette inched their way to the end of the wall and peered around the corner.

Lava poured out of the cathedral through the center and right *portails*, flowed across the southeast corner of the square, and drained into the Seine west of Pont au Double. The heat had seared the cathedral's front façade and burned the southern tower into a charred hulk. From this distance, the left *portail* looked fine, although it stood too close to the lava to risk entering Notre Dame that way. They would have to make their way to the cathedral's northern façade and find an entrance. Crossing the square would be easier said than done. It stretched for more than three hundred feet with scores of flesh eaters milling around. The distance was too great, and the their numbers too many, for them to make the run without being swarmed. They would have to fight their way to Notre Dame.

What caught Jason's attention was the pair of Demon Spawn that stood motionless in the center of the square. They were monstrosities, over thirty feet in height with massive torsos. The demons crouched on thick, muscular legs. Their bulky arms were almost the same length as the demons' entire bodies and dangled by their sides, with the knuckles resting on the pavement. Each had a bulbous head that merged with the shoulders, with no signs of a neck. There were no visible ears, noses, or throats, only a pair of coal black eyes on either side of a ridge that ran down the face and substituted for a nose. Their skin appeared dark red, almost as if the flesh had been stripped off to expose the underlying muscles.

A flesh eater wandered near the closest monstrosity. It lifted its right arm across its chest and swung out, slapping the flesh eater. The demon flew seventy-five feet across the square before landing with a thud against the pavement. A blue eddy of light flowed from the body and dissipated into the sky.

"What are those things?" Jason asked under his breath.

"Golem," Jeanette answered.

"I thought Golem were made of stone."

"They are, according to Jewish legend. The rabbis of Prague created the Golem to be the policeman of the Jewish ghetto and prevent anti-Semitic attacks. These demons are made from body parts of the condemned."

That explains the overpowering anguish he sensed. He pushed a strand of blonde hair back behind his ear. "How do you know all this?"

Jeanette breathed in deep. "My uncle heard reports about them from Tokyo before the city went silent. The Japanese Self Defense Force studied their behavior and engaged them in combat. They examined one that they killed. These Demon Spawn are incredibly strong and aggressive. Their job is to protect the portals and to make sure the other Demon Spawn stay under control."

"It almost makes me miss the giant, slow-moving tarantulas."

"For all we know, they're waiting inside." Jeanette grinned. When Jason didn't respond, she became serious again. "Sorry. I shouldn't joke like that."

Jason peered around the corner again. "How do we get past them?"

"According to the Japanese, they're not very quick or agile, so avoiding them should be easier than avoiding the flesh eaters. Their reach is long, so tell the others to give the Golem a wide berth."

Jason motioned for Jeanette to get back against the wall and then waved for the others to join them. He briefed them on what stood between them and Notre Dame.

"What's the plan?" asked Sasha.

"Cross the square and make our way to the northern side of the cathedral. There's an entrance there. Once inside, one of us throws the anti-matter device into the portal. Then we run like Hell is after us."

"Because it probably vill be," added Reinhard.

A few awkward chuckles passed through the group.

Jason nodded. "Okay, this is what we came here to do. Let's roll."

CHAPTER FIFTY-ONE

B OTH GOLEMS SPOTTED the group as they ran across the street and into the square in front of the cathedral. The closest lumbered toward them, legs bent and walking on its knuckles, much like a gorilla. As Jason approached the nearest Golem, he noticed that every limb or torso section was made of scores of corresponding human limbs stripped of their flesh and stitched together. Most disturbing was the monstrosity's head. Hundreds of skinless faces stared at him, each mouth contorted in a silent, soulful wail. The anguished aura peaked within Jason's head.

The second sentinel hovered in the background, judging where these puny things were going. It tilted its head, gazing at them with a sense of curiosity. Then it stepped to the right, trying to cut off Jason and the others.

Attracted by the commotion, the flesh eaters stared in the group's direction. Upon seeing food, they moved en masse toward the humans.

Jason suddenly realized that crossing the square would be more difficult than he realized. If they stayed together, half of them would be taken down before they even reached Notre Dame. "Split up!" he yelled. "We'll meet by the north entrance."

Without hesitating, the group spread out. Jason made a dash between the Golems, hoping to sneak through the gap and draw their attention away from the others. Lucifer and Lilith ran beside him.

JEANETTE BROKE TO the right, trying to give the closest Golem a wide berth. It lumbered toward her as she ran past it. That put her dangerously close to the lava flow. A dozen flesh eaters blocked her path, and five more approached from her left. They were less than ten feet away and closing, threatening to trap her. Jeanette stopped and spun around, deciding to go back and circle around the square. She gasped when she saw the Golem behind her, its right arm raised across its chest, ready to strike.

SASHA BROKE LEFT and raced along the outer perimeter of the square where there were less Demon Spawn. Antoine and Sook-kyoung stayed close to protect her. A flesh eater staggered in front of them. Sook-kyoung raced ahead and launched into a roundhouse kick. Her foot connected with the demon's head, sending it spinning backwards onto the ground.

A flesh eater in a *gendarme* uniform emerged from a clump of trees and grabbed Sasha as she passed. She tried to break free but was hampered by the weight of the minigun. The demon hung on tight and plunged its mouth toward her neck. She raised her left arm, catching the flesh eater across its throat. This one possessed more strength than the rest, or maybe she was just worn out. In any case, she would only be able to hold it back for a few seconds at best.

DOC RAN DOWN the center of the square, clutching to his chest the saddle bag with the anti-matter device. He made it halfway across when a naked flesh eater swerved in his direction and lunged. Doc gasped, unable to fight it off with his one arm clutching the bag.

A gunshot rang out from behind him. The flesh eater's head jerked back as a bullet entered its forehead and blew off the back of its skull. It dropped to the ground as an eddy of blue light flowed skyward. Neal raced up beside Doc, the barrel of his FAMAS still billowing smoke. He grabbed Doc by the arm and pushed him forward, heading for a spot where the Demon Spawn were fewest.

JEANETTE SPRAWLED TO the ground as the Golem struck out. Its hand swiped above her prone body and connected with the flesh eaters surrounding her, throwing the horde aside with one blow. Bodies tumbled into the lava. Jeanette jumped to her feet before the last carcass hit the molten river and bolted forward. The Golem swung its arm back, missing her by inches. It lumbered after her, but she was already half away to Notre Dame.

THREE FLESH EATERS converged on Jason. He pulled his machete from its sheath, ready to take them on.

Lucifer and Lilith leapt forward. They pounced on the outermost demons, knocking them down and tearing into them with fangs and claws. The flesh eater in the middle paused, its gaze switching between the fallen Demon Spawn, which gave Jason the time he needed. Swinging the machete, he sliced through its neck. Its head lobbed off and sailed through the air, allowing a blue eddy of light to escape. Jason shoved aside the decapitated corpse and continued toward Notre Dame. The werehounds released their prey and gave chase.

JOSH AND SHANE also made their way down the center of the square, more careful to avoid the Golem than the flesh eaters. Josh weaved among the Demon Spawn as if he was on the football field. Shane took a more direct approach, using his FAMAS to crush the heads of anything that got in his way. Reinhard, Ray, and Haneef stayed twenty feet behind them, taking advantage of the path their friends cleared and covering their backs in case any of the demons circled around. With most of the Demon Spawn distracted by the others, it took this group only a minute to reach the other side of the square. The nearest flesh eater was more than fifty feet away.

Doc and Neal raced up, the former hunched over, gasping for breath.

"You okay?" asked Josh.

"I'll be fine," Doc wheezed. "I just need to catch my breath."

The group checked on the others.

SASHA BRACED HERSELF to be bitten by the flesh eater when the demon groaned. She opened her eyes to see Antoine's machete piercing its face. The flesh eater's grip loosened. It slid off the blade onto the pavement, leaving chunks of bone and brain on the metal. Antoine grabbed Sasha's arm and dragged her along.

"Keep moving unless you want to become one of them."

ONE BY ONE, the group coalesced around the front façade of Notre Dame. The twin Golem plodded toward them, still too far away to pose an immediate threat. The few flesh eaters that got close were taken down with single shots to the head. Jason couldn't believe their luck. They now stood in the shadows cast by Notre Dame's twin towers. Only a short dash and they'd be inside the cathedral.

When Jeanette joined them, Jason led the group around the corner.

CHAPTER FIFTY-TWO

A HANDFUL OF flesh eaters wandered along the cathedral's northern façade, so it took only a few seconds to reach the entrance. As they ran up the steps, Jason stopped the others.

"Wait here."

"For what?" asked Doc. "We should push ahead while we have the chance."

"I want to check inside first. We don't know what's in there. I'll only be a minute."

As the others formed a perimeter around the stairs, Jason rushed up to the heavy wooden doors, relieved to find that they were not locked. He pushed open the one on the left enough to slip through and entered Notre Dame.

The stench nauseated him. A pungent odor of rot and decay mixed with brimstone assaulted his nose, making his sinuses water. He wiped the tears from his eyes and forced down the bile rising in his throat.

Jason stood in the northern transept across from where it connected with the nave. The portal stood off to his left in the area reserved for the choir. The moment he saw it, memories of CERN raced through his conscious. This portal measured seventy feet in circumference, with the lower portion buried in the floor. Everything within five feet of the outer edge of the portal had disintegrated as a natural result of its formation. Most of the nearby plate glass windows had been shattered and the choir stalls had been ripped apart. Extensive damage to several of the support columns on either side of the cathedral caused the upper balcony to sag. Like at CERN, this portal also shimmered as if gazing through a layer of water.

The landscape on the other side looked grey and barren, contrasting sharply with the blood red sky. Raging infernos burned in the distance and lit up the horizon. Within the light of the fires stood a dark outline of what appeared to be a city. Flesh eaters stretched as far as he could see, although none of them seemed interested in crossing to this side. The biggest danger was posed by four Golem that stood on the opposite side of the portal and faced inward toward the landscape. These monstrosities were spread out one to two hundred feet from the portal and could pose a problem if they tried to stop the group.

A stream of lava flowed through the right side of the portal and across the nave, burning its way toward the front of the cathedral where it cascaded through the southern and central doors and into the square. The intense heat had scorched the southern interior. Across from Jason stood a mound of charred wood, which he assumed had once been the altar. The only portion of the interior his people could walk on was a strip along the northern wall thirty feet wide that paralleled the lava flow and stretched from the front of the cathedral into the portal, leaving only a small path for Demon Spawn to travel through. The temperature approached one hundred and thirty degrees because of the molten mass oozing past him. More than a hundred flesh eaters milled around inside the cathedral, packing the space not rendered impassable by the lava. Jason cursed under his breath. They had made it this far only to fail in the last hundred feet.

Before any of the flesh eaters noticed him, Jason slid back outside and closed the door behind him.

"What's it like?" asked Doc.

"We're screwed." Jason couldn't hide the depression in his voice. "There's over a hundred flesh eaters inside."

Reinhard cursed in German. Antoine punched the stone column.

"We're not going back after coming this far," said Jason. "We're just going to have to fight our way through them. Doc, when we rush in, you and Neal head straight for the portal and plant the device. The rest of us will hold them off for you as long—"

"Let me go in and take care of the flesh eaters," interrupted Sasha.

Jason could not believe what he heard. "There's too many. You won't be able to take them down by yourself."

"I know that. But I can distract them and lead them away from the portal."

"No." Jason shook his head so that the strands of blonde hair waved across his face. "It's suicide."

"It's the only way." Sasha's voice had a tender edge to it. "I'll buy you enough time so Doc can close the portal."

Jason started to protest but stopped. He knew Sasha was right. The mission could succeed only if she led the flesh eaters away long enough for Doc to get close and use the device. He also knew it would be the last time he saw Sasha. He wanted to say something profound, to tell Sasha how he felt about her, to explain why he had acted the way he did. There was no time. He boiled down eight months of emotion toward Sasha, the woman who had been his first love and his comrade in arms through the apocalypse, into two simple words.

"Be careful."

"I will." Stepping up to Jason, Sasha placed her hands on his cheeks leaned forward, and brushed her lips against his. She kissed him long and deep. It didn't feel like anything he had felt before. Sasha sighed contentedly into his mouth. When she broke the embrace, her eyes locked on his. "I'm doing this for you. I love you, Jason."

Before Jason could reply, Sasha became all business. "Antoine, Shane, Ray. You're with me. Stay close. We're going to send these Demon Spawn back where they came from."

Rushing past Jason and flashing him a loving smile, Sasha entered Notre Dame with her suicide team.

CHAPTER FIFTY-THREE

S ASHA MOVED INTO the northern transept and assessed the situation. They had only one chance of getting out of this alive, as slim as that would be. She waited for the others.

"We're going to make a run for the front of the cathedral and lead them out of the nave."

"You mean outside where the rest of those things are waiting?" Ray asked.

"No. We're going to head for the top of the tower and let them follow us. That way they can't swarm us and we have a better chance of controlling their advance. Follow me and use ammo only when you have to."

Without waiting for their reaction, Sasha ran down the northern aisle. Half a dozen flesh eaters blocked her path. Firing up the minigun, she let loose a five-second burst that cleared the path. The noise attracted the attention of the remaining demons. As one, the horde sauntered toward the group.

When Sasha reached the base of the tower, she pushed the others into the spiral stairwell. "Head for the top and clear out anything ahead of us."

"What about you?" Shane asked.

"I'll be right behind you. Followed by them." She gestured over her shoulder toward the advancing flesh eaters. Sasha spun around and faced the approaching horde. "Come on, you bastards. You don't want to pass up the only meal you've had in months."

She waited until the demons were ten feet away and fired the minigun, spraying it back and forth across the horde. The concentrated fire tore into the first two rows, splattering body parts across the nave and sending dozens of blue eddies of light toward the arched ceiling. Those in back stumbled over the carcasses and closed in, their hands outstretched. Sasha backed into the stairwell, climbed ten steps, and waited. When the first flesh eater centered itself in the opening, she fired a one-second burst that blasted it apart. Others swarmed past the remnants. Sasha climbed ten more steps and fired another one-second burst, taking down the next two demons in line, and then climbed ten more steps to give the others a chance to follow.

Come on, Jason. You can do this.

"THEY'RE GETTING CLOSER." Haneef stood in the center of the street, keeping his eye on the flesh eaters approaching from the square.

"We have to wait for Sasha to clear out the nave otherwise this isn't going to work."

Haneef shook his head in resignation. "We are keeping Allah busy this afternoon."

The remainder of the group stood in a semi-circle, their weapons at the ready.

Jason waited until he could no longer hear Sasha's minigun, hoping that it meant she had successfully led the flesh eaters away. Pushing open the door, he cautiously stepped inside and stepped over to the nave. The last ones were pushing their way into the tower's stairwell. He waved for the others to join him. Haneef entered last, pausing long enough to lock the doors.

Jason pointed toward the portal. "Okay, Doc. Close it down. The rest of you spread out and keep your eyes open for danger."

While Neal hovered near Doc, the others formed a circle

around him. The werehounds stayed with Jason.

We might do this, thought Jason. *We might actually—*

Lilith's growling broke into his trend of thought. "What's wrong, girl?"

Lilith stared up at the balcony that ran above the northern aisle. Six soul vampires crouched on the railing, glaring down at the group.

ON THE OPPOSITE side of the portal, the commotion inside Notre Dame attracted the attention of the closest Golem. It swung its massive head to one side and surveyed its realm. Unusual sounds emanated from the cathedral and the flesh eaters were on the march. Swinging its body around, the Golem shambled toward the portal to check on the disturbance.

ANTOINE REACHED THE roof first and crossed over to the western edge. Glancing down into the square, he mumbled under his breath, "Shit."

Those flesh eaters in the square were converging on the front façade of Notre Dame. Even worse, the noise had attracted every other demon in the vicinity. Hundreds emerged from side streets throughout Ile de la Cite, with scores more crossing the bridges spanning the northern Seine. The two Golem had climbed the stairs in front of the one remaining door and were pounding on it to gain access.

Shane stepped up beside him. "What's wrong?"

Antoine motioned toward the square. "We've got company."

Shane leaned out over the wall and whistled. "You know, that sucks big time."

"Tell me about it. At least we're safe up here." The Moroccan headed toward the stairs and saw only Ray standing there.

"Where's Sasha?"

"She's still drawing those things toward us."

SASHA COULD SEE the sunlight pouring through the opening to the roof. She had been holding off the flesh eaters for five minutes, climbing ten steps at a time and releasing short bursts to keep them following her. She figured she had killed close to fifty, although twice that number remained. Even worse, by her estimate she had already expended half her ammunition.

Spinning around, she ran the last few yards up the stairs and burst into the sunlight. The others waited for her.

"What now?" Ray asked.

Sasha faced the stairwell and aimed her minigun at the opening. "Now we make our last stand."

THE SOUL VAMPIRES launched themselves off the balcony into the nave.

Lucifer and Lilith, now morphed into their demonic forms, pounced on two of the demons as they landed, pinning them to the floor. Lilith's jaws clenched around the soul vampire's neck and bit down. It growled and tried to break free. She arched her stinger over her head and plunged it into the struggling demon's chest. The soul vampire cried out and thrashed around, its movements becoming weaker with each passing second. Once Lilith subdued it, she whipped her jaws to the side and tore off its head.

The other soul vampire scratched at Lucifer's sides, succeeding only in ripping out its talons on his scales. With his right paw, Lucifer slapped the demon off the side of its head, snapping its neck. A third soul vampire jumped on Lucifer's back, hoping to attack his spine, and instead became impaled on the three-inch spikes around the werehound's shoulder. In desperation, it vomited acid on Lucifer, covering the werehound's back. The acid sizzled against the scales. Lucifer yelped and bucked, dislodging the soul vampire and throwing it to one side where it lay shriveled, coddling its wounds. The werehound rolled around on its back, trying to wipe away the acid and ease the burning.

The fourth soul vampire landed in front of Jason. He raised the crossbow and pulled the trigger. The soul vampire ducked. Instead of striking its heart, the arrow lodged in its neck. The demon dropped to its knees and howled, trying to remove it. Jason replaced the arrow and fired again. This time it struck the soul vampire's chest a few inches from its heart. Jason reached for another arrow, only to discover that he had run out. Throwing the crossbow aside, he slid out his machete and stepped toward the demon. It glared at him and snarled. Jason brought down the blade on its skull, cleaving its head in half.

That's when Jason heard Lucifer whine. He turned to see the werehound covered in acid, and the offending soul vampire on the floor, several holes punched into its chest. Jason rushed over. The soul vampire arched its head toward him. Jason could smell acid vomit on its breath. Raising the machete above his head, he brought the blade straight down, slicing into the demon's skull where the eyes would normally be. It convulsed. Jason twisted the machete to the right, scrambling the soul vampire's brain.

The fifth chose Jeanette as its target. Jeanette waited until the demon attacking her had gotten within range and then plunged her machete into its abdomen. It sliced through the skin with a dull squish. The soul vampire froze. Jeanette pulled up, slicing the blade along its torso, and jumped back. Its skin opened with a sickening tearing sound and its internal organs snaked out and plopped onto the floor. The acid vomit sack ruptured on impact, sending corrosive liquid splattering across its disemboweled organs. Jeanette stepped forward and swung her machete sideways, slicing through the soul vampire's neck.

Slava shot at the last soul vampire when it landed in front of him. The demon moved too fast, and only a few rounds thudded harmlessly into its abdomen. It circled around and charged. Slava aimed again and fired. Two rounds left the FAMAS when the bolt stuck in the open position. Before Slava could react, the soul vampire ran into him and knocked him to the ground. The Russian tried to keep the FAMAS between himself and the demon, pushing the weapon against its chest. He had a tenuous grip on the soul vampire that would not hold for long, so he closed his eyes and waited for the inevitable.

Sook-kyoung appeared out of nowhere and kicked the demon in the head, knocking it off Slava. When it stopped rolling, she fired a sustained burst from her FAMAS that ran up its chest. The last three rounds ruptured its heart, and the soul vampire toppled over backward. The young woman reached out a hand and helped Slava to his feet. "Are you all right?"

"Yes. And thanks." He reached into his ammo bag for another magazine, only to find it empty. "I'm out."

"Same here."

The two looked around, hoping no one other Demon Spawn were nearby.

NEAL CROUCHED AND held open the saddle bag as Doc, who knelt in front of him, used his hand to undo the flap and slide out the anti-matter device.

"Hurry up."

"Don't rush me," Doc chided his assistant. He checked on the battle with the soul vampires, relieved that none of the demons were interested in them. Doc removed the device with his good arm and, as he did, Neal tossed aside the saddle bag. One way or another, it would all be over in a minute.

BEING PREOCCUPIED BY the soul vampires, no one noticed the

Golem step through the portal into the cathedral and lumber toward Doc.

THE FIRST FOUR flesh eaters exited the stairwell onto the roof of the tower.

"Fire!"

Sasha sighted in on the lead flesh eater and squeezed the trigger. The demon blew apart, showering those behind it with chunks of decayed flesh and gore. She lifted her finger off the trigger, switched her aim to another and fired again, decimating it. The others each took careful aim, lining up their shots before firing. At first the tactic worked fine, bringing down ten flesh eaters in the first few seconds. Soon the mass pushing its way up the stairwell became too heavy and an increasing number made their way onto the roof. Some stumbled over the remains of the other demons, spoiling the humans' aim. Others staggered off to the sides, spreading across the roof and threatening to outflank the team. Sasha and the others increased their rate of fire. They succeeded in taking down all the flesh eaters that reached the roof yet were going through their ammunition at an alarming rate.

The flood of flesh eaters continued.

JASON CHECKED ON Doc and Neal as the Golem stepped up behind them, its arm raised above its head.

"Doc, look out!"

The two men glanced over their shoulders. Neal jumped out of the way. Doc was still on his knees and could not move fast enough. The Golem slammed its fist on top of Doc's head, crushing him into the floor. His body ruptured, sending internal organs and blood spewing across the tiles. The anti-matter device flew out of Doc's arm and rolled across the floor, heading for the lava. Because of its oblong shape, it wobbled to one side and curved back toward the center of the floor, coming to a rest ten yards from Jason. The Golem ignored Neal and moved toward the device.

JOSH WATCHED DOC'S death with a sense of sadness and anger. It sucked that he had to die so close to completing his mission. To fail now was inexcusable. He knew he had one chance to save the situation, and without hesitating Josh dropped his FAMAS and ran toward the Golem. The Golem raised its right foot, ready to stomp on the device. Crouching, Josh crashed into its left leg and shoved, wrapping his arms around the limb to get a better grip. Caught off balance, the Golem staggered to its left toward the lava. Josh kept on pushing until the monstrosity toppled over and plunged into the molten river. Josh released his grip, but momentum carried him forward and he tumbled into the flow. He hoped his sacrifice wouldn't be in vain.

The pain when he hit the lava was excruciating yet brief.

SASHA KEPT HER finger on the trigger, splaying the minigun from side to side to stem the unending flow of flesh eaters. Beside her, the others switched their weapons to full-automatic mode and emptied them into the swarm, replaced their empty magazines, and resumed firing. The noise from the weapons was deafening. Even out here in the open air, the combined smell of burnt gunpowder and rotted flesh was overpowering, making their eyes water.

Shane was the first to expend all his ammunition. "That's it. I'm out."

"Me, too," added Ray a moment later.

The bolt on Antoine's FAMAS locked back, signifying he had used up his last round. He tossed the assault rifle aside.

Sasha kept up the assault, swinging the minigun from side

to side. There were too many flesh eaters to stop them all. Eventually, the last of her ammunition was used up. The only sounds were the whir of the minigun's spinning barrel mount and the moans of the remaining demons. Close to two dozen had survived and they moved across the roof and circled the humans.

"We're screwed," said Shane.

"Not yet." Sasha unbuckled the chest straps to her minigun and slid the device and backpack off her shoulders. Sliding her machete from its sheath, she held it in front of her, her knuckles tightening around the grip. "Come on, boys. It's time to get close and personal."

JASON WATCHED AS Josh's body fell into the lava and ignited. He closed his eyes as the burning corpse flowed past. He would say a prayer for his fallen comrade later, if he lived that long.

A crash at the front of the nave caught his attention. The door to the remaining entrance fell to the ground. The two Golem from outside entered the cathedral, accompanied by a swarm of flesh eaters.

Jason rushed over to the anti-matter device and scooped it up, then raced to the portal.

SASHA'S TEAM SLASHED their way into the approaching horde as if their lives depended on it because, in fact, they did.

Sasha stepped forward and plunged her machete into the face of the closest flesh eater. It stiffened as the blade sliced into its brain. Placing her foot on its chest, Sasha pushed. The demon slid off the blade and tumbled into another demon, knocking it to the ground.

Antoine moved in between two flesh eaters and slashed to the right and then to the left, decapitating them both.

Shane gouged one in the abdomen, tearing open its guts. It

stumbled and fell on its own intestines.

Ray went to slice a flesh eater across the neck. It moved at the last moment. The blade lodged deep in its shoulder. He tried to pull the machete free, but it stuck in the rotted flesh. Rather than abandon his weapon, he continued yanking at it. The blade would not move. The flesh eater grabbed Ray by the shirt and pulled him close, sinking its teeth into his neck. Ray cried out for help. Two more converged on him and dragged him to the ground. His screams echoed across the roof as the flesh eaters feasted on him.

The others took down flesh eaters one by one, yet there were too many and exhaustion slowed down each team member. The remaining demons soon had the humans back against the wall. Eight trapped Sasha and Shane along the west wall. The two slashed away. Shane stood in front of Sasha, swinging madly from left to right. He managed to slice one across the face, ripping out its eyes. Two more grabbed him and dragged him down. The last five swarmed Sasha. They closed in around her, pinning her arms by her side and pushing against her. A set of teeth dug into her shoulder, biting through the flightsuit and piercing the skin. A decayed hand clawed at her face, the fingers gouging at her eyes. Rather than be eaten alive, Sasha tumbled backward over the edge of the wall, plummeting three hundred feet to the ground below, and taking three of the flesh eaters with her.

With the last of their food supply almost gone, the surviving flesh eaters converged on Antoine, who was surrounded in the northeast corner.

JASON PAUSED FIFTEEN feet from the portal to check the device and make sure it was intact. In the nave, Jeanette, Haneef, Sook-kyoung, Slava, Neal, and Reinhard had formed a tight line, their machetes drawn, ready to meet the oncoming threat from outside. The two werehounds stood amongst them. He had to act now if—

"Jason?"

A chill raced down his spine. He knew the voice, although he had not heard it in months. It came from the last person he expected to see at this moment. Jason stared at the portal, his mouth agape.

"Mom?"

CHAPTER FIFTY-FOUR

J ASON'S MOTHER RAN toward him from the other side of the portal. Three other Golem lumbered toward the portal to stop the commotion inside the cathedral, placed between her and safety. She was much thinner than when he had seen her last at CERN. Her clothes were soiled and torn. Her long hair had been chopped short. She had that weary, emotionless expression of someone who had seen too much for the mind to grasp. Despite everything, she waved frantically to get his attention. He had never been so happy to see anyone in his entire life. When their eyes locked, a smile spread across her face. She paused to catch her breath.

"I knew you'd find a way to get me," his mother huffed.

My God, he thought. *She's alive. She's been waiting for me to rescue her all these months.*

The closest Golem on the other side of the portal would be inside the cathedral well before she could pass through, assuming she could make it by them. Jason turned back to the nave. The Demon Spawn from outside had closed to within fifteen feet of his friends. When he faced back to the portal, the first Golem started to cross over, its right leg pushing through the shimmering surface into the choir section. Jason made his decision quickly, and it was easier than he had thought. He couldn't risk the mission for his mother. Not for the woman who caused this apocalypse in the first place.

Lifting the anti-matter device in his right hand, Jason tossed it into the portal.

His mother's scream of "No" was drowned out the moment

the device touched the surface of the portal. The outer casing disintegrated on impact, releasing the anti-matter inside. A blinding flash of light and a thunderous roar crashed through the cathedral, much brighter and louder than the explosion at CERN. Flames engulfed the portal, incinerating the Golem passing through into this realm. The portal burned intensely for a few seconds, consuming itself in the conflagration until it collapsed on itself. With nothing left to support them, the weakened pillars gave way, and the arched roof at the east end of Notre Dame caved in, filling the choir section with debris and dust.

Jason observed none of this. The shock wave from the detonation had blown him across the nave into one of the support columns along the northern aisle. He lay sprawled across the floor, motionless.

A HAND SHOOK Jason's shoulder and then gently slapped his face, slowly bringing him back to consciousness. He heard a soft feminine voice asking, "Jason, are you okay? Please talk to me."

"Mom?" he slurred.

"No. It's Jeanette."

His mind recalled flirting with Jeanette on the floor of the bunker as they played with Lucifer and Lilith. That had happened days ago. He sorted through the jumble of thoughts. The last thing he remembered—

Jason sat up abruptly, panic coursing through his body. "The Demon Spawn? Where are they?"

"They're dead." Jeanette placed her hand on his chin and stroked his skin. "They died when you closed the portal."

A fleeting image of the explosion flashed through his mind. "I-it's closed?"

"You did it, boss." Slava patted Jason on the shoulder.

"Help me up," said Jason.

Jeanette and Slava each took an arm and lifted Jason to his feet. The room spun when he tried to stand. He closed his eyes for a moment. When he opened them again, he had regained his balance. His body, however, still felt like he had taken a punch from one of the Golem.

A pile of rubble from the collapsed roof filled the space where the portal once stood. With its source cut off, the last of the lava flowed out the front doors of the cathedral and into the square. Then he noticed the pile of dead Demon Spawn near the front of the nave.

"What happened?" asked Jason as he pointed to the carcasses.

"When the portal exploded," said Neal, "every one of those things collapsed where they stood. I guess that without the link to their dimension, the Demon Spawn couldn't survive in this world. Doc was right after all."

Jason stepped over to the spot where the physician had been slaughtered by the Golem. His shattered body lay in a heap. Jason wanted to do something to show respect, but there were no eyelids to close, no arms to cross, and too large of a bloody splatter to cover with a jacket. The man had sacrificed so much to save the world. It didn't seem fair his final resting place would be out in the open amongst the Demon Spawn. The only memorial Jason could offer was to close his eyes and mentally tell his friend, "You did it, Doc."

A large tongue lapped at Jason's hand. Lilith stood beside him, her tail wagging furiously. Lucifer limped over and nudged him in the leg. First-degree burns etched across his back from where the soul vampire had vomited on him. Thankfully, his thick scales prevented him from getting hurt too badly. Jason reached down and patted his pets on the head.

Oh my God! Sasha! Jason didn't see her or the rest of her team. "What about the others?"

Slava appeared embarrassed. "We haven't checked on

them yet."

"Why not?"

Slava tried to find the right answer.

"Because everyone thought we were dead." Antoine exited the stairs leading up to the tower and walked over to them. He held a gore-covered machete by his side. "Frankly, I'm surprised any of us are alive."

Jason felt his sprits sink. "Is Sasha…?"

Antoine placed a hand on his shoulder. "I'm sorry. Those things pushed her off the roof. I'm the only one who made it."

Jason experienced a crushing emptiness in his chest. It felt as though someone had grabbed his emotions, twisted them in a knot, and ripped them from his heart. He wanted to cry. No, he wanted to wail. Turning his back to the others, his face grimaced and tears flowed down his cheeks. For a moment, he wanted to die, anything to stop the torment raging inside of him. As suddenly as the torrent of emotions had begun, they stopped. Jason bit his lip hard enough to draw blood. He tamped down the grief, pushing deep inside him the physical pain and emotional anguish. He couldn't afford to show weakness right now. There would be time later for mourning. Right now, he had a mission to complete. Sniffing back the tears, he wiped his face with his palm.

"I would have been dead myself if the Demon Spawn hadn't suddenly dropped," Antoine continued. "What happened?"

"Jason closed the portal," said Jeanette. "When he did, all the Demon Spawn collapsed."

"Thank God for that." Antoine nodded. "Did it happen in here or all over Paris?"

"There's only one way to find out." Jason made his way to the front of Notre Dame, carefully maneuvering through the mass of dead Demon Spawn, and stepped outside.

The sun had begun to set, disappearing behind the buildings of Isle de la Cite. Scores of immobile flesh eaters lay scattered across the square and side streets. Jason listened. He heard the last of the lava as it made its way down the Seine, but nothing else. It suddenly dawned on him that they had done it. They had succeeded in closing the portal as well as eliminating the threat caused by the Demon Spawn. They had saved Europe from certain destruction and given the continent a chance to rebuild.

At what cost? Twenty of them had set out from Mont St. Michel eight days ago. Only seven survived. They had lost good people and good friends, and even loved ones. Andre. Christophe. Renato. Philippe. Petra. Bill. David. Franco. Josh. Doc. Shane. Ray. His beloved Sasha. All of them had put their faith in him and none of them were around to savor their victory.

At the base of the tower lay the crumbled body of Sasha. He could see a river of blood flowing across the pavement toward the gutter. He wanted to go over and say goodbye, yet he could not bring himself to do so. He wanted to remember Sasha as she was, the vibrant young woman he had loved and who loved him back. He wanted to remember the way she kissed him before running off to face the Demon Spawn, and not the shattered body. Jason closed his eyes to fight back the tears. Everything had been so repressed into his psyche that they did not flow. He looked away.

"Vat should ve do about our comrades?" asked Reinhard.

"Nothing." Jason's tone had a harsh quality to it. "We need to get back to Nanterre before the Enclavers leave without us. There'll be time to bury the dead and mourn their loss later."

Jason descended the steps and headed across the square. The others fell in behind him.

CHAPTER FIFTY-FIVE

IT TOOK THE group all night to walk the eight miles from Ile de la Cite back to the warehouse in Nanterre, with a slight detour back to the Louvre to retrieve Haneef's minigun. Only this time, they made the trip above ground. Even though the Demon Spawn were dead, Jason did not want to revisit the nightmare that had taken place in the Metro. He could not bear the idea of seeing the bodies of those lost battling the giant centipedes and tarantulas. Besides, most of the group had lost their flashlights in the earlier underground battle or inside Notre Dame, which would have made traversing the Metro impossible. Even topside, with the streets pitch black, the going was slow.

The survivors had spent the first several hours checking over their shoulder or searching every doorway and side street for danger, afraid that the Demon Spawn farthest from the portal may not have been affected by its closure. Jason knew they were dead. Not because his group passed the carcasses of thousands of fallen flesh eaters and soul vampires littering the streets of Paris. For the first time in months, his mind was clear. No tortured souls hummed in his psyche. The only thing that swam around in his brain were his own thoughts and emotions, both of which he could tamp down. Not having that sixth sense constantly buzzing felt lonely and isolating, and Jason reveled in the sensation.

They reached the warehouse as dawn broke, the dawn of the first day without Demon Spawn. The Enclavers greeted them with hugs and a warm breakfast. If the Enclavers were appalled by how few had survived the ordeal, none of them showed it. When the Enclavers heard about their success in closing the portal, they broke out bottles of wine to toast their victory. The survivors joined in, mostly out of politeness. None of them were in a mood to celebrate.

Later that morning, the group set out for the Enclave.

THE TWO-DAY JOURNEY passed without incident. The group stuck to the main roads to save time. The carcasses of flesh eaters and soul vampires littered every town they passed through. At one town bisected by the Seine River, which now flowed with water, the group came upon the remains of a magma monster. It lay on its back on the riverbank, a pile of cracked stone and ash with its arms spread out and its legs immersed in the river.

Back at the Enclave, Reno welcomed them with open arms, thankful that they had succeeded and that his niece had survived. The group endured endless rounds of congratulations, praise, and a huge feast in their honor. Jason's people forced a smile and accepted the honors good-naturedly, albeit with little enthusiasm. Slava was the most popular member, regaling the Enclavers with tales of what they faced in Paris. To his credit, the Russian paid tribute to his fallen comrades, going into detail about how each had died heroically.

RENO HAD GIVEN up his private quarters so Jason could get a good night sleep. Taking advantage of the chance for privacy, Jason slipped away from the celebration early. Lucifer and Lilith stayed with the others, who constantly slipped the werehounds scraps from the table. Jason did not take offense. He brought a bottle of wine back to his room. If he slept, he would dream, and he wanted to be drunk enough so as not to remember those dreams.

Jason unzipped his flightsuit and slid the top portion down around his waist. Only then did he realize how filthy and worn his uniform had become and how much he stank. He developed a new-found sense of respect for the Enclavers. Anyone who showed such hospitality to a smelly, unkempt group such as his team deserved admiration.

He had uncorked the wine and taken the first long drink when someone knocked on the door. "Is this important?" he growled.

The door opened and Jeanette slipped her head inside. "I don't know. Am I important?"

Jason's demeanor softened at the sight of the young woman. "Sorry. I'm exhausted and not in the best of moods."

"Understandable." Jeanette slipped into the room without an invitation and closed the door behind her.

Jason was too tired to be embarrassed at having Jeanette see him half naked. "Are you sure you want to be in the same room with me? I smell like a Demon Spawn."

"We all do. That's one of things I came to tell you. My uncle is arranging hot showers and a change of clothes for us in the morning."

"That's nice of him."

"It's the least he can do. You're a hero."

Jason took a swig of wine to wash away the bad taste that word left in his mouth. "Heroes don't wind up getting two-thirds of their people killed."

"You saved Europe in the process."

"I had to do it."

"No, you didn't. You could have aborted the mission at any time, and no one would have thought any less of you."

I would have, thought Jason.

"Like it or not, Jason, you are a hero," admonished Jeanette, although her voice still possessed a tenderness to it.

"You're going to have to deal with it."

Jason turned from Jeanette so she wouldn't see his sneer. He knew the name McCreary would be talked about for the next hundred years, although he thought it would in relation to the abomination his mother created rather than his own efforts. "What was the other thing you wanted to tell me?"

Jeanette beamed. "I talked to Uncle Reno, and he's willing to let me go back to Mont St. Michel with you."

Jason's surprise must have been evident in his face. Jeanette instantly became crestfallen. "You don't want me to go back with you?"

"That's not it," said Jason.

"It's Sasha." Jeanette seemed on the verge of tears. "You love her, not me."

"No," he partially lied. How could he explain to Jeanette that he loved them both, each for different reasons, but that he chosen her over Sasha? And how could he explain to Jeanette that he felt guilty about his choice, especially after Sasha loved him enough to sacrifice her own life to save his?

"Then why can't I return with you to Mont St. Michel?"

"I didn't say you couldn't. It's just… well… why do you want to go back with *me?*" His emphasis on the last word expressed a degree of self-doubt he had not intended.

Jeanette smiled. "For all your heroics, you're still a boy at heart."

"Excuse me?" Although he knew she did not mean it as an insult, some how he felt offended.

"I want to go back to Mont St. Michel because I like you. Now that the portal is closed, we're going to have to rebuild this world." Jeanette stepped forward, slid her hand behind his neck, and pulled him close. "And repopulate it."

Her lips slid across his. The kiss was awkward, yet Jason didn't care. For a moment, he forgot about the pain and anger bottled up inside of him. Before he could kiss back, she stepped away, letting her hand tenderly slide across his cheek.

"Get a good night sleep." Jeanette glided toward the door and opened it. She had a gleam in her eye. "See you in the morning."

RENO ALLOWED JASON'S group to stay a full day to rest up. The Enclavers were less profuse in their praise of the Demon Hunters, as they had started calling Jason and his group. As time distanced Jason's people from the events in Notre Dame, they grew more comfortable with what they had gone through, although no wanted to talk about their experiences yet. When they departed on the morning of their third day, they received a warm send off. Jason promised Reno he would take good care of his niece. Reno hugged them both, fighting back the tears.

The journey to Mont St. Michel proved as uneventful as the one to the Enclave. Jason had opted to follow the same route they had originally traveled to ensure that the Demon Spawn were gone. As anticipated, every demon they came across had dropped where it stood when the portal imploded. The group's growing pride at their success was tempered by horrible memories as they passed the locations were members of their group had fallen. Notre Dame de la Garenne. The copse of trees where Petra had been mortally wounded. Falaise. The field outside of Ger where Christophe had become a flesh eater. For Jason, the latter location still engendered feelings of guilt he had difficulty repressing.

THE GROUP ARRIVED at Mont St. Michel on the afternoon of their ninth day out of Paris. Word had somehow reached the walled city of their success. Refugees raced to the roadside as they passed, clapping and cheering the Demon Hunters.

Several rushed forward, reaching up to shake their hands. One mother bent over and kissed Jason's shoe as he rode by.

Slava saddled up beside Jason. "How do you Americans say it? We're rock and roll stars."

"We gave them hope, something they didn't have before."

Slava patted him on the back. "Enjoy this. This is for you."

"It's for all of us, Slava. Especially those who didn't make it back."

"No. We would have come back after Falaise if it wasn't for you. They don't know that, but we do. You deserve this more than us." The Russian swung his horse around. "Andre would have been proud."

As Slava rode to the rear, the six-year-old girl with curly blonde hair who had waved to them as they left ran into the street and came up to Jason. Her eyes glowed with adoration as she said, "Thank you."

Jason sat up straight in his saddle and smiled. This was why they had gone of the suicide mission in the first place—to protect these people and give them hope for the future.

For the first time in months, he felt that such hope no longer seemed unfounded.

ONCE INSIDE MONT St. Michel, the locals treated Jason's people like conquering heroes. The gate guards swarmed them as they entered, shaking hands and patting legs. Even the head guard snapped to attention and gave Jason a crisp salute. The girls who tended to the horses hugged each of the Demon Hunters as they dismounted. All the men received a barrage of kisses, which made Antoine and Reinhard uncomfortable. As the others drifted away, a young man Jason recognized by face, but whose name he did not know, rushed up to Jason.

"Excuse me, sir. Jacques requested that you come see him at once at the abbey."

"I'll be there in a minute."

The young man's eyes widened. "Ah… Jacques was very insistent. He told me to tell you—"

"In a minute." Jason dragged out each word, making it clear the discussion had ended. The young man backed off and milled around King's Gate.

Jason faced the group. They stood in a semi-circle, waiting on him. Jason had no idea what to say.

"Thank you. I never could have done this without you. I wish I could have brought the others back, too."

An awkward silence ensued. Then Antoine broke out into a hearty laugh. "Brief and to the point. My type of leader." The Moroccan stepped forward and wrapped his arms around Jason's shoulders, holding him for several seconds. Breaking the hug, he walked off into the *Le Mere Poulard*, chuckling all the way into the lobby.

Reinhard gave Jason a single nod of approval. "Good job." He followed Antoine into the hotel.

Sook-kyoung bowed at the waist. When she straightened, she said, "I'm sorry I doubted you."

"You had every reason to."

The Korean shook her head. "You are stronger than you give yourself credit for. It was an honor to serve with you and I'll gladly do so again."

"Thank you."

Sook-kyoung gave Jason a brief hug and entered the hotel.

Haneef offered his hand and Jason gave it a firm pump.

"So, I guess it was Allah's will after all that we succeed," said Jason.

"I knew it was Allah's will that we would succeed when he allowed you to lead us." Haneef motioned for Slava to follow him. "Come on, my friend. I need a drink."

"I thought Muslims didn't drink alcohol," said the Russian as he fell in behind his friend.

"We don't." Haneef smiled. "Considering what we have

accomplished, I think Allah will forgive me this one indulgence."

Neal sighed. "What do I do?"

"What do you mean?" asked Jason.

"With Doc gone, what's going to happen to me?"

Jason placed a hand on his shoulder. "You have more medical experience than anyone else here. And you're the only person who knows how to construct the anti-matter device."

"You're saying I'm the new Doc?"

"Congratulations," offered Jeanette.

Neal sighed again. "I have some pretty big shoes to fill."

"Now you know what I felt like."

Neal thought about it for a few seconds and shrugged. "I guess you're right. Thanks."

The young man walked off, passing through the King's Gate on his way to the abbey.

When they were alone, Jeanette asked, "What should I do?"

Jason motioned to the hotel lobby. "Go inside and tell them you're with me. They'll get you a room. I'll come and get you when I get back."

"You better hurry." Jeanette pointed to the young man who paced back and forth a few yards away. "He's about ready to start climbing walls."

When he looked over, the young man stopped and motioned with his hand for Jason to hurry. Jeanette leaned over and kissed Jason on the cheek, and then entered the hotel. She paused to call Lucifer and Lilith, who bolted after her, their tails wagging.

Jason watched her until she passed through the lobby and then stepped over to his impatient guide. "Come on. Let's get this over with."

Along the streets of Mont St. Michel, people came out of their homes and shops to greet him. Some applauded, while several offered briefs words of congratulation. Others whispered behind his back as he passed.

"That's him. He's the one who closed down the portal."

"Thank God he made it out alive."

"He saved us."

The irony was not lost on Jason. Several weeks ago, the citizens talked about him, only back then they muttered condemnations about his being the son of the woman who had loosed the demons on mankind.

Jacques greeted Jason in his private quarters with a bear hug and a pat on the back. Even Bishop Fiorello seemed uncharacteristically pleasant. For the next three hours, while feasting on roasted rabbit and vegetables, Jason related the details of their journey to and from Paris. When Jason concluded his story, Jacques leaned back in his chair.

"You're sure all the Demon Spawn are dead?"

"I am."

"God be praised," Bishop Fiorello bellowed in between sips of wine.

God had nothing to do with it, thought Jason as he tamped down his disgust for the fat cleric.

Jacques detected the animosity in Jason's mood. "You saved our city from certain annihilation. You saved all of Europe."

"*We* did, sir. And we lost a lot of good people doing it."

"Of course, you did. And we'll never forget them." Jacques leaned over toward the bishop. "Have the town council rename some of the city streets to commemorate those who gave their lives on this mission."

Bishop Fiorello belched. "It would be an honor."

Jason had all he could do not to punch the cleric.

Jacques turned back to his guest. "You should be proud of yourself. All of you should be. Thanks to you, we can start rebuilding and making a better life for ourselves."

"What about the refugees outside the gate?"

"Them, too," Jacques said as an afterthought. "And let me be the first to apologize for underestimating you."

"Yes," chimed in the obsequious bishop. "Fine job, young man."

Jacques waved off the bishop with a flick of his right hand. "Jason, I want you to officially take over as the head of Andre's unit."

"What's left of it," said Jason.

"We'll rebuild it. You pick whoever you want on your team and Franco will train them."

"Franco is dead. Remember?" Jason made no attempt to hide his contempt. "He died in the subway battling the centipedes."

"That's right." Jacques tried to conceal his embarrassment. "We'll have Reinhard train them, if that's okay with you?"

"Whatever." Jason intended to let the subject drop, but at the last minute asked, "Why do we even need the team if the Demon Spawn are gone?"

"It's a dangerous world out there. We'll need a police force to protect us from those who want to take away what we have. You're perfect for the job." Jacques lifted his glass of wine in the air. "A toast to a bright, new future."

Jason didn't join in. *It's amazing*, he thought. *Some things will never change.*

CHAPTER FIFTY-SIX

LATER THAT NIGHT, Jason had a quiet dinner with Jeanette. They didn't talk about the portal or their experiences; they concentrated on making plans for the future.

The hotel concierge had placed Jeanette in Petra's old room down the hall from his own, saying it wouldn't be right for two teenagers to share quarters. Jason didn't argue. Although he cared deeply for Jeanette, deep down he didn't feel proper having them do anything with the memory of Sasha's death still so vivid in his mind. He loved Sasha, although not in the same way he loved Jeanette. He only wished he had told Sasha how he felt before she gave her life to save him and the others.

After dinner, Jason escorted Jeanette to her room. She paused at the door and gave him a long, warm kiss that melted his heart.

"I love you," she whispered in his ear.

"I know." It was the only sentiment he could muster.

"I know you had feelings for Sasha and feel guilty about her death."

"It's not—"

"Yes, it is. And that's okay. You need to sort through your emotions. I'll be here when you're ready." Jeanette's face beamed with affection, yet she could not hide the pain in her eyes.

Jason wrapped his arms around Jeanette and hugged her tight. "Thank you."

As the young French girl disappeared into her room and

closed the door, he felt an emptiness and loneliness wash over him.

STANDING IN FRONT of the mirror to his bathroom, Jason pushed back a strand of hair. The image that stared back at him was not the teenager he once knew, but that of a man. The youthful innocence had been replaced by a steely determination. His face had become lean and tough. His soft eyes had hardened with the cold fortitude of someone who had made life and death decisions, decisions that often ended in death. He knew he would be making those same decisions in the future and burying more friends and loved ones as a result. Jason the man was up to the task, not Jason the teenager. All traces of the latter had to disappear.

Lifting the razor from off the vanity, Jason held it upside down, placed the blades against the hairline above his forehead, and stroked back. Several clumps of hair fell into the sink. He continued the process for several minutes until he had shaved his skull bare. Looking back into the mirror, he nodded his approval. He no longer stared at Bait. He stared at the commander of the Demon Hunters.

Going back into the room, Lucifer and Lilith were in their usual position by the window. They sensed a change in him and seemed apprehensive. He knelt between them and scratched each one behind the ears.

"Don't worry, guys. My feelings for you haven't changed." Standing up, the two werehounds gave him a face bath.

Climbing into bed, Jason pulled the covers over himself and laid his head against the pillow. He still could not get over the narrow sightedness of Jacques. Yes, they had saved Europe and wiped out the Demon Spawn on the continent. However, there were still four other portals throughout the world, and two more continents suffering the ravages of these demons. Those people needed saving, too. Thanks to Doc, Jason had the means to close those portals. He couldn't let the rest of the world suffer while Jacques and the elite of Mont St. Michel thrived in their glorious isolation.

Besides, his mother was still alive. If she had survived this long in the other dimension, the chances were good she could survive a while longer. At least until he found a way to get her out. Someone had to close those other portals and rescue his mother.

Jason knew that someone was him.

Preview of *Shattered World II*

RUSSIA

CHAPTER ONE

Red Square, Moscow, nine days after the opening of the Russian portal

TEN FLESH EATERS broke through the line and swarmed General Budenny. They were even more frightening up close, like the zombies from American horror films, emaciated corpses with gray leathery skin and dull, milky white eyes. They also had a taste for human flesh. These were the tortured souls condemned to eternal damnation that now walked the Earth because of the portal, the gate to another dimension. Unlike their movie counterparts, a bite from one of these demons would not turn the victim into a flesh eater, although that didn't mean enough of these creatures couldn't strip a man down to his bones if given a chance.

Budenny raised his 9mm Makarov pistol at the flesh eater rushing toward him and fired three rounds into its face. A blue eddy of light, the creature's lifeforce, separated from its body and drifted skyward. The carcass went limp, forward momentum carrying it a few feet until it collapsed and tumbled onto the pavement. The other flesh eaters maneuvered around the body and swarmed the general. He shifted his aim to the next closest and fired three more rounds. The bullets punched into its chest and head, freeing its lifeforce and dropping the corporeal shell. Budenny continued his attack, taking down two more flesh eaters before the breach of his Makarov locked in the open position.

Major Rozhenko stepped in front of Budenny, his AK-47 automatic rifle raised. The major fired into the heads of the last six onrushing flesh eaters, bringing each down. The last fell in front of the major and rolled. Rozhenko stepped back so the carcass wouldn't knock him over, ejected the weapon's empty magazine, and loaded a fresh one.

Rozhenko's eyes pleaded with his commanding officer to end this carnage. "You have to order a retreat."

"No," barked the general.

"But…."

"We can do this." Budenny added under his breath, "We must."

"We" referred to the five thousand soldiers of the Russian Ground Forces surging across Red Square to close the portal that had opened in front of the State Historical Museum in the wake of the scientific accident at the Institute for High Energy Physics in Protvino, seventy miles south of Moscow. The portal measured seventy feet in diameter. The bottom five feet lay buried beneath ground level, melting the surrounding stones and forming a trough. Its circumference shimmered, creating a distorted boundary between the two realms. An endless column of flesh eaters stumbled through, their numbers stretching back into the other dimension as far as the eye could see. They had been pouring into Red Square and spreading out across Moscow since the portal first opened.

The electromagnetic pulse generated during its formation had burnt out all electronic circuitry for thousands of miles, rendering most of the military equipment useless. Not that it mattered. Budenny had scoured armories throughout the Urals to find "old school" weapons to arm his troops—AK-47 Kalashnikov automatic rifles, Makarov semi-automatic pistols, and a dozen TPO-70 heavy infantry flamethrowers left over from the Cold War. He also possessed four ten-man squads, each armed with a Special Atomic Demolition Munition, more commonly known as a "suitcase bomb," a portable low-yield nuclear weapon they would use to blast shut the portal. The general had thought his command would be able to deal with this threat.

To paraphrase von Moltke, no battle plan ever survived first contact with the enemy.

The flesh eaters threatened Budenny's force by their sheer numbers. As his troops advanced up Red Square, they ran into a seemingly impenetrable wall of the demons that slowed their pace. For every flesh eater brought down, twice as many took its place. It had taken nearly an hour to move only a few hundred feet. Their left flank was anchored by Lenin's Mausoleum in front of the Kremlin, with the line of advance stretching across Red Square before swerving north in front of Gum Department Store where the right flank pushed three hundred feet ahead. Two of the nuclear squads had fallen in behind this surge to get closer to the portal. Budenny had used his left flank to distract the bulk of the flesh eaters and give his right flank a chance. As a hedge, he had ordered the remaining two nuclear squads to maneuver toward the mausoleum to make an end run if the opportunity arose. Budenny hoped this would work because his men had already expended more than half their ammunition. Once they were out, the flesh eaters would overwhelm them.

A commotion came from the troops off to his left. Budenny focused his attention beyond the portal toward the northeast corner of the Kremlin, expecting to see more flesh eaters bearing down on them. Rozhenko expressed the disbelief both men felt when he muttered, "You've got to be kidding."

A dragon had emerged from behind the Kremlin wall and centered itself between the citadel and the State Historical Museum. It did not resemble the mythical creatures from the childhood fairy tales his grandmother had told him about dragons protecting the Motherland from foreign invaders. This monster had the shape of a lizard, albeit one that stretched two hundred feet from nose to tail, and did not have wings. Its colorization was a deep red streaked with tints of orange. The scales were as thick as armored plates, especially around the head where the chin, nose, and brows extended outward in bony structures, and along the chest and spine where the skin peeked into thick ridges that glowed crimson. The beast crouched as if to lunge yet remained still and observed the battle through a pair of glossy, pitch black eyes.

Rozhenko moved beside Budenny. "General, we have to fall back now while we still have a chance."

Before Budenny could respond, two soldiers, each carrying a flamethrower, raced up on the dragon's flanks and doused it in flames, the one on the right aiming for its head, the other focusing on its massive chest. The behemoth reared up on its hind legs and screeched in agony. When the attack ceased, the dragon had not even been singed. It dropped onto all four legs, lowered the front part of its torso, and leaned its head forward. The glowing ridges along its chest and spine shone in intensity. Budenny sensed the panic that raced through his men.

Rather than fire, the dragon exhaled a cloud of lime green smoke tinted with thousands of crystals. The behemoth swung its head from side to side, producing a cloud that stretched for five hundred feet and expanded above Red Square, forming above the heads of flesh eaters and humans. It floated for several seconds before settling onto the troops. When the first crystal touched a hard surface, it ignited a flame no larger than the head of a lit match, which then kindled the lime green gas around it. The cloud became a raging inferno that burned itself out within seconds, incinerating flesh eaters and Budenny's men, leaving thousands of charred corpses sprawled across the square. A few remaining green crystals smoldered on the blackened skeletons and scorched pavement.

The left flank of Budenny's front panicked and broke into a

horde of terrified men, including one of the nuclear squads, all of whom dropped their weapons and ran for the Moskva River. Colonel Yurchenko, who led the other nuclear squad, headed for shelter behind Lenin's Mausoleum. Budenny, Rozhenko, and a dozen soldiers followed, stopping only when they reached the relative safety of the tomb's southern wall.

Several of his men stood their ground inside the square, many aiming for the ridges along the dragon's chest and spine. The behemoth glared at them. A guttural growl emanated from deep within its throat. One of the flamethrowers circled to its right and released a stream of fire that engulfed its head. The growl became an agonized screech. Budenny braced himself for another gas attack. Instead, the dragon lifted its left leg and smashed its foot on top of the flamethrower. The fuel tank exploded, splashing liquid fire on the nearby troops. Those not burnt alive were crushed as the behemoth lowered its head to the pavement and swung it sideways, flinging a score of Budenny's men into the air to be smashed against the Kremlin walls. One brave comrade rushed forward and emptied his AK-47 into the dragon's face, only to be scooped up in its mouth. As the man screamed in pain and terror, the dragon lifted its head and swallowed. The final shreds of discipline among Budenny's left flank collapsed and a panicked escape ensued. Surging ahead, the dragon rampaged through the fleeing men, crushing them under its weight or hurling them aside.

The right flank remained intact and took advantage of the confusion. Moving toward the center of Red Square where the dragon's fire cloud had cleared away the flesh eaters, the other two nuclear squads, protected by one hundred troops, raced for the portal. A handful of new flesh eaters had passed through it to replace those wiped out, more than enough for the Russians to handle. They had closed to within fifty feet when a roar came from Nikolskaya Street, which ran alongside Gum Department Store and entered Red Square near Kazan

Cathedral. A second dragon thundered into the plaza. The ridges along its chest and spine glowed crimson. Upon seeing the humans, it exhaled a lime green cloud over the advancing soldiers. The two nuclear squads rushed ahead, trying to plant their devices in the few remaining moments left to them. The crystals struck a hard surface and ignited. In seconds, the cloud became an inferno that incinerated another hundred troops and a score of flesh eaters. An explosion erupted from the fire cloud as one of the nuclear devices misfired, detonating with the equivalent of between ten and fifteen tons of high explosives.

Budenny and the others ducked behind the wall moments before the shock wave slammed into the mausoleum. The entire structure shook. Chunks of red marble broke loose and fell on them. Budenny felt his internal organs compress, fearing for a moment that they might rupture. The mausoleum took the brunt of the force, and the general suffered nothing more severe than a ringing in his ears. Leaning with his back against the wall, he shouted, "Is everyone okay?"

"Yes," Rozhenko responded. Budenny didn't hear the words but instead read his aide's lips.

"Wait here." The general made his way to the corner of the mausoleum and checked on the situation in Red Square. The blast had devastated everything within a two hundred foot radius. Those soldiers on the right flank not killed outright had been crushed or maimed from the concussion. Every flesh eaters in the square had been ripped apart, the blue light of their life forces mixing with black smoke as both drifted skyward. Even the dragon had not come through unscathed. The blast had thrown it against the front façade of Gum where it lay amongst a pile of debris. A gaping wound in its abdomen oozed blood and the torn remnants of internal organs. It tried to raise its legs and swing its tail, an effort that ended in a pathetic mewl before the behemoth went limp. For all the destruction it caused, the blast had one positive effect. It had cleared away all obstacles between them and the portal.

"Yurchenko," Budenny ordered. "Move while you have the chance."

The colonel did not waste time responding. He circled Budenny and rushed into Red Square, knowing the others would follow. The general watched as the squad raced toward the portal, confident they would make it.

AS YURCHENKO'S SQUAD approached the portal, half a dozen flesh eaters wandered through onto their side, only to be taken down by a barrage of automatic weapons fire. The squad stopped twenty feet from the opening, most providing suppressing fire against the demons that came through. Yurchenko slid off his backpack, lowered it onto the pavement, and unzipped it to reveal a cylindrical-shaped device eighteen inches in length by four inches in diameter. An LED display and keypad were built into one side. He would set the timer for two minutes, place it against the portal, and then get as far away as possible before the one kiloton explosion detonated and, in theory, blasted shut the portal. Yurchenko unlocked the keypad. The six spaces on the LED device lit up in a series of 0s. Once he typed in 120, he would—

A distorted roar shot across Red Square. The way his squad backed away from the portal told Yurchenko in which direction the sound came. A third dragon raced toward them from the other dimension. It rushed the opening, though still a thousand feet distant, crushing or pushing aside the flesh eaters heading in the same direction. Another roar came from behind him near St. Basil's. The first dragon had reversed direction, abandoning its pursuit of the fleeing humans to defend the portal. It had already approached to within one hundred feet, the ridges along its chest and spine a radiant crimson. The behemoth stopped, crouched low to the ground, and exhaled a cloud of lime green gas.

Yurchenko had a few seconds at most. He set the timer on the LED display to 1. Picking up the device, Yurchenko stepped up to the portal and initiated the countdown.

The first crystal touched one of Yurchenko's men, erupting into a spark that ignited the expanding cloud.

The LED counter switched to 0.

BUDENNY SHUT HIS eyes and ducked behind Lenin's Mausoleum as blinding light flashed across Red Square. Rozhenko scrambled over and threw himself on top of his commanding officer.

The dragon reared back, screeching as wisps of smoke formed on the skin and scales exposed to the fireball. A moment later, the shock wave slammed into the behemoth, tearing it apart and flinging the shattered carcass across the square to land in a bloody heap in front of St. Basil's.

The same shock wave slammed into the mausoleum, shearing off the top layers of marble and the reviewing stand, and dropping the fragments onto those hidden along the southern facade. Rozhenko groaned when a chunk fell on him. Budenny did not hear the major, being only vaguely cognizant of his surroundings for the next minute, sliding in and out of consciousness. When he regained his senses, he heard a low rumbling, and immediately knew what caused the sound.

"Rozhenko, get up. It's over."

The major did not respond. Budenny reached up to shake his shoulder. A warm liquid covered his palm. Rozhenko's body slid down the general's back and onto the marble debris surrounding them. Blood flowed from the torn skin around his crushed skull. His blank eyes stared up. Budenny placed two fingers over the major's lids and closed them. When the general stood, he could not see out of his right eye and the skin on that side of his face felt warm and numb. He would worry about his wounds later. Right now, he needed to confirm that Yurchenko had closed the portal. Placing his left hand against the mausoleum's wall, Budenny stumbled through the debris until he reached the corner of structure.

Smoke and dust shrouded most of Red Square. The rumbling came from a cloud that billowed skyward, the top forming into its familiar mushroom shape. Budenny could not see the section of Red Square where the portal once stood. He leaned against the wall and waited as the dust settled. His heart sank when he saw something shimmer on the other side of the smoke. The blast had not affected the portal. The explosion had penetrated the opening because the dragon and the closest flesh eaters on the other side had been cut down. The portal, however, remained intact. He had lost almost five thousand men to seal off this portal and had been unsuccessful.

Budenny slid down the wall and sat on the rubble from the mausoleum. He laid his head back and closed his eyes, wishing he had died along with the rest of his men. His failure meant that nothing would stop the demons from flooding into Moscow.

A Thank You to My Readers

I know it's unusual for writers to thank their fans for reading their book, but this is a heartfelt appreciation. The publishing industry has changed dramatically over the past ten years, and there are now thousands of young adult post-apocalypse novels on the market for readers to choose. I appreciate the fact that you took a chance on *Shattered World*. I hope you enjoyed reading it as much as I did writing it.

If you liked *Shattered World*, please tell your friends about the book and review it on Amazon. The review does not have to be long—just a rating and a sentence or two about why you enjoyed it. The more reviews *Shattered World* receives, the more opportunity other readers have of discovering the book.

Shattered World is just the beginning. Future books will take the Demon Hunters to Russia, Asia, and the United States. The locations they will visit will be more exotic. The people they encounter will be more colorful and, in some cases, will pose as much of a threat as the Demon Spawn. And the demons they face will be more fierce and terrifying. I can't promise that your favorite characters will survive, but I can promise action, thrills, and surprises.

Acknowledgments

Writing is very solitary and lonely. Getting a book published, on the other hand, is a complicated process involving many people, and they deserve to be recognized.

A huge thank you goes to Jess Iverson who reviewed the scientific aspects of antimatter and its applications. His input was crucial in making the scene inside CERN as accurate as possible. However, Jess has assured me that antimatter cannot exist outside its containment chamber and that the concept of a portable antimatter device is purely fictional. Without an antimatter device, there would be no reason for the Hell Gaters to travel to Paris; without their traveling to Paris, there would be no book. So the scientific portions of this book that read true are thanks to Jess; the rest is from my imagination.

I want to thank my beta readers, Virginia Smith and Alison Beightol, for reviewing the first draft of the manuscript and providing their feedback. I also want to express my appreciation to Michele Thompson for her excellent editorial skills, and for catching those things I missed in the original draft.

The cover art for this book was done by Uwe Jarling and Julie Nicholls. Their work is phenomenal and I cannot wait to see what they come up with for the rest of the series. Many thanks to Petar Dekic for providing the map so my readers can follow the adventures of the Demon Hunters.

Finally, a major debt of thanks goes to my family, both human and furry, for putting up with my self-imposed isolation while I write. Sure, it's hard to maintain my writing discipline when Walther is sitting by the desk, his favorite pull toy in his mouth and his big brown eyes pleading with me to play, or when Archer stands in front of the computer screen until I pet him. Yet my family gives me the time I need to write and never holds it against me. I couldn't do this without their love and support.

Author's Bio

Scott M. Baker was born and raised in Everett, Massachusetts and spent twenty-three years in northern Virginia working for the Central Intelligence Agency. Scott is now retired and lives just outside of Concord, New Hampshire with his wife and fellow writer Alison Beightol, stepdaughter, two rambunctious boxers, and two cats who treat him as their human servant. He has written *The Vampire Hunters* trilogy, about humans fighting the undead in Washington D.C.; *Rotter World*, *Rotter Nation*, and *Rotter Apocalypse*, his post-apocalyptic zombie saga; *Yeitso*, his homage to the giant monster movies of the 1950s that he loved watching as a kid; as well as several zombie-themed novellas and anthologies. He is currently working on a new zombie survival series focusing on a young woman learning how to stay alive in a world overrun by the living dead.

Please check out Scott's social media accounts for the latest information on future books, upcoming events, and other fun stuff.

Blog: scottmbakerauthor.blogspot.com
Facebook: facebook.com/groups/397749347486177
Twitter: @vampire_hunters
Instagram: scottmbakerwriter